Beloved Woman

Appalachian Journey
Book 3

CC Tillery

Spring Creek Press

First Edition

ISBN 098946413X
ISBN-13 978-0-9894641-3-0

Published by:
Spring Creek Press

As always, this one is for our dad, John Tillery who continues to share his "Aunt Bessie and Uncle Fletch" stories with us. We are blessed to have you, Daddy, and we love you very much!

And, of course, to our great-aunt Bessie and our great-uncle Fletcher who lived the stories and were kind enough to share their hearts and home with our dad.

Authors' Note:

The title of Beloved Woman comes from the story of Nan'yehi, a Cherokee woman who earned the honored Cherokee title of *Ghigau*. *Ghigau* is the highest distinction given to a Cherokee woman and carries with it great responsibility, as well as immense respect from the tribe. Nan'yehi was first honored as a "War Woman" at a very young age when she took up her husband's weapon after he was killed in battle and continued fighting the enemy. She was given the right to sit on the War Council, made a leader of the Woman's Council, and granted a power even the Chiefs didn't have; the right to determine the fate of captives. After many years as a respected "War Woman" she was given the title of *Ghigau*, or Beloved Woman. In that capacity, she continued with her duties as a War Woman and also served as a peace negotiator between the Cherokee and the white settlers, as well as with other tribes. To find out more about Nan'yehi's story, please visit http://www.nanyehi.com.

.

CHAPTER ONE

Winter 1914

She can just get glad in the same britches she got mad in.

The mountain people claim there's a mystery to the way God works, one we'll never be privy to, but I often found myself wondering why His way always hurt so much.

I spent a good many months after Sadie and her girls left studying my Bible, looking for an answer that couldn't be found, not even in the Good Book. In the end I learned the answer only existed in my heart.

I had been angry with God for the longest time, ever since George had died, followed by Sadie's stillborn baby, and finally, Sadie and the girls leaving our farm to go to Virginia.

I told myself I understood why Sadie felt she had to leave us, but oh, how I hated it. Hated it more than the vicious group of Red Shirts who were the cause of her departure, more than George's death, more even than the memory of his and Sadie's tiny stillborn baby—a baby I couldn't save.

And I hated God most of all for letting it happen.

I forgave Sadie fairly quickly, but as for God, it would be a long time before my broken heart would learn to trust Him again.

At that point in my life, I couldn't see ever forgiving Him for what he'd taken from me. But life, of course, would always go on. And God, it seemed, would always be there. No matter how I hated it in my heart and how I wished things could be different, the simple fact was I had to accept Sadie's decision. She made the only choice she could under the circumstances and God, in His infinite wisdom and, to me at least, baffling ways, had approved.

I knew Sadie had only been doing what she felt was best for her girls and it was a great comfort to me when Liza kept her promise to write and let me know how they were doing. Her first letters were stilted and consisted of only a few lines—she was, after all, only eight years old—but I was delighted to note that her writing improved with each one. I could see that she and Ruth were happy in their new home and intuited Sadie, if not happy, was at least not as scared as she'd been here on the farm after George died.

They were with family. I knew in my heart that, given enough time, family could soothe the hurt and mayhap heal it completely.

And life, as I said, does go on. While our serene existence on Stone Mountain didn't change much, the outside world was experiencing its fair share of upheavals. Across the ocean, an earthquake in Italy had killed 150,000 people, Japan's Prince Ito had been assassinated, the Turks had rebelled against the Ottoman Empire, and in China, a 3-year-old boy was made Emperor, followed a few years after that by a bloody revolution.

Over here on our side of the world, Henry Ford invented the Model T automobile, and though it took a while for those speedy horseless carriages to catch on here in the mountains, we sometimes saw one of them zipping down the roads in Old Fort—well, as much as they could zip given that the roads at that time were all hard-packed dirt filled with potholes that sometimes grew to craters. Robert Peary made history by being the first man to trek to the North Pole. That one befuddled me. Why in the world would you want to go to a place covered in ice and snow? It was, I reckon, dictated by a sense of adventure or maybe even just to be the first man to accomplish such a thing.

On March 25, 1911, a fire at the Triangle Waist Company in New York City killed 146 people, 123 women and 23 men ranging in age from 43 to 14. The only good thing to come of that tragedy was it called attention to the unsafe working conditions in high-rise factories which led to legislation requiring safer working conditions for workers. It also spurred the growth of the International Ladies' Garment Workers' Union.

And in 1912, even as the world was introduced to the Oreo cookie by the National Biscuit Company, a treat that would grow in popularity over the course of my lifetime, the Titanic, a luxury ocean ship touted as being unsinkable, sailed on her maiden voyage from England to New York. Somewhere in the northern Atlantic Ocean, it struck an iceberg and, in spite of the owners' claims, sank, killing over 1500 people. Lives lost for no other reason than the owners trusted in their supposedly unsinkable ship and failed to properly outfit her with lifeboats, leaving most of the passengers to drown in the cold ocean waters.

Tragedies continued into 1913, with the Italian Hall Massacre on December 24th when 73 men, women, and children were crushed to death in a stampede after someone falsely yelled "fire" at a crowded Christmas party at the C&H Mine in Calumet, Michigan. It was never discovered who shouted the warning but many believed it to be a friend of the anti-union management in retaliation to the strike that had been going on since July.

It seemed my old friend Death was as busy as ever and I was grateful Its attention was elsewhere.

Or so I thought until my Cherokee great-grandmother visited me in my dreams on a cold February night in 1914, her appearance a gift sorely needed at the time.

On that night, the winter winds howled outside with gusts strong enough to rattle the windows and send the smoke rushing in a reverse course down the chimney, making it hard to breathe at times. The pings of frozen ice pellets hitting the tin roof accompanied by the keening wind serenaded me into sleep and I remember thinking that the morning chores would be a misery the next day if winter continued her furious assault throughout the night. Thankful for my husband Fletcher's warmth beside me, I snuggled closer and longed for spring as I so often did during that unpredictable and frigid winter when it seemed warmth and sunshine would never grace our mountain again.

My thoughts turned to a summer walk with my great-grandmother Elisi who had stayed with us in Hot Springs after my little brother Green died. I remembered with longing the warm sun caressing my shoulders and the air carrying the delicate scent of wildflowers mingled with the slightly musty scent of a wild strawberry bush past its prime and ripening peaches, backed up with the sharp tang of ozone. I had looked up at the clear blue sky and despite the absence of clouds knew it would storm later that afternoon. It had been Elisi who taught me to smell the rain, one of the many and varied things I learned from her as we gathered wildflowers and herbs during her time with us.

We had talked of mundane things; the bountiful blackberry harvest we would have later in July, the antics of the kittens the barn cat had birthed only a few weeks before, the unexpected offer of a temporary teaching position at Dorland Institute where I had graduated that past spring. And as she so often did, Elisi listened patiently as I babbled on about my life.

I was 18, teetering on the verge of womanhood—a late bloomer when it came to that particular area of life—taking my first cautious steps in the unexplored and mysterious dance of love, and wondering, as young women often do, what would become of me now that I was out of school.

"You will find your true path in time, *ayoli*." Elisi took my hand as we came to the curve in the creek where my little brother Green had been swept away in a flash flood back in May. The water in the creek was muddy and full of sticks and leaves as it had been after the flood.

I shivered. For some reason the sight of that dirty water frightened me.

I remember shaking my head. Confusion seemed to

walk with me back then. How could I find my true path if I couldn't even figure out what I would do now that I had graduated from school? I knew I wanted a full-time teaching position but in order to have that dream I would have to move away from my home and family and I wasn't sure I could do that. Dorland was the only school in Hot Springs, and though I had been asked to teach there for the first few months of the school year, I knew I would be replaced as soon as Miss Amelia returned from her latest treatment at the Asheville tuberculosis center.

"I don't know, Elisi. It seems to me if I was going to find my path, I would have stumbled upon it by now. I'm 18 years old and some of the girls I went to school with are already married. By the end of this summer, I'm certain a few of them will already have babies on the way."

Elisi chuckled. "Yes, but have they found their true path in life or do they walk in the easiest direction simply because it is there?" She patted my hand. "You are the smart one. You take your time and observe all that is around you and in the end you will be rewarded by finding the path you are meant to walk. That is how it should be."

"I reckon, but I sure do wish someone would point me in the right direction."

"No one can choose the path for you, *ayoli*, it is something you must find on your own. Remember what I told you about Miss Cordy being a whistling woman?"

I nodded. "Yes, you said she lived her life however she pleased and didn't care what anyone else thought of her. But does that mean I have to live as long as Miss Cordy before I find my path?"

"Not at all. The path is yours and it will come to you in time." She hesitated then smiled before going on. "I will tell you a story and maybe then you will understand better."

"What's the story about, Elisi?"

"A woman named Nancy Ward, but when the story begins she was Nan'yehi."

"She changed her name like me?"

"No, Nan'yehi is the Cherokee name she was given at birth. She was born long ago in Chota to a Cherokee woman named Tame Deer and a mixed-breed father named Fivekiller." She shrugged. "It was when she was older that she married a man named Bryant Ward and the white people started calling her Nancy Ward. But to the People, she will always be Nan'yehi."

"Nan'ye-hi," I repeated after her. "It's a pretty name. What does it mean?"

"It means she who walks among the spirit people."

"Oh, I like that. And did she?"

"I will tell you the story first. Since Tame Deer was of the Wolf Clan and Cherokee society follows the mother, all of her children would be of the same clan. On the day Nan'yehi was born, a white wolf appeared on the horizon. The People saw that as a momentous sign because they considered white the color of peace.

"When Nan'yehi was young," she patted my hand and smiled, "younger than you, little one, she married a great warrior named Kingfisher. When the People went to war against the Creek, she went with him even though she was only 17. She stayed by his side, preparing his weapons and ammunition and rallying the other warriors when their strength and courage flagged. During the battle of Taliwa, Kingfisher was killed and Nan'yehi took up his weapons and fought in his place. It is said she sang a war song while she fought and that her bravery encouraged the other warriors to fight harder and eventually led them to triumph.

"Because that victory was an important one, Nan'yehi was honored as a 'War Woman' and given the right to sit on the War Council. She was also made the leader of the Women's Council and given a power not even granted to the Chiefs, whereby she could determine the fate of captives, whether they be killed, enslaved, released, or adopted into the tribe."

"And she was only 17?"

"Yes, little one, only 17. She found her true path early. But it is not always so. There are many who find it much later in life and there are some who never do."

"Like me."

Elisi patted my hand again as she shook her head.

"There is no way of knowing when you will find it, *ayoli*. All you can do is live your life and do what you think best." She smiled. "You will find it if you are patient."

"What happened to Nan'yehi, Elisi?"

"Oh, she had a long life, and because she was such a good negotiator with the other tribes and the white men, the People eventually honored her with the title of *Ghigau*."

"*Ghi-ga-u*," I said slowly, rolling the syllables off my tongue. "What does it mean, Elisi?"

She smiled. "Beloved Woman. It's the highest position a Cherokee woman can have. She was given a shawl of white swan feathers and it remained a symbol of her authority for the rest of her life. The title brought with it even more rights and privileges as well as a great deal of responsibility.

"A Beloved Woman is looked on with much respect. She is allowed to speak and even vote at the General Council, she is a leader in the Women's Council, and has the honor of preparing the Black Drink for ceremonies and to give to warriors before they go into battle. She also has the right to save a prisoner from execution, no matter what the men say. Most importantly, she serves as sage and guide to the People."

"Did she ever save a prisoner from death?"

"She did, a woman named Mrs. Bean. Nan'yehi stopped them as they were tying Mrs. Bean to the stake. She took the woman into her own home, treated her injuries and nursed her back to health."

I smiled. "Not only brave but kind, too."

"Yes, gentle and caring. On the day she died, they say a white light rose from her heart and swirled around the room, taking the form of a swan and flying out the window toward Chota where she was born. Nan'yehi found her true path in life and she walked it with pride. She was the last *Ghigau*."

"The last one?"

"Yes, the last of the Cherokee Beloved Women. Up to now, anyway. There's always the possibility of a woman in the future earning the title. Or even someone living now."

"You should be one, Elisi. You're the wisest woman I know."

She laughed then shook her head. "Why would I want to be a *Ghigau*? That is not my path."

"You're a healer, right? But you're still the smartest woman ... no, the smartest person I know." I put my arm around her waist and hugged her to me. "You're a Beloved Woman to me."

"And you to me, little one." She smiled. "Did you know that back when the white men first settled here they scoffed at the way the Cherokee treated their women?" She shook her head. "They called us a 'petticoat government' because they didn't understand the respect the Cherokee men had for the women, much less the power the woman has in her tribe. A Cherokee woman can choose the man she wants to marry. She owns the house where they live and all of the possessions, and if she decides she does not want to be married to her husband anymore, she only has to pack his things and place them outside the house."

Warmed by this memory, I drifted into sleep and into a dream about Spring Creek, usually tranquil and serene, now muddy and violent, sweeping along its banks carrying debris and a small blue shirt. I must have cried out because suddenly Elisi was there, with me, and I knew she had come to comfort me. I smiled at her, so happy to see her. She returned the smile as she hugged me close but when she pulled back I saw her eyes were clouded with sadness.

"Keep looking for your true path, *ayoli*, and you will find it," she whispered. "When you do, remember you are a Cherokee woman and what that means. You are strong and brave, and though it may not always be easy or pleasant, you must walk your path no matter what. In time, the path will lead you to a child, and when it does, you must stand up and do what you know is right for him." She laid her head on my shoulder as the sun slipped behind a cloud. "Be true to yourself, that's the best advice I can give you. I must go now, *ayoli. Gugeyu.*"

I knew what that meant, Elisi had taught me that word long ago, "I love you." Though she rarely said it, I always knew it was true. A chill raced up my spine at the same time a warm feeling settled in my heart and I hugged her closer to me. "No, Elisi, no. What will I do without you?"

"You will walk your path, little one, as you are meant to do." She placed her hand over my heart. "You feel the warmth?"

"Yes, Elisi, *gugeyu*," I whispered as I placed my hand over hers.

She smiled even as her body seemed to fade away. "That is me. I will always be with you in your heart, my *ayoli*."

I awoke in my own bed, tears running down my cheeks into my hair as the first light of dawn brightened the window. The wind had died and the sleet had turned to snow sometime during the night, the flakes piled in a fluffy bolster across the bottom of the frosted glass of the windows. Fletcher snored softly beside me and Fritz chuffed as he struggled to get up, his old bones protesting the cold. He walked to the side of the bed and rested his chin on the mattress at my hip.

I placed my hand on his head, thinking about the dream and remembering how the water of the creek had looked muddy as if it had recently flooded. I shivered as I had in the dream and pressed the heels of my hands to my cheeks in a futile attempt to dry the tears streaming from my eyes.

Elisi herself had taught me that muddy water in your dreams meant one of two things; bad luck or someone had died. And I knew for sure what this dream portended: my beloved great-grandmother was dead.

Moving slowly, I eased from the bed and went out into the living room. I tossed a couple of logs onto the fire Fletch had banked the night before, stirring it with the poker to get the flames going again. Then I picked up my guitar from the rocking chair where I'd left it. I thought about playing something, it always soothed me, but after a moment set it aside. With the snow, Fletch had a long day waiting for him and I wanted him to sleep as long as possible. Added to that, I needed a few minutes alone to mourn Elisi. Dragging the chair over to the window, I sat down and watched the full moon set even as the sky tinged a delicate pink with the sunrise.

Fritz settled at my side and laid his head in my lap. I

scratched behind his ear and he moaned, bringing to mind a funeral dirge.

"She's gone, Fritz. Elisi's gone," I whispered.

My eyes watched the moon as it slid behind the mists riding low along the tops of the mountains, bringing a reluctant smile to my lips. It was, I thought, Elisi's farewell to me.

The Cherokee called the full moon in February the Bony Moon. I considered it fitting that Elisi had died under that beautiful moon, a time when the People traditionally set an empty plate at the table to honor loved ones who had passed from this world. I would do that for her, my adored great-grandmother, the woman who had taught me so much about life and love and being someone I could be proud of. I closed my eyes and pictured her walking the trail to the Darkening Land, the next step in her life's journey. She straightened, dropped the walking stick she had taken to using in her later years, and reached out her hands. Green bounded up, Mama close behind, and each took one of her hands to walk with her. It made a beautiful picture and I dried the last of my tears then rubbed my hand over my heart. Opening my eyes, I stared out at the brightening sky and whispered, "Safe journey, Elisi. *Gugeyu*, always."

She was gone yet she would always be with me in spirit and I would do my best to honor her memory. I would find my true path and walk it safe in the knowledge that she traveled with me.

Bowing my head, I closed my eyes and prayed, stumbling over the words as I gave thanks to God for bringing her to me one last time. It was a gift, I knew, a gift that should be recognized and I accepted it with joy. Humbled that He'd seen fit to share Elisi with me at the end of her life, I raised my head and smiled.

Grief seemed a distant echo as I watched the colors the dawning sun swirled across the tops of the mountains. Elisi was gone though I held her in my heart, and for the first time since Sadie and her girls had left, I felt entirely at peace.

God does indeed, as the mountain folk say, work in mysterious ways. They also believed it wasn't for them to question His dealings but to accept them and go on with the life He'd given them.

Pondering that, another quote from the book of Job in the Bible came to me; "the Lord gave, and the Lord hath taken away; blessed be the name of the Lord." I had forgotten that somehow but it came home to me with Elisi's visit and I vowed I wouldn't forget it again.

I heard Fletcher stirring in the bedroom so got up and moved the rocking chair back to its place beside the hearth, propping my guitar on the seat cushion. Fritz stayed right by my side as if he sensed my sadness and wanted to cheer me up.

I rested my hand on his head then ruffled his soft, floppy ears. "I guess we should get the coffee going and get this day started, huh, boy?"

He woofed cheerfully in agreement.

CHAPTER TWO

Summer 1914

It's so hot the hens are laying hard-boiled eggs.

Fletcher offered to take me to Hot Springs when I told him Elisi had died but I didn't see the point in it. I wanted to be with her but couldn't see any way to get there in time as Cherokee custom called for a quick burial, whether it be outside or inside the person's house. I knew Elisi had Aunt Belle and other family around, grandchildren, cousins, nieces and nephews, and they would see to the burial as soon as possible.

Instead, remembering the story Elisi told me about how the cedar tree was born as a reminder to the Cherokee to honor the spirits of their ancestors, I went into the woods, found a small cedar tree, and marked it with a bright yellow ribbon. In the spring, I would come back, dig the little tree up and transplant it closer to the house where I could visit it every day and honor Elisi's spirit. And I thought about what Elisi had taught me when Druanna died. Death isn't an end to the person. Their spirit lives on.

A couple of weeks later, I received a package in the mail from Aunt Belle. The letter she included confirmed what I already knew; Elisi had passed away in her sleep on a cold winter night. Aunt Belle wrote of how she'd enjoyed a long and happy life and that she had died as she had lived, quietly and peacefully.

Yes, she had, I thought, and though I hadn't been there to see to her burial, Aunt Belle assured me that one of her grandsons and his wife had taken care to follow the Cherokee tradition of burying her the next day in her little cabin, beneath the hearth as was customary. They'd also buried her possessions with her. There weren't many, Elisi had never developed the habit of collecting things she had no use for, only her dried herbs and wildflowers which she used for healing.

The package also brought several tins of those herbs tucked in a beautiful blanket of soft white wool Elisi had woven herself. It made me think of the shawl the Cherokee people had given to Nan'yehi when they'd honored her as a *Ghigau*. It wasn't swan feathers but it was soft and warm as the finest goose down and I would treasure that final gift from my beloved great–grandmother all my life.

Summer arrived early that year, shoving spring out the door in mid April with soaring temperatures and hardly any rain. My garden suffered just as the wildflowers and plants, producing little in the way of edible goods despite my efforts to keep the plants alive with pails of water from the well and from the creek later in the summer when I worried about the well drying up.

Even the trees took on a wilted look in the blazing heat with leaves that drooped forlornly and branches dry enough to snap in a heavy wind.

The barn cats were often seen lazing in the stingy shade underneath the water trough, too slothful to move and with no interest at all in chasing the dry leaves that fell from the trees, a favorite pastime before the heat set in. And poor Fritz stayed close to home instead of joining Fletch on his daily treks around the farm or into Old Fort.

I swan, it was so hot and dry even the cicadas and birds couldn't drum up the energy to sing.

And surprisingly, I found myself longing for winter as I had longed for spring and summer just a few months before.

Shaking my head at my contrary nature, I carried the

dishwater left over from doing the breakfast dishes outside and dumped it on the little cedar tree Fletch had dug up and planted for me outside our bedroom window. I ran my fingers over one of the branches and watched in frustration as dry needles drifted to the ground. Despite a good dose of water twice a day, it was barely clinging to life, and depending on my mood, I cajoled, scolded, urged or begged it to stay strong and grow.

Off in the distance thunder rumbled, interrupting today's pleas, and Fritz whined as he scurried off to hide in the barn, seeking refuge there as he always did when he heard loud noises. I looked up, sniffing the air and hoping for the smell of rain. The heat of the day blanketed all but a whiff of drying plants and the cloudless skies quickly dashed any hopes of much-needed rain. What we could really use, I thought, was a good steady downpour that lasted more than a few minutes. One of our mountain frog-stranglers, usually heralded by claps of thunder and punctuated with flashes of lightning, wouldn't be of much use as the ground was so dry that the water would simply bounce off the hard-packed earth and evaporate in the heat on its way back down.

"Lawsa mercy, it's hot as blue blazes out here," I said to Elisi's tree as I stood up and ran my forearm across the sweat on my forehead. "And we haven't even reached the dog days yet." Looking up at the sky, which appeared a white blue as if the sun had leached all the color from it, I wondered how hot it could possibly get before the whole world simply went up in a blazing inferno.

It was still early morning, we weren't even into the hottest part of the day yet, but it already felt as if I was standing in the center of a bonfire. I rolled up my sleeves, searching for a little relief but it wasn't to be found that day.

Fritz slunk back around the side of the house, looking embarrassed at his faint-heartedness and panting as if he'd galloped a mile through the fires of Hell. I sympathized. Though his fur had thinned with the passing years, the thought of wearing any kind of coat in this heat was enough to have another line of sweat breaking out on my brow.

And it was about to get hotter yet. Today was Monday

and Monday was always wash day.

"Let's get to it, boy. Those clothes aren't going to wash themselves."

Fritz moaned but followed along beside me as I walked around the house to the back, pausing on my way to stir the iron kettle of soap I'd placed in the full sun beside the porch. Its pale golden color brought a satisfied smile to my face. In a couple more days, it would be time to pour it into molds then set the soap aside for a few months, allowing the lye to thoroughly blend with the other ingredients so it wouldn't be too harsh. Soap making was a long, exacting process but one I enjoyed as it could be done in stages. Unlike laundry which took a full day of continuous labor every week. And it wasn't even finished then, as the next day would be spent ironing what I'd washed, another hot and backbreaking chore.

I checked the tub of water Fletch had set over the outdoor fire he lit for me that morning. It was boiling at last so I ladled half into another tub sitting to the side. After that water cooled a bit, I would add the colored clothes and let them soak before scrubbing them against the rippled washboard. The whites would go directly into the boiling water with a healthy dose of soap added to make the scrubbing easier.

In the kitchen, I took the time to peek into the pot of beans I had simmering on the stove and gave them a quick stir. Then I scooped up the dirty clothes waiting in two piles, whites and coloreds, on the kitchen table and headed outside to deal with the laundry.

An hour later, while scrubbing the last of the bed sheets and singing a rousing rendition of "She'll Be Comin' 'Round the Mountain" to take my mind off the boring chore, I smelled smoke. Thinking at first I'd stood too close to the fire, I looked down at my skirt, fully expecting to see a scorched hem or maybe a burned spot where a spark had leapt out of the fire and caught, charring a bit of the material.

Dropping the sheet back into the tub, I turned this way and that, trying to see the back of my skirt. But there were no scorch marks and no smoke to indicate an accidental spark.

I turned and looked at the house. No smoke emanating from there but I went inside and took a quick look around to be sure. Like everything else that summer, the walls of our little log cabin were as dry and brittle as a sinner's heart.

I found no fire and shook my head. "Imagining things," I muttered to myself and went back to scrubbing the sheet. But the smell stayed with me and I hunched my shoulders against the chill that ran up my spine.

I suppose by that time in my life, I should have understood that the smell was a warning sign from my subconscious that something bad was about to happen, but it never occurred to me. Instead, I assumed someone had a fire going somewhere and the smoke had drifted to me on some capricious breeze, even though there wasn't so much as a puff of air to be found that day unless it came out of Fritz's panting mouth.

As I hung the sheets to dry, lightning coursed through the sky way far away over the mountains. Automatically, I started counting, "One one thousand, two one thousand, three one thousand," trying to gauge the distance, but the storm, if there was indeed a storm and not merely heat lightning, was too far off to hear the thunder. Still, judging from the angry clouds roiling over the mountains, some lucky soul somewhere was getting some much-needed rain. I didn't like thunderstorms but I wished fervently that the storm would track this way if only to relieve the heaviness of the air. Breathing was almost painful with this kind of heat, the air so weighty and wet it seemed to smother rather than relieve your lungs when you breathed it in. It was like trying to inhale hot molasses—smoke-scented molasses.

I looked off into the woods, checking once more for smoke. The sky seemed to wiggle and dance in the heat and I rubbed my hand over my forehead as I wondered if maybe I should go in and cool off for a while. But it was as hot inside the house as outside, even with all the windows open, so I went back to hanging the sheets.

When I finished, I set my hands on my lower back and stretched, trying to relieve the stiffness that came with bending over a washtub all morning. I made a bargain with myself; I'd finish hanging the rest of the white clothes on the line and set the colored clothes to soak in the tub and then I'd take my lunch down to the creek and stick my feet into the cool water while I ate. Or maybe I'd just plop my entire body down in the middle of the creek and let it wash some of the heat away. My clothes were drenched with sweat anyway and could probably do with a good rinsing. And I just might soak my head too and see if I could get the smell of smoke out of my nose.

Almost as soon as I pegged the last shirt to the line, Fritz barked from beneath the branches of a Mountain Laurel beside one of the paths leading into the woods where he'd been catching a nap. Scrambling out of the shade, he looked into the trees and cut a gleeful jig. I knew without looking that meant Fletcher was nearby. Shielding my eyes from the bright sun with the flat of my hand, I watched my husband emerge from the trees. I raised my hand and waved. He smiled and walked over to me, wiping his face with a bandanna he pulled out of his back pocket.

"Whoo-wee, sure is a right miserable day, Bessie-girl. Why, it's so dry, I think I heard one of the trees whistling for a dog." He bent down and rubbed his hand over Fritz's back which sent the dog into paroxysms of delight. "I thought I might take my lunch down to the creek and sit in the shade of that weeping willow tree."

Pleased his thoughts ran parallel to mine, I smiled. "Great minds think alike. I had the same thought a few minutes ago only I was planning to sit in the middle of the creek and maybe even lie down if that was what it took to get cool."

He held out his hand to me and nodded in the direction of the washtub. "You at a stopping place?"

"I am, yes. Just let me throw a little soap in with the colored clothes and swish it up a bit to get them started. I've got biscuits and some fried ham left over from breakfast. We can have that and some of the pears you picked yesterday."

"All right, that sounds right good. You go on and do what you need to do with the washing and I'll go get us a quilt to spread underneath that willow."

We walked hand in hand toward the washtub and then Fletcher veered off to go into the house.

I added the soap to the tub, swished the water around halfheartedly then went inside, mopping my face with my handkerchief. I spied Mama's magic quilt Fletcher had draped over the back of one of the chairs and started to take it back to the parlor where it customarily decorated the back of my favorite rocking chair then get another quilt from the cedar chest but shrugged my shoulders and let it go. The quilt could stand to be washed and I could do it after we had our lunch.

The smell of smoke was still with me and I walked through the house doing a quick check for fire. Finding nothing, I went back to the kitchen where Fletch was packing one of my baskets with biscuits and pears. "Fletcher?"

He looked up. "Yeah, Bess."

"Do you smell smoke?"

He sniffed the air. "Nope, all I smell is those beans you've got on the stove." He walked over and lifted the lid, inhaling loudly. "They smell right good, too." Picking up the spoon, he stirred then hummed appreciatively and lifted it brimming with beans and fatback out of the pot. "I hope that means beans and cornbread and maybe some fried potatoes and onions for supper."

I put my hands on my hips as he blew on the spoon to cool the beans. "Mercy sakes alive, don't you dare eat those, Fletcher Elliott, they're for supper."

He grinned, let the beans fall back into the pot and replaced the lid. "Yes, ma'am, they are, but they smell good enough to eat right now."

"Well, they're not finished cooking and they'll taste that much better if you wait. You'll probably get a belly-ache eating beans that aren't fully cooked."

"Mayhap I would, mayhap I wouldn't. The way they smell, it might be worth it." He lifted the lid again and gave the beans another quick stir.

I knew he was only teasing me but I huffed out a breath. "Fletcher Elliott," I said warningly, "those beans are for supper, they are not fit to eat yet, and that fatback hasn't had time to fully cook either. If the beans don't make you sick, the fatback will." When he raised his eyebrows and grinned at me, I laughed. "Come on, let's go down to the creek and have ourselves a picnic in the shade."

We lingered over our lunch, enjoying the cool shade and refreshing ourselves by wading in the creek for a bit after we'd finished our meal. Fritz, always happy to have his master home, jumped in with us and frolicked like a puppy, shaking enough water off to drown a rat. It always amazed me how the water could be so cool during the heat of the summer. Fletcher said it was because it was a spring-fed creek and the water came from deep in the mountain where the sun couldn't reach and so it never got truly warm like the water up in Hot Springs.

A light breeze was blowing by the time we'd packed up our basket and headed back to the cabin. A flock of crows hiding in the thick shade of the leaves suddenly took flight, rising to the sky in a tight-knit silent group, as if fleeing in terror from an unseen, but deeply sensed, monster. I hunched my shoulders instinctively and when I looked up at a sky suddenly gone dark, I gasped and reached out for Fletcher. An angry cluster of thunderclouds was directly over us, covering the sun with a purple-black bruise, heavy with rain and charged with lightning, framed by the dazzling white-blue of the summer sky. The hair on the back of my neck stood straight up and my fingers closed, tight enough to bruise, around my husband's upper arm. I opened my mouth to say something, a warning perhaps or maybe only another gasp, but before I could get a word out, lightning crashed through the clouds and speared down to the huge dying white pine in our side yard, immediately followed by the loudest clap of thunder I'd ever heard.

The thunder died away to be replaced with an ominous sound. It happened so fast I still to this day can't believe I saw it with my own eyes. The pine tree Fletch had been talking about cutting down before it fell and damaged something split clean in two as if Almighty God had taken a massive ax to it, cleaving it right down the middle. Too late, I thought as, with a thunderous roar, one half plummeted toward the woods, taking out a wide swath of trees and plants, and the other half fell toward us.

Pine cones flew through the air, one hitting me on the arm right before Fletcher shoved me to the side and fell on top of me, shielding me from the topmost branches. Fritz yelped and took off for the barn as if the hounds of Hell were after him.

Luckily, the tree was so tall that when it landed with a mighty rumbling boom, shaking the ground as if Satan had reached up and punched the ceiling of Hell, the branches reached clear across the creek and missed us completely. The house wasn't so lucky. The wide trunk crushed the chimney and completely demolished the living room and front porch.

"Well, hell," Fletcher said when he rolled off me and stood up. He reached a hand down to help me to my feet. "You all right, Bessie?"

I took a deep breath. "I am." My voice shook and I cleared my throat. "I'm fine. Are you all right?"

"Yep, got clobbered by a few pine cones but that's all." His hat had flown off when he jumped to protect me and he walked over, picked it up and slapped it on his thigh, knocking off pine needles and bits of broken pine cones. "I thought for a minute there we were a couple of gone geese." Scratching his head, he surprised me when he chuckled at the furious barking emanating from the barn. "I didn't know that damn dog could move that fast."

I laughed. "Poor thing high-tails it to the barn every time he even suspects it's going to thunder. He probably thought the world was coming to an end when that tree fell."

"Well, I know I did for a minute there. It sure sounded like it." He looked up at the sky and then back at me. "You sure you're all right?"

I nodded and he said, "Good. Seems mighty unfair that we didn't even get a drop of rain after all that, but maybe it's for the best since the only roof we have right now is the sky." He pointed toward the cabin and shook his head as he bent down to pick up the picnic basket and Mama's magic quilt. "Heck of a thing..."

The wind gusted. "I don't think it's through with us yet, Fletch, but oh, that breeze sure does feel fine."

"Yep, guess we should be grateful for small favors."

I took his hand and squeezed it. "We have each other and our lives to be grateful for, too."

"That we do," he said, giving my hand a squeeze in return. "Yep, that we do, Bessie-girl. Well, let's go see what's what."

As we walked up the bank, I said a silent prayer of thanks to God for keeping us safe. We might not have a roof over our heads for the foreseeable future but we were alive and we had each other. And if I knew anything, I knew Fletcher would work himself to the bone to see that we had shelter as quickly as possible. We really didn't need much since it was summer and warm enough to sleep outside if we had to. But I knew it wouldn't come to that as there was always the barn or one of the old slave cabins.

Fletcher stopped suddenly. "Would you look at that, Bess? God was looking out for us after all."

It was as if our little house had been sliced in two. The back half of the cabin with the kitchen and our bedroom, though now open to the elements, stood unharmed. The front, consisting of the parlor, fireplace, extra bedroom, and front porch, was almost smashed flat.

I sniffed the air, catching the comforting scent of beans cooking from the kitchen. "Looks like you'll have your beans and cornbread and those fried potatoes after all, Mr. Elliott. And I set a pitcher of buttermilk in the spring box this morning. It should be good and cold by suppertime."

Fletcher took my hand and bowed at the waist like the finest English gentleman addressing the Queen. "You sure do know the way to a man's heart, Bess, especially mine."

I laughed. "Oh, you're a charmer when it comes to something to fill your belly, you are, and I'm willing to oblige you but I have laundry to finish first and," I pointed to the house, "you have a parlor and spare bedroom to build."

He snapped his fingers. "Ain't going to happen in a day but I reckon I can get some of the men folk around here to help and we'll get her done soon enough. You ain't going to make me wait that long for my supper, are you?"

"I imagine if you were to promise to build me a porch swing to put on the new porch you're going to have to build, I could promise to keep you fed while you do it."

He grinned. "Well, I guess before I start promising anything, I should take a look at the damage and see what needs to be done. Reckon I can drape a few of those tarps I've got in the barn over the front of the bedroom and kitchen to keep out the weather. Might keep out the wildlife, too, but I'll need to get the walls back up soon as I can." He took off his hat and scratched his head. "Why don't you go on around back and finish your washing? I don't want you inside until I know it's safe."

I nodded as I took Mama's magic quilt from the top of the picnic basket and shook it out. Another blessing, I thought. If Fletcher hadn't grabbed it from the back of my rocking chair in the parlor, I might not still have it.

As I walked around to the backyard, I glanced at the slave cabins and thanked God we wouldn't have to live in one of them until the house was fixed. It wasn't that they were unstable or anything, I just didn't want to face the memories of Sadie and her girls they would bring.

As it turned out, those memories would soon fade when we were blessed by another couple of friends who needed a place to stay. Not that they were wiped completely out, I could never forget Sadie, Ruth, and Liza, much less George, but they softened with the arrival of the Berryhills.

CHAPTER THREE

Summer 1914

There but for the grace of God...

The Berryhills came to us on Tuesday, August 4, 1914, a little over a week after the pine tree fell on our house. That alone was enough to mark the day in my mind but when Fletcher brought them home with him he also brought dismaying news from across the ocean that would eventually reverberate in our country, echoing through all 48 states, especially North Carolina, particularly my old home town of Hot Springs.

And it would, of course, touch the lives of many of the families living on Stone Mountain, including the Elliott family.

Trouble had been brewing in Europe since June 28th when the heir to Austria-Hungary's throne, Archduke Ferdinand and his wife, Sophie, were assassinated by a Serbian nationalist while visiting Sarajevo.

Shortly after the assassination, Austria-Hungary declared war on Serbia. I could understand that but it baffled me when Germany seemed to use that unfortunate event as a stepping stone to enter into conflict with the rest of the world, declaring war first on Russia and then on France.

On August 4th, Germany decided to take their battle a step further when they invaded Belgium. This caused Great

Britain to enter the fray, issuing an ultimatum to Germany, giving them until 8:00 that night to pull out of Belgium or they would find themselves in combat with the British. That was all Fletcher knew when he came home that afternoon. We later learned that Great Britain did indeed declare war on Germany when they let the deadline pass without withdrawing their troops. Eventually, the whole world would be involved in World War I, or the Great War as it was sometimes called. Four years later, after it was over, President Woodrow Wilson referred to it as the War to End All Wars in a speech and that name caught on. It was, to my way of thinking, a purely wishful phrase; the only war that would end all wars was one that wiped out the whole of mankind.

The night before that fateful day, Fletcher convinced me it would be better to tear down our house and start new. He had originally planned to simply rebuild the front part of the house that had been demolished by the tree falling on it but changed his mind and told me it would be as easy to build a completely new house than to try to fix what was left. I, imagining months and months of living either in the barn or in one of the slave cabins, protested his decision. For all the good it did me. One thing about my husband, he was a world-class horse-trader and could talk an Eskimo into building a front porch on his igloo so he'd have a place to sit and enjoy the nice weather.

And when he started explaining why he wanted to build a new house, it didn't take long before I was nodding my head in agreement and anticipating evenings spent on my new front porch much like that imagined Eskimo. Fletcher showed me the plans he'd drawn up, pointing out all the advantages to doing it his way. And with each one he listed, it became harder and harder to disagree with him.

First, he pointed to the weather, chiefly the fact that our little branch of Cedar Creek had almost flooded during the four days of heavy thunderstorms that followed the freak storm which demolished the front of our cabin. If he built a new house, he planned to construct it so that the floor wouldn't be flush against the ground but elevated slightly.

That way, we could have real floors, even some of that new-fangled linoleum in the kitchen, instead of rough wooden planks that I had to sweep and sometimes mop every day.

He would add a few more windows, making it easier to keep the house cool in the summer heat and bringing in welcome sunshine during the winter. The walls would be smooth instead of bumpy and we could paint them. "Why," he said, "you can even have wallpaper if you want, Bess."

The list went on and on and fairly soon I was leaning in the direction he wanted me to. And when he said it wouldn't take any longer to build the new house than it would to fix the old one, I relented. To cap off his victory, he told me he planned to build the new house in pieces, starting with the front half first and then tearing down the back and rebuilding it when that was finished.

I admit, I didn't fully understand how it could be done but I had faith in my husband. After all, I saw what he had been able to do with the old barn every time I walked outside. And when he said he wanted to put clapboard on the outside, well, I decided not to protest and let him do it. I would be thrilled to have a house without walls made of rough logs and set to dreaming about what color we would paint the outside.

By the time we went to bed, he had a list of what he needed from town to start the project and the next morning was up with the sun and raring to go. He hitched our two red mules to the wagon, kissed me good-bye and left right after daybreak to go to Old Fort and pick up the supplies. I went out to water Elisi's cedar tree to the steady clip-clop of the mules' hooves moving over the bridge in front of the house. Fletcher waved and called, "Be back soon as I can, Bessie-girl."

I waved back and called out, "Safe trip, Fletch," my standard farewell from the many times I'd watched Papa leave for Marshall or on one of his other business trips. It made me feel a little teary-eyed remembering that. It also felt right somehow, carrying on that tradition with my husband as he left our home.

Never dreaming what he would bring back with him, I

went about my daily routine. Today, being Tuesday, meant I needed to set my irons to heating and get busy with pressing the clothes I had washed the day before. Ironing wasn't so much of a chore as washing, and truth be told, one I enjoyed much more. It wasn't back-breaking by any means, and though the heat could be a problem in the hottest part of the summer, it was always a pleasure to me to smooth the wrinkles out of my linens and our clothes. Ironing was one of those tasks that gave you a sense of satisfaction to see that growing stack of freshly-pressed clothing.

I expected Fletcher back around mid-afternoon that day but, as it turned out, he arrived home much later. Town had been hopping with the news of what was happening in England and Europe, and when he finally started home, he was detained by another of the ferocious thunderstorms that seemed to happen daily that summer ever since lightning struck our house. Halfway up the mountain, he caught sight of smoke pouring from the trees and, when he went to investigate, found the Berryhills standing in the field beside their house watching as it burned to the ground. The storm clouds, while not producing any measurable rain, had packed enough lightning to strike their tiny house in several places. Like ours, theirs was a log cabin and, also like ours, the walls had been as dry as a pile of tinder.

With a crack of thunder and a flash of lightning, they lost near everything they had and my tenderhearted husband just couldn't stand to leave them there. They were left with hardly more than the clothes on their backs and those Mrs. Berryhill had gathered together in a large flour sack and set on her kitchen table as she ironed. When the lightning struck, she'd grabbed the sack and one of her flat irons and ran for the front porch where Mr. Berryhill had been napping in his rocker.

When Fletcher pulled up, the Berryhills were sitting beside him on the seat of the wagon. I didn't ask any questions, just walked over to the mules and held their harnesses as Fletcher helped the old man and woman down, both looking as if they'd been through a war.

Mrs. Berryhill, normally a soft, billowy sort of woman with

shiny dark hair streaked through with silver and a delicate musical laugh that always made me think of Mama's and Aunt Belle's voices drifting down the hall at our house in Hot Springs, clutched a handkerchief in her fisted hand, crying softly. Mr. Berryhill, a rotund, stately looking man with a full head of flowing white hair, patted her on the back, mumbling nonsensical words in an effort to calm his wife.

It was one of the few times I had seen Hoyt Berryhill without a smile on his face. He had a booming laugh and loved to tell tall tales to anyone who would sit and listen. He always ended his stories with, "Ain't that right, Miss Maudie?" To which she would always reply, "Wuss than that, Little Berry, wuss than that." And then they'd look at each other and laugh. It was obvious to me theirs was a love that, while it may have mellowed over the years, had grown with each day and was stronger now than when they first came together. A love that would, I often thought, survive even death.

When Fletcher helped Mrs. Berryhill down, she stood on shaky legs and continued to cry. Fletcher looked at me helplessly. Like many men, a crying woman always bewildered him. I put my arm around Mrs. Berryhill's shoulders and led her to the oak tree in the front yard where we'd placed the rocking chairs from the front porch, murmuring a few nonsensical words of my own. Things like, "There, there," and "Shh, don't take on so, Mrs. Berryhill," platitudes that seem to fall from people's mouths when they want to help but aren't sure what's wrong or what to do about it.

I led her to one of the rockers and eased her down then knelt before her, taking her handkerchief from her hand and replacing it with my own dry one.

Mr. Berryhill came and sat in the other rocker, reaching out to pat her on the shoulder. "Here now, Miss Maudie, you'll make yourself sick crying like that. We're alive and that's all that matters."

I looked up at Fletch. "What in the world happened?"

Fletch shook his head. "Their house burned to the ground. They don't have anything left and need somewhere to stay. I told them they could have one of the old cabins until we can get their house rebuilt."

"Well, of course they can, that isn't a problem." I took Mrs. Berryhill's hands in mine and pulled them away from her face. When she looked at me, I gave her a reassuring smile. "We'd love to have you stay with us, Miss Maudie," I said, using Mr. Berryhill's pet name for her. "We're delighted to have you and I hope you know you're welcome to stay for as long as you like. I'm just sorry we don't have better than one of those old shacks to offer you. Still, we'll fix it up right comfortable, you and I, and Fletch and Mr. Berryhill will see to the roof and outside so you'll be as snug as a bug in a rug."

She blew her nose daintily, squared her shoulders and tried out a smile. "That's right nice of you, Bessie." She looked up at Fletch. "And you too, Fletcher. We'll do our best not to impose too much on your hospitality."

When the tears threatened again, Fletcher cleared his throat. "No thanks needed, Mrs. Berryhill." He wrung the brim of his hat in his hands as she buried her face in the handkerchief and sobbed.

"Merciful heavens, Mrs. Berryhill—Maude," I said, drawing her attention back to me, "what are neighbors for if not to help each other in times of trouble?" I patted her hand and looked at Mr. Berryhill intently, hoping he'd get the message I conveyed with my eyes. "Can you tell me what happened, Mr. Berryhill?"

He scratched his chin and nodded as the twinkle came back to his eyes. I knew he'd gotten the message; embellish the telling as much as possible and maybe that would bring a smile to his wife's face.

"I reckon I can, Miss Bessie," he said and launched into a tall tale that would have made the devil laugh. The fury of the lightning spearing out of the sky had near blinded him, the heat and ferocity of the fire would have put Hell itself to shame, "Why even standing way far out in the field, it nearly peeled the skin from my bones," the speed with which the house burned, "there one minute, gone the next," had "flat-out flummoxed my brain" and when the trees around the house caught fire, "there weren't nothin' God nor all his angels could do 'cept stand there and watch her burn."

I silently blessed his heart when he took his wife's hand and ended the telling with the words, "Ain't that right, Miss Maudie?"

Her lips twitched as she wiped her cheeks. She blew her nose and then smiled at him. "Wuss than that, Little Berry, wuss than that."

That's when I knew it would be all right. "Why don't you come into the kitchen with me and we'll make us some tea. When Fletch finishes unloading the wagon, he and Mr. Berryhill can go take a look and find a suitable cabin for y'all to stay in...unless you'd like to do the choosing yourself."

She smiled at her husband. "I guess I can trust Little Berry to find a fittin place for us to stay. We're much obliged to you and Fletch, Bessie. I don't know how we can ever repay you."

I stood up and put my hands on my hips. "Mercy sakes, Maude Berryhill, you hush now. There'll be no talk of repaying because there's no need. We're just doing what any Christian neighbor would do." I winked at Fletch. "Sides, I'm sure Fletch is looking forward to hearing more of Mr. Berryhill's tall tales. I know I am. Friendship and fellowship are all we ask in return except..." I narrowed my eyes and turned to look at Mr. Berryhill. "Hoyt Berryhill, I only have one rule you need to follow."

He harrumphed. "Just like a woman, always settin rules for men to follow." He shook his head. "Well, let's hear it, Miss Bessie, and I'll see if I can oblige you."

I pointed a finger at him. "You spit that wad of tobacco out when you come inside and sit down at my table. I might only have half a house right now but there'll be no spitting at the table or anywhere else in my home."

His booming laugh teased a smile out of me but I did my best to contain it.

He shook his head. "You and Miss Maudie, what is it you women folk have against a good chaw? I bet you don't let them young'uns at school get away with nothin, do you?"

"No, I don't and don't try to distract me. The rule is no

spitting in the house and it isn't the chaw I object to. Lord knows, you're entitled to your pleasures and it's not for me to tell you not to indulge. That's between you and God but I don't cotton to the expectorating of tobacco juice in my home. No spitting inside, you hear?"

"I ain't deaf, Miss Bessie, and I reckon I can last through mealtime without a chaw in my jaw. Maudie don't allow no chewing at her table either."

"All right, then. I reckon we'll get on without any problems." I held out my hand to Mrs. Berryhill. "Come along with me, Maude, and we'll have us some of that fancy English tea Fletcher brought home from Old Fort the other day. Mr. Berryhill, you should go on around back with Fletch. I'm sure he could use some help unloading that wagon and when you're finished you two can go and see if one of those cabins will work for you and your wife."

Mr. Berryhill hoisted his round body out of the rocker, hitched his pants and expanded his chest. "Well, now, Miss Bessie, my rheumatiz's been actin up but I'll do what I can to help."

"Well, now, Mr. Hoyt, I'm sure Fletcher can find something for you to do that won't devil that rheumatiz any. Think you can handle a box or two of nails?"

"I reckon I could."

I nodded. "Well, then, go around to the back and get to it. When you're finished, I'll make you some Stinging Nettle leaf tea that will take care of that rheumatism. Come along, Maude, I need to check on the chicken I have in the stew pot. Oh, Mr. Berryhill," I called sweetly, hoping to ensure my husband a little help, "supper will be chicken and dumplings, and the sooner your chores are finished, the sooner you can eat."

With that, I led Mrs. Berryhill around the back of the house and into the kitchen.

The next day at church, we could still see black smoke rising in the air from the direction of the Berryhills' house. Fletch watched it for a moment, shaking his head. "Fire's still burning," he told Mr. Berryhill.

"Oh, you reckon so?" he said, scratching at the back of

his neck. "How you know it ain't out yet?"

"'Cause the smoke ain't white. I reckon that thunderstorm we had last night didn't put it out completely."

Reverend Redmon, inspired by the foul-smelling air, had the windows to the church propped open and he preached a powerful sermon about hellfire and brimstone and the importance of accepting Jesus Christ into your life. Pacing in front of the pulpit with one hand raised in the air and his eyes on Thorney Dalton and pointing at the smoke outside the window, he ended his sermon with the warning that those who weren't saved in the eyes of the Lord would be damned to an eternity of the same.

Reverend Redmon had been trying ever since he'd come to Stone Mountain to get Thorney and his sons baptized but Thorney had been adamant all these years that he didn't see the sense of it. "Hell," he would say, "you dunkin my head in some water ain't gonna make no difference. Way I see it, God knows I'm His and He won't bar me from the gates of Heaven when I die." He had allowed Mrs. Dalton to have the girls baptized seeing as how "womenfolk were weaker than men" but he'd held out for years when it came to him and his boys.

The fire on the mountain and the open church windows finally did the trick. Thorney stood up and walked down to the pulpit, his boys trailing along behind him to accept the Lord into their lives.

Half the congregation muffled their laughter behind handkerchiefs or their hands and the other half sat in stunned silence. Sitting at the organ, I shuffled through my music and chose a fairly new hymn, "Joy Among the Angels", playing and singing the words softly as Thorney and his boys made their way down the aisle. It was, judging by the self-satisfied look on Reverend Redmon's face, a joyous occasion and most likely one of the high points of his preaching career.

After church was dismissed, we gathered outside and I knew exactly how Reverend Redmon felt. Most of the congregation had come bearing gifts for the Berryhills, clothes, dishes, pots and pans, and numerous quilts and blankets. I had given them some extra linens and quilts the day before to make a pallet on the floor until we could get them a bed. Fletcher's brother Doc and his wife Laura had a wagonload of furnishings, including a bed. Laura's mother had recently passed away and she needed somewhere to put the furniture she didn't have room for in her own home.

The generous nature of the people and the way neighbors looked out for each other, particularly when someone was in need were, to me, two of the best things about living on the mountain.

But, as I was to find out in the near future, it wasn't always that way and their concern and care did not extend to every person on the mountain. There were certain circumstances where they turned their heads and looked away knowing full well one of their neighbors was in dire need of help.

CHAPTER FOUR

Summer 1915

Lower than a snake's belly in a wagon rut.

Fletcher, with the help of neighbors and friends, was able to finish the house before I went back to school in the fall of 1914. It was, as he had promised, beautiful and so much more comfortable than our cabin. The next spring, he built a full front porch running the width of the house with the promised swing on one end, a couple of rocking chairs, and a garden of flowers and herbs spilling out of containers.

I had practically worn the Burpee catalog out when it arrived back in February, dreaming over the pages filled with colorful flowers, tasty vegetables and luscious fruit. I even ordered a few seeds though, for the most part, Fletcher and I took seeds from the garden each year and saved them over the winter to be planted in the spring. And, if there was a plant we didn't have in our vegetable and flower gardens, it never hurt to ask our neighbors, particularly the women, before ordering from a catalog. Seeds and cuttings were often traded or simply given away among the mountain folk.

To go along with my abiding love for growing vegetation was an intense hatred for weeding. But one went with the other so early one summer morning, with the dew still glistening on the grass like tiny crystals on a bed of green velvet, I forced myself out the door, hoe in hand, determined to rid our garden of the weeds which seemed to grow twice as fast and as dense as the vegetables. I took a moment to appreciate the sky, a pretty cerulean blue with white wispy clouds drifting across like dandelion seeds floating on the wind. Thanking God for such a pretty sight, I resigned myself to the task at hand and set to work.

I had found that focusing on other things made the work go faster, so as I moved along the first row of plants, ignoring the grasshoppers springing up in alarm when I neared, my mind settled on the slaves who once worked this land, which was only natural since I had heard them the night before shuffling along beside our house, singing in their soft, sad melodious voices. Although I had never seen them, I had a good sense of what they may have looked like and many times wished there was some way I could convey to them that their slavery was a stain upon our nation that would never go away no matter what cleansing efforts were made to remedy this wrongness. I sighed. It seemed to be the way of this world. Look at what had been done to my people, the Cherokee, who had been forced to pledge never to speak of or claim their heritage in order to remain in the mountains. And the Melungeons, ostracized even more than the Cherokee and Negroes and used as a means to make children behave by threatening them with the Melungeon boogie-man. Two more wrongs that could never be atoned.

The sound of a jingling harness drifted my way as I worked between the tomato plants, and I straightened up, shading my eyes with my hand. I spotted a wagon pulled by a horse that looked worn and bedraggled traveling over the bridge. A tall, thin man held the reins in his hands and beside him, huddled into herself, was a woman with what looked to be dirty blond hair partially covered by a shawl she had wrapped around her even though the day was beginning to give in to the fierce heat that would settle in once the sun got far enough above the mountains to shine down on us. As the wagon drew nearer, I counted five children in the bed, bouncing along with its movement. Could that be Sally Laughter, I wondered. Sally had been to see me a good while ago, asking for something that would keep her from having anymore babies, and I'd given her Queen Anne's lace seeds and told her where to find them. She had begged me not to tell her husband, claiming he wouldn't understand, and I'd assured her I didn't discuss my patients with anyone, not even my own husband.

The man's posture changed when he spied me among the plants, his head rising above his shoulders like a turtle peeking out of its shell, making him appear even taller and skinnier than he had at first notice. I stepped out from between the rows and waited for the wagon to stop, wondering what the entire family had come here for. Were they all sick and in need of medicine? But something seemed very strange about the way Sally sat, head hanging, eyes downcast, her arms wrapped around herself as if shielding her body from some unknown danger.

The man drew back on the reins and said something undecipherable to the horse and it stopped on command, standing still with a miserable look. Its hair was coated with dried mud and its mane and tail tangled and dirty. I could count each rib and wondered how in the world a horse could starve with so much grass and fauna in abundance on the mountain.

I watched who I presumed to be Sally's husband set the brake on the wagon and swing down off the seat. I stepped closer to Sally, saying, "Good morning to you, Sally. It's awful good to see you and your babies." She didn't respond, only clutched the shawl tighter around her face. "What in the world are you doing with that shawl wrapped around you on such a hot day? Are you ailing?"

"You the one they call Moonfixer?" the man said, stepping around the horse and stalking toward me.

I noticed the distressed look in Sally's eyes as she raised her gaze to meet mine. She barely shook her head at me before glancing away.

I turned to face the man. "I'm Bessie Elliott. And you are?"

"I'm her husband, that's who I am."

I looked him over, noting his tattered clothing, unshaven

face, the hard press of his lips as he glared at me, and thought rather unchristianly, why, he's so skinny it looks like he traded legs with a wasp and got cheated out of the stinger. Ignoring him, I turned to Sally once more. "Why don't you and your young'uns come on in and have something cold to drink, Sally? It's awful hot out here and I imagine you must be miserable in this heat."

She sat up straight, the shawl falling away from her face, and I gasped with shock. A large bruise covered her right cheek, all yellow and purple and blue, and her nose was so swollen it looked like a large mass of pulp sitting in the middle of her face. Her lips were puffy and broken open and I imagined it must hurt like the dickens to try to talk or eat.

"Mercy, Sally, what happened to you?" I reached for her, saying to her husband, "Help me get her down from there. She looks to be awful hurt."

"You don't touch her," the man shouted at me. "You done enough damage as it is."

The children in the bed of the wagon cringed and seemed to fold into themselves, much like Sally. A small girl who looked to be five or six began to whimper.

"What in the world are you talking about?" I stared at him and knew in an instant what had happened to Sally. When I spoke, my voice was low and harsh. "You did this to her."

"She only got what she had comin." He turned to the side and spat a stream of tobacco juice on the ground.

I touched Sally's skirt. "Sally, come on inside and let me treat those wounds. I know you must be hurting something fierce."

Her husband stepped between us and I searched my memory for his name. Was it Nate?

"You keep away from her," he said. "We don't want none of your help."

I glared at him. "Then what do you want…Nate, is it? Is that your given name? Seems to me you came here for a reason and I'd sure like to know what it is without all this blustering and bullying you seem to favor."

He hesitated, something flickering in his eyes, and I realized this man was not used to being challenged, especially by a woman.

"State your business then go your way," I said in as strong a voice as I could manage, wondering where Fletcher was if things got out of control.

His mouth moved and he opened and closed his fists several times and I thought, you're nothing but a bully and I've dealt with my fair share, including those evil Red Shirts, and you don't scare me. I arched my eyebrows. "Well?"

When he spoke, his voice was low and choked. "I come here to find out what you give my wife to keep her from catchin."

"Catching?"

"She ain't had a baby in two years now and I heared a rumor on this mountain that you been helpin women who don't want no more babies." A toddler with golden blond hair and big blue eyes stood up in the bed of the wagon, sniffling and wiping at his nose. Nate pointed one long finger at him and said, "Sit down or you won't be able to for a month of Sundays." The child immediately dropped onto his backside and my fists clenched with anger.

I tried to keep the words from passing my lips but could not. "So it's not enough that you bully and beat on your wife, you have to do it to small, innocent, defenseless children?" I spat at his feet. "You're not a man, you're a beast and you should be ashamed of yourself."

His face turned red and I gripped my hoe handle tighter, thinking if he came for me, he wouldn't leave without some sort of injury.

He noticed the movement of my hand, his eyes darting to the hoe and back to me. "She won't tell me what she's been takin to keep from havin anymore young'uns and I'm here to tell you she don't need your help no more and if I hear you been helpin her, why, I'll—"

"You'll what, Mr. Laughter? There's not a thing you can do to me even if I was helping your wife, which is no business of yours or anyone else's. And why in the world do you want another mouth to feed?" I blatantly looked at his tattered shirt and britches, the emaciated horse, the children in the back of the wagon who wore dirty, ragged clothing.

"Looks to me like you can't take care of the ones you do have."

"I reckon I take care of 'em well enough. Ain't lost one yet." He pointed at the bed of the wagon. "Them young'uns is what keeps us alive. I need 'em to work my farm, tend to my garden, take care of my animals. And the more young'uns I got, the more can git done."

"While you do what, sit on the porch and bluster? You look fit enough, why aren't you working your farm?"

His jaw clenched and he moved toward me. I brought the hoe up, ready to strike him if he touched me.

Behind me, Fletcher said, "You take one more step toward my wife and I'll kill you." I tried not to let the relief I felt show on my face as I looked at Fletcher, walking toward us with Fritz at his heels, growling low in his throat.

When Fletcher reached me, he grasped my arm and drew me slightly behind him. Fritz stepped up next to Fletcher and bared his teeth at Sally's husband, another barrier for my protection. Although well advanced in age, I knew Fritz to be a loyal dog, one who would gladly give his life for Fletch or me, and I have to admit I felt much the same for him. Fletcher's rifle rested in the crook of his elbow. When he spoke, his voice was low and hard. "I reckon you better get back in that wagon and get on out of here. I don't cotton to anyone threatening my wife."

"Sally," I said, "why don't you get down from there and let me take care of you?"

She gave a furtive glance toward her husband then shook her head.

"You and your children can stay here, Sally. You don't need to go with him. We've got room and food enough for you all."

Oh, the look on her face as she considered this, filled with hope and desire before Nate spoke. "You want her? You can have her, she's no-count anyways, but you ain't taking my young'uns. You don't got the right to take a man's young'uns from him."

I watched Sally's face fall, the look of despair come back into her eyes. "I'm going to report you to Sheriff Nanny, Mr.

Laughter," I said. "These children and your wife don't deserve to be treated this way."

He cursed under his breath. "My family belongs to me and I got the right to do any damn thing I want to them, and I don't reckon there's nothin you or nobody else can do about it, includin the sheriff. And I'm gonna tell you again, you better not be helpin my wife to keep from whelpin or there'll be hell to pay."

"You threaten my wife one more time and you're gonna feel my fist against your teeth," Fletcher said, his voice a low growl. The hackles on Fritz's back rose and he showed his teeth again, emitting a low rumbling sound as Fletch stepped closer to Nate. "You want your wife and children to see you bested? See what a coward you really are? Say one more word."

Nate looked at Fletcher and I watched fear flicker in his eyes. He turned and glared at Sally. "Well, make up your mind, woman. You stayin here? If so, get down off'n the wagon but I better not see you on my property or I'll shoot you for trespassin."

Fletcher made a disgusted sound in his throat. Nate straightened at that and I watched as he hurriedly walked around the horse and began to climb in the wagon.

"Sally, come with me," I said. "We'll take care of you, help you get your children away from him, give you a place to stay."

She glanced at her husband, then to the children behind her, and leaned down to me, speaking in a whisper. "Oh, Miss Bess, don't you understand? If he don't have me to beat up on, he'll do it to my young'uns. I can't leave 'em by theyselves with him."

"Do you want me to talk to Sheriff Nanny? See if he can help y'all?"

"Best not." She darted a look at her husband, staring at her. "I reckon I'm fine enough, Miss Bess," she said in a loud voice. "I'll just go on home with my husband and young'uns. Don't you worry about me, everything will be all right."

Nate flicked the reins against the horse's scrawny back and it began to lumber away.

My heart skipped a beat as I watched the wagon cross the small bridge over the creek, a gray cloud hovering above Sally and her husband. I had seen a cloud similar to this before, oh, yes, but at that time it had been black and foretold death. But gray ... even so, I knew this to be an ominous sign. I grasped Fletcher's hand. "Oh, Fletch, I fear what he's going to do to her once he gets her home. I can see danger there."

"A man like that's a danger to himself and everyone around him." Fletcher shook his head. "I swear, ain't nothing lower than a man beats his wife, young'uns or animals. Makes me want to pound him senseless." He patted my hand. "But she chose to go with him, Bess. Ain't nothing you can do about that now except pray for her."

"I'm still going to talk to Sheriff Nanny, see if he can't do anything about Nate Laughter."

"I sure hope so, Bess, but I fear he's right. They're his family, they belong to him."

"We'll see."

I took Sheriff Nanny's presence at Stone Mountain Baptist Church the next day to be a good sign. As sheriff, he rarely attended church, too busy dealing with the aftermath of Saturday night drunkards to spend Sunday mornings in worship. As the congregation milled about afterwards, visiting with one another, I managed to catch his attention and asked if I might speak with him in private.

"Why sure, Moonfixer," he said with a smile. He led me outside to the shade of a large oak tree and I thought ironically it was the same one Bull Elliott and Possum Gilliam had pulled me behind to confide what they'd done to that evil Orson Belle after he and his Red Shirts had killed George. "What can I do for you?" Sheriff asked, taking off his hat and wiping moisture off his forehead with the back of his shirt sleeve.

I relayed to him Nate Laughter's visit to our farm and his threats and mine back to him. "Can you do something for Sally, Sheriff? I'm fearful he's going to kill her one day." I didn't tell him about the gray cloud I saw hovering over Sally and Nate and would later regret keeping that information from him.

Sheriff Nanny's face grew grim. "You ain't the first that's told me about his mean ways." He shook his head. "Others have witnessed poor Sally's bruised face and heard the way he talks to her and them kids. He even broke her arm once, I've been told. I've paid him a visit more than a time or two, told him the way of the world, that he ain't got the right to beat on his wife like he does, but Sally always tells it different, says she fell or bumped into something and that's why she's all bruised up and hurt. When I asked her about her arm, she said she tripped over a chair leg and hit it against the side of the fireplace and broke it." He shrugged. "I can tell she's scared of him, what he might do to her if she tells the truth, but until she makes the accusation, there's nothing I can do, and I can't tell you how frustrating that can be. That Nate Laughter's nothing but a no-count, lazy bastid who needs someone to knock his feet out from under him."

"You can't legally do anything?"

He lifted his shoulders. "Well, there is legal precedent. The North Carolina Supreme Court ruled that a man ain't got the right to chastise his wife and I've told Nate that but Sally has to claim he's done the damage before I can arrest him."

"Well, at least the Supreme Court has ruled on this," I said. "Maybe we can talk her into accusing him of abuse. It's worth a try."

Sheriff snorted. "Them jurists didn't do much by way of making that ruling. They went on to qualify it by stating it'd be better if the husband and wife worked things out for themselves 'stead of making it a concern of the law."

My hands itched with frustration. "A ruling made solely by men, I'm sure."

"Well, you're right there, Moonfixer. I reckon it might help things if we let women influence our legal judgments, although I got to tell you, I don't see that happening in the near future. Look at the fight you women have got on your hands just to get the right to vote."

"That's one fight I support fully, Sheriff."

"Figured you would, Bess, right along with my sweet

wife." Who must have caught his eye because he looked that way and nodded. "Speaking of, I reckon I'm needed for something or other." He stuffed his hat back on his head. "I've got my eyes on Nate Laughter, Moonfixer, don't you think I don't, and the minute he steps out of line in my presence, he'll be spending a good amount of time in my jail. That I promise you." With a final nod, he strode away.

CHAPTER FIVE

Summer 1915

Her face looked like 9 days of bad weather.

The air in the house seemed hotter than that outside, so I took my fried chicken, sliced tomatoes and biscuit to the porch and settled in my chair, placing a tin cup of buttermilk on the floor by my feet. I darted my eyes around, making sure no one was nearby to see, then gingerly raised the skirt of my dress to just below my knees, sighing as the air swirled around my legs, thinking I just might take off my shoes in a moment and, after I finished this fine meal, go down to the creek and wade a bit.

As I ate, I tried to recall the dream I'd had about Sally Laughter the night before that at the time seemed so ominous and alarming but had vanished when I woke. As the morning wore on, snatches of the nightmare drifted through my mind, and when I would try to seize them, they would vanish, leaving behind a feeling of something terribly wrong. I hoped Fletcher got back from cutting lumber before nightfall, as I felt an urgent need to go to Sally's cabin to make sure she was all right but didn't feel safe going by myself, with the way Nate felt about me.

Fritz pressed his nose against my arm, giving me an expectant look. "Well, I guess I've eaten enough of this chicken, old boy," I said and began feeding him my leftovers. A horse's loud snort drew my attention and I looked toward the dirt road, sighing with disappointment when I saw Sheriff Nanny riding his sorrel toward me. Fritz glanced that way, gave a lazy wag of his tail, and returned to his meal. I eased my skirt down my legs and placed an expectant smile on my face, wondering what brought him out this way on such a hot and miserable day. Then remembered my dream last night and thought I knew.

He drew back on the reins and tipped his hat at me. "Mornin, Moonfixer, or is it afternoon yet?"

"Not sure, Sheriff, but I'm hoping it's afternoon so this heat won't hang around much longer." I studied his face. "Something's happened?"

He grimaced. "I need you to come with me to the jailhouse, if you don't mind. It's – it's Sally Laughter. She's hurt bad. I offered to go get Doc Widby but she's asking for you, says she won't let nobody treat her but you."

I had risen to my feet while he talked. "I'll get some herbs together and be right back. There's water or buttermilk inside if you're thirsty," I called over my shoulder as I rushed through the door.

"I'll saddle your mare while you get your things," he said.

In the kitchen, I set the kettle on to boil then hurried to the bedroom for my medicine bag. Back in the kitchen, I went to my herb shelf and began pulling jars and tins of medicines, packing them in the small valise, stuffing rags around the glass jars to keep them from breaking, my thoughts flashing, finally remembering last night's nightmare, thinking, Nate's the one who got himself killed, thank God it wasn't Sally. Once the water was boiling, I poured it into a glass jar and added willow bark, figuring it'd be good and steeped by the time we got to the jail.

When I stepped outside, my mare stood next to the sheriff's horse, both looking miserable in the sun. I petted Fritz, told him to stay, hooked my bag over the saddle horn and allowed the sheriff to boost me up into the saddle, then waited for him to mount.

As we trotted down the road at a fast clip, I asked,

"Where's Nate?"

He shook his head. "Dead. Sally bashed his skull in with an iron skillet."

"Well, that doesn't really surprise me, Sheriff, not after the way he's treated her and those young'uns of theirs."

"Me neither, just hate I'm gonna have to hold her for trial."

Shock coursed through my body. "You arrested her? Surely you don't think she deliberately killed him, Sheriff. I'm certain it must have been self-defense."

"She tells it different, Moonfixer."

I stared at him. "She confessed?"

"Says she's the one who killed him. But I think I'll let her tell you herself what happened, if you don't mind. Be easier all the way around if she does. As sheriff, I don't need to hear it again." He rubbed his hand over his face. "Might be I misheard her the first time, if you get my meaning."

I nodded, thinking not for the first time we were awful blessed to have a sheriff who was willing to give a woman the benefit of the doubt. I knew there were men in authority who would have strung her up at the first chance for killing a man even though that man might have deserved such a fate.

"How did you find out?" I asked.

"Sally showed up at the jail on that raggedy ol' horse of theirs. She was so hurt she could hardly hold on. It's a wonder to me she managed to ride down the mountain like that but she somehow did. I helped her down, asked her what happened and she told me she reckoned I best get on up to their cabin and see to Nate, that she'd..." He glanced my way. "She asked me to fetch you on my way back. I left her in Otis's care and took their horse with me. Made sure Ned was dead then came straight to your place. She's hurt bad, Moonfixer. I sure hope you can help her."

"Who's taking care of Sally's children, Sheriff?"

"They weren't home when I got there. Sally said she sent 'em down the mountain to her ma's place with her oldest son before Nate got home so she could talk to him about..." He hesitated then continued "Well, I'll let her tell you. She said her ma'd take care of 'em till Sally comes back home."

"And the children, did they see...?"

"No. Sally made sure they were gone before it happened. I don't even know if they're aware what she did yet though I suspect they might have figured it out."

When we arrived at the small jail, I slid off my horse and hurried inside, leaving the care of my lathering mare to Sheriff Nanny. I found Sally lying on a small cot inside the first of the two jail cells, Deputy Otis, cousin to Thorney Dalton, standing outside with a worried look on his face. When he saw me, he opened the door to her cell with a grateful nod. I hurried inside and knelt beside the bed.

"I reckon I'll be a-heading up to Sally's place till Sheriff can get back up there," Otis said. He waved his hand at a damp cloth plastered to Sally's forehead. "Wasn't sure what could be done for her but figured that wouldn't hurt."

"You did fine. Thank you, Otis."

Sally opened her eyes when I removed the cloth and placed the back of my hand against her forehead, the only part of her face that wasn't bruised or bloody. So far, no fever, I noted with relief.

"I was prayin he'd find you," she said, her voice raspy.

"I'm here, Sally. I see he got your face, he hit you anywhere else?"

She shifted a bit, wincing with pain. "He kicked me in the stomach a few times. Don't think he caught a rib this time. Least it don't hurt to breathe like it did afore."

"You coughing up blood? Feel heat in your abdomen or back?"

Tears sprung to her eyes. "I hurt all over, Miss Bessie. He was good and mad." She turned on her side to face me and I tried not to let concern show as I studied her damaged face.

"Oh, Sally, you didn't deserve this." I opened my bag, began removing jars and tinctures. "I'll help you feel better, Sally, I promise." I poured willow bark tea into a tin cup and offered it to her. "Drink this. It'll help with the pain."

She dutifully drank the tea, although it took a while. Her lips were so swollen, it was an effort to get the liquid into her mouth. I blotted the excess off her chin and neck when she finished, then applied St. John's wort soaked in vinegar to a laceration on her arm, relieved when the bleeding began to slow.

She waited until I put the rag down and looked at her. "I killed him," she said, her voice strong.

I glanced out the jail cell, hoping Sheriff Nanny wasn't around to hear this, even though she had already told him so. "You don't need to be talking about that right now, Sally. Someone might hear."

"I don't care who hears me, Miss Bessie. He deserved what I done to him." Tears tracked down her cheeks. "Found out he's been at my oldest girl, that's what did it." She shook her head. "I could handle the things he done to me, figurin it kept him away from my young'uns but when I found out he's been..." her mouth worked for a moment "...touching my Emily, I knew there weren't no other way except to make sure he never did it again." She swallowed, grimacing with pain as she shifted. "I meant to kill him, I surely did, but I don't remember it, Miss Bessie. I recall him laying on the bed passed out drunk and I just went away, I guess. When I come to myself, I was standing over him with my big ol' iron skillet all bloody and his ugly, vile face just, just gone." She sighed when I put a decoction of tobacco roots on her cheeks to control the inflammation. "I'm glad I done it, even though I might go to Hell right alongside of him."

"You protected your children, Sally, nobody can blame you for that. And you won't go to Hell for sending someone there who should have been there a long time ago."

She put the back of her hand against her mouth, trying to control the sobs.

I smoothed her hair back off her face. "Let it go, Sally, crying helps sometimes." I tended her as she wept, biting back my own tears, fearful for what would happen to this poor young woman who felt she had no other choice but to kill a man who deemed it his right to beat and brutalize his wife and children. And what would become of all those children? Would her mother feel up to caring for them if Sally was found guilty of murder and imprisoned, or even worse? But I couldn't worry about that now, not with Sally so hurt.

Sheriff Nanny returned to the jail shortly before I finished with Sally. He didn't come back to the cell area, instead remained in his small office at the front of the building. When I left, Sally had drifted off to sleep, helped along by the oat straw tea I gave her, which had a calming effect. I had managed to tend to the outside physical injuries but worried that Nate might have damaged her internal organs in some way. If he had, there was nothing to be done but wait and see and hope Doc Widby would be in town to tend to her.

Sheriff Nanny waved me into a seat when I stepped into the front office area. I sat down, wiping perspiration off my face with my apron.

"She gonna be all right?" he asked.

"Unless he did some damage internally, she'll mend well enough. He hurt her pretty badly. She's got enough bruises over her body to cover a cow. Had a deep cut on her arm which looked to be where he gouged her. I got it to stop bleeding. I left some tea that will help with the pain and help her relax but she's probably going to have a miserable night. I hope you'll excuse me for saying so, Sheriff, but that man needed killing. I'm just sorry Sally's the one that will have to pay the price."

He nodded. "I ain't gonna ask you what she said to you, Miss Bessie, but I think it'd be best if we could find a lawyer for her. There's gonna be a trial, ain't no way of gettin around that."

"But does she have to stay in jail? Her children need her and Sally can't mend very well in a jail cell, you know that as well as I do. It would be best for her to stay here tonight in case she has internal injuries. Any sort of jarring is liable to make it worse. But she'll need daily tending and I know you don't have time for that, Sheriff."

He leaned back in his chair, considering. After a few moments, he said, "Ol' Judge Hawkins is the one who decides that sort of thing but he's presiding over a trial in Graniteville, probably won't be back for a week or two. Seeing as how she needs medical attention, I reckon I can place her in your custody till she's well enough to return to jail. Maybe by then the judge will be in town and we can get her trial heard and disposed of."

Relief flooded through me and I sank against the chair. "Oh, thank you, Sheriff. I'll send Fletch with the wagon tomorrow." I smiled at him. "You have a good soul, Sheriff Nanny. I hope you know that."

"I try, Moonfixer, but I got to tell you, if I'd been in her shoes, I reckon I'd've done the same thing Sally did although a lot sooner. That man deserved what he got and more. Only wish I'd gotten the chance to deal with him so poor Sally wouldn't have to."

"I think a lot of the mountain folk will agree with you, Sheriff."

He sighed. "Exceptin for Nate's pa, Holcomb. I'm afraid we might have a problem with him."

I had only met the man once and knew of his reputation for angry outbursts and bullying ways, much like his son. It seemed the apple didn't fall far from the tree in that family. "Well, he'll just have to deal with it," I said rather brusquely as I rose to my feet. "Where might I find my sweet horse, Sheriff? I'm afraid Fletcher's going to be worried about me and I best be getting home to him."

He pushed his chair back and stood. "I had Otis brush her down for you and give her some water. She's tied up in the shade back of the jail."

As we stepped outside, I glanced up at the sky, gauging the sun's position, figuring the time to be close to four o'clock. "Will you be here in the morning when Fletcher comes?"

"I'm heading up to Sally's cabin, collect any evidence I can find, make sure Orvil's..." he squinted at me. "You know Orvil, the mortician, Bess?"

"Yes, I think so. A tall, thin man, kind of looks the part, I think."

He snorted laughter. "I need to make sure he's taken the body to his mortuary, things of that nature. I may have to go back tomorrow, but if I do, I'll make sure Otis stays behind so he can give Fletcher any help he needs." He stopped and stared at me. "I'm trusting you to keep her with you, Bessie, not let her take off for parts unknown."

"She wouldn't leave her children, Sheriff, you know that. I'll stop by her ma's place tomorrow, tell her Sally will be at our place, see if those young'uns might want to stay, too."

"You sure you're up to taking care of that many folks? Five young'uns can be a world of trouble at times."

I smiled at him. "Sheriff, you forget, I deal with three times that many most days. We'll handle it. I've got Fletcher to help if I need him."

"Fletcher's a good man, Bessie." He studied me for a moment. "Y'all are good folks. We're lucky to have you on the mountain. Don't know if anyone's told you that or not but it's the truth."

I smiled, pleased to hear this acknowledgement. "We feel the same about you, Sheriff. Not many law enforcers would be as understanding and kindhearted as you are. We're blessed to have you."

He nodded, rubbing his chin. "Just wish old man Laughter felt the same way, Bess."

I found Fletcher pacing the front porch when I arrived home. He greeted me with a worried look and followed me around back to the barn. As he helped me off Pet, I quickly told him about Sally and that I had agreed for her to stay with us.

Fletch nodded as he rubbed his chin, glancing at the sky. "Too late to go to Old Fort today to collect her. I reckon I'll take the wagon and head that way first thing in the morning."

"You don't mind, do you?"

"Nope. Just wish we'd been able to do something for Sally afore it got so out of hand."

"I know, Fletch. I'm worried about her having to face a trial and Sheriff said Nate's pa's going to be a problem for Sally."

"I reckon we'll deal with that when we have to." He took Pet's reins and began to lead her into her stall. "I'll take care of ol' Pet here, you go on in the house and splash some water on your face, Bess, you're red as them tomatoes over yonder in your garden."

I smiled, thankful I had a husband who was so caring. "I'll get supper started, Fletch. You must be starved."

"Just worried about you."

At breakfast the next morning, I told Fletcher I planned to walk over to Sally's cabin to gather some of her things and make sure her young'uns hadn't gone back home looking for their ma.

"Might make Sally feel better having her young'uns around her," Fletch said, biting into a biscuit.

"I reckon we'll see what Sally wants, but in the meantime I want to make sure they're with her ma and pa like she thinks."

I set out right after breakfast, hoping to return home before the day got too hot, thankful for the coolness beneath the trees as I tread across the mountain. Fritz accompanied me and I was glad for his companionship. He didn't seem to mind the hymns I sang as we made our way through the woods, occasionally bounding off after some scent or other. But he would always return, a happy look on his face, and not for the first time I thought what a wonder it would be to live life as a dog. To me they had a much better way of looking at life than humans did and this world just might be a right better place if we mimicked our furry friends' ways.

Sally's pa, Lucien Davis, stood in her yard, one hand holding the reins of the poor bedraggled horse that had been pulling the wagon the day Nate paid a visit to our farm, the other holding a rifle. When he spied me, he said, "Mornin, Moonfixer. You here to fetch something for Sally?"

"Good morning, Mr. Davis. Sally asked me to get a few of her things for her and I wanted to see about her children. She said you and her ma were going to take care of them but I wanted to make sure they got to your place and were welcome." I put my hand beneath the horse's coarse mane and stroked her long, elegant neck. "Sheriff Nanny's released Sally into my custody and she'll be staying with us till her trial. Her children are welcome there as well. We've got enough room and food to take care of them if you and your wife would rather."

He spat tobacco juice on the ground. "Aw, I reckon they're well enough where they're at. 'Course, it's a bit crowded but we'll get along all right. You tell Sally they're well and cared for but if she wants 'em with her, we'll bring 'em on over to your place."

"Thank you, Mr. Davis. That's good to know. Fletcher is fetching her from Old Fort as we speak."

He shook his head. "'Tis a terrible thing she done," he said in a low voice.

"I don't think she had any other choice, Mr. Davis, the way he treated her and those children."

"He was a no-good, that's for shore. I told Sally that the day she married him but he got her with child so she figured the best thing to do was to get hitched and give her baby a good and proper name." He sighed. "I shoulda done somethin, I guess, tried to stop his ways, but my old woman told me it weren't none of my business, to stay out of it. Said I might possibly make it worse on Sally and her young'uns if I interfered."

I wondered to myself if things would have been different if he had. But then Sheriff Nanny had talked to Nate several times and it hadn't seemed to help. The horse whickered softly, seeming to like the touch of my hand. "You taking this old gal here to your place?"

He shook his head. "Nah, ain't got pasture enough for her. Sides, look how sickly she is. Why, she's so weak she can hardly stand on her own feet. Nate always said she weren't good for nothing so I figured I'd take her into the woods there, put an end to her misery."

My hand froze as shock coursed through my body. "I can take her to our farm, doctor her, get her healthy. There's no need to kill her just because she's sickly."

He waved his hand at her. "She looks like she's et up with worms, no tellin what else is wrong with her. Why spend time and money on an old hoss?"

"Because she's one of God's creatures, Mr. Davis. Besides, I suspect the way she looks has more to do with the way Nate treated her than illness. Why, you can count every rib in her body and look how dirty and grubby she is.

I'd say her physical state probably comes from Nate working her to the bone and not feeding her enough to keep her in good health. I've got herbs for worms if that's what's wrong with her, some good food and good pasture for her. I'll get her healthy."

He moved tobacco around in his mouth.

"Besides, Sally might want the horse. Lord knows, she'll need her if she decides to stay and farm this place. Or sell her perhaps and get some money. It won't hurt anything for me to try to get this old gal healthy again." I rubbed my hand along the white strip on the horse's muzzle, determined to save her even if it meant shoving Mr. Davis to the ground and running off with her. "Why, I bet she's a beauty when she's all filled out."

Mr. Davis dropped the reins and stepped back. "I reckon if you've a mind to do it, you're welcome to it. Sally's always had a soft spot for animals and I reckon she might want to keep this one if she lives."

I stared in the horse's large, doe-like eyes and thought I saw a flicker of gratefulness there. I hoped she understood that I would see to it she had a better life from here on out.

"Well, I ain't gettin nothin done a-standin here. I reckon I best get on home now, get to my chores. Good day to you, Moonfixer." Mr. Davis hefted the rifle over his shoulder and took his leave. "Tell Sally we'll be down to see her directly. You can let us know if she needs anything."

"I'll do that, Mr. Davis." I looked around, found a bucket, filled it with water from the well and gave it to the horse, who slurped thirstily. Intending to bring her back with me, I'd brought along a bag with oats and corn and fed it to her, hoping it'd sustain her till I could get her home. She ate every bit, nuzzling my hand for more. I dug in my pocket and produced an apple I'd brought as a snack and fed it to her. After I tied her reins to a small sapling, leaving the bucket of water nearby in case she wanted more, I stepped inside the cabin, trying to keep my focus on finding Sally's shawl and a tintype of her young'uns she said was the dearest thing in the world to her.

The cabin was small and consisted of one room, and I

imagined it must have been awful crowded with Sally, Nate and their five children inside at one time. The table was crude and ill-made, without chairs. I noted Sally hadn't the luxury of a woodstove but had had to use the rather large fireplace to cook their meals. A wooden rocker sat before the hearth, but that was the only place in the cabin to sit except for the bed, butted up against the far wall. I tried not to look that way but it would have been impossible to miss the blood-splattered wall behind the bed and large reddish-brown splotch on the floor. The coppery-rust smell of blood clung to the room so strong that I imagined I could taste it. At least Orville had taken the body away, I consoled myself, but I could still feel the presence of something evil and vile lingering in the room. I shivered as goose bumps rose over my body and a sensation of spiders crawling up my spine overcame me. I tried to tell myself I was being over-imaginative but I knew better.

I rushed outside and breathed in the mountain air, thinking what a terrible thing it was it had taken this to stop a man from abusing his family. The horse raised her head and neighed at me, forcing my concentration on her. As I untied her, I said, "I'll take you someplace you'll be much happier, you sweet girl. We'll get you feeling good and show that old man you're worth something."

As we left, I could not stop myself from glancing behind me until I could no longer see that small, rundown cabin, expecting each time to see a bloody, faceless Nate lumbering behind me, hands outstretched, groping for me. I prayed his spirit would not linger at the cabin, especially if Sally wanted to return there with her children.

The mare trod along behind me as we made our way home, Fritz bounding along happily beside us. He seemed to take to the horse and the two would occasionally touch noses as if conversing with one another. I wondered what Fritz was telling her and hoped he was assuring her she'd be well taken care of. The trip home was a longer one as we had to stop several times for the horse to rest. But finally we were in sight of the house and Fritz ran ahead, barking loudly. Fletcher hadn't returned with Sally yet, so I led the horse into the barn and into a stall. I gave her fresh water and hay and told her after she'd had a good rest, I planned to groom her proper and see to whatever ailed her.

I was brushing down the horse when Fletcher arrived with Sally. I put down the brush and stepped into the yard to meet them, watching as Fletch helped Sally out of the wagon. Her stiff movements and grimacing expression told me she was in a lot of pain. I took her arm and guided her toward our house, saying, "I'm glad you'll be staying with us, Sally. Come on inside and I'll fix you a nice cup of tea to help ease your pain." I smiled at Fletcher as he led our mules toward the barn so he could unharness them.

"I thank you, Miss Bessie," she said, tears in her eyes.

"I imagine that wagon jostling over that rocky road didn't help any."

She wiped her face. "I'm just thankful to be out of the jail. Sheriff Nanny's a nice man and his wife Melanie was awful good to me, bringing me food and water, but I ain't never been in a jail before, all closed in like that." She looked at me, panic in her eyes. "I can't go back there. If that judge finds me guilty and sentences me…"

I patted her arm as I guided her into the kitchen and pulled out a chair. "Hush now, let's not worry about that just yet. That judge just might see things the way most of us do, that you had no choice in the matter and were only protecting yourself and your children. You concentrate on getting strong and healthy so you can tend to your young'uns and make yourself a better life."

She nodded, biting at her lip. "I'll try, Miss Bessie, I'll try hard."

I made willow bark tea for Sally and, placing the cup in her hands, urged her to drink till it was empty.

She took a sip and sighed. "Oh, this is what you brung me yesterday, Miss Bessie. It shore did help ease my pain."

"And will now," I said, moving around the kitchen, putting together lunch for her and Fletch.

Fletcher stepped into the kitchen, removing his hat and slapping it against his britches to get the dust off. "That horse Sally's?"

"Yes." I smiled. "I brought your horse back here, Sally. She looks underfed and sickly and I thought I'd doctor her and try to fatten her up in case you want to work that farm or mayhap sell her for some money."

The smile on Sally's face told me I had done the right thing. "Oh, Miss Bess, I been so worried about her. I knew Pa wouldn't want her and he ain't one to help a sickly animal, he'd just as soon shoot 'em and be done with it."

"Well, he won't shoot that sweet gal."

Her face fell. "Nate treated her so poorly. Worked her half to death and wouldn't give her hardly nothin to eat. Even kept her from grazin when she found a good enough patch." Sally sighed. "I'd sneak out sometimes and give her an apple or carrot if I had one to spell. He caught me once and made me watch while he near beat her to death."

My hands clenched, and I thought again that a man who beat on women, children and animals did not deserve life on this earth. I hoped he was in Hell, getting his just rewards. I knew that to be an unchristian thought but did not feel the least bit remorseful about it.

After lunch, Fletch and I helped Sally settle in one of the cabins across the creek. We offered her our guest room but she declined, asking instead if she might stay in a cabin by herself. "I got me some thinkin to do and some grievin and don't want to trouble you none," she said, looking embarrassed.

"It's your choice, Sally. If you change your mind, just come on over to the house," I said as I made a pallet on the floor. "Your pa said to tell you your young'uns are well and being cared for but if you'd prefer to have them here he'll bring them on down to you."

"For now, I reckon they're where they need to be." She eased into a chair at the small wooden table. "Maybe when I'm feelin a bit more pert."

"He also said to tell you they'd be down to visit you before too long."

"I miss my young'uns." She looked at me, pain in her eyes. "Do you think they'll forgive me for what I done, Miss Bessie? Do you think they'll understand?"

I sat down across from her, took her hand. "Sally, children are more perceptive than we give them credit for. I'm sure they'll understand and love you all the more for protecting them. From what I saw, Nate didn't spare any kindness for his young'uns, and that's what they'll remember. When they visit, talk to them about this, let them talk to you, and you'll see, it will be all right."

She nodded. "I can't thank you enough for your help and understanding."

Something blocked the sunlight coming through the door and I turned to see the Berryhills standing there.

"Oh, Sally, you know the Berryhills, don't you?"

Mr. Berryhill stepped inside, his eyes widening when he saw Sally's bruised face. He glanced at me, his eyebrows raised in question. I barely shook my head at him in warning and his shocked expression transformed into a smile as he looked back at Sally. "Why shore she knows us. We've known Sally since she was knee-high to a grasshopper."

Mrs. Berryhill followed her husband in, the smile on her face fading as a small gasp escaped from her lips.

Before she could say anything, I rose to my feet and stepped in front of Sally. "Sally's going to be staying with us for the next little bit." I locked gazes with Mr. Berryhill, trying to signal that Sally needed to be alone.

He nodded in acknowledgement and gave his wife a pointed look. "Well, that's right nice, ain't it, Miss Maudie?"

Maude had recovered enough to smile at Sally with warmth and welcoming. "It shore is, Little Berry. It shore will be nice having you here, Sally."

"I thank you," Sally said in a soft voice, her head turned away to hide her injuries.

Mr. Berryhill yawned with great exaggeration and took his wife's arm. "Well, Miss Maudie, I reckon it's about my naptime."

I inclined my head to the Berryhills. "I'm fixing chicken and dumplins for dinner, Hoyt, and I expect y'all to be on time."

"You can count on it, Miss Bess. Nobody makes chicken and dumplins like you." He winked at Sally. "We'll see you then, Sally."

I watched them leave then turned back to Sally and patted her hand. "You go on, lie down and get you some rest. You drink some of that oat straw tea I brought you, it'll help. I'll call you when supper's ready." I hesitated then took her hand in mine and went with my gut feeling. "Sally, I want you to promise me one thing."

"What is it, Miss Bess?"

"This next bit of time's going to be rough on you, you know that, don't you?"

She nodded.

"Good. The fact that you do might help you prepare for it, in a way. But it will be trying and I want you to remember, you didn't do anything wrong, not in the eyes of Sheriff Nanny, not in my eyes, or Fletcher's." I squeezed her hand. "I don't care what anybody says about you or to you, you remember that and hold your head high. The Bible may say to turn the other cheek but that doesn't mean you should just bow down and take the kind of treatment Nate was so fond of handing out, especially when it comes to your children. You did what you had to do to protect the little ones, and while I can't tell you God approves, I believe ... no, I know He has forgiven you."

She drew in a long breath, let it out slowly then nodded her head. "Thank you, Miss Bessie. It means a lot to hear you say that and I promise I'll do my best."

"I know you will, Sally, I know you will. Now, go on and drink that tea and have a bit of a lie down."

She stood up and I smiled when I saw her square her shoulders and lift her chin. I had no way of knowing, of course, but I had a feeling everything would be all right.

CHAPTER SIX

Early Fall 1915

At cross-purposes.

Our small mountain community seemed split right down the middle over Sally Laughter and how she'd killed her husband Nate. Some mountain folk screamed she was guilty of murder and ought to pay the price for it while others lauded what she had done and said she should be set free. Nate's pa stoked the fire of her guilt, visiting saloons and extolling the price his son had paid simply for "straightenin out his willful wife and young'uns on occasion." Some of the mountaineers forgot Sally's bruises and broken bones as they took up Holcomb's cause, insisting Sally be taken from our home and jailed till her trial. Sheriff Nanny stood firm on his decision, telling the community Sally needed medical attention and would remain where she was.

It seemed every day Fletcher was running someone off our property who thought it their right to see that justice was served. Because of this, Sally elected to have her children stay with her ma and pa, who were surrounded by good friends that would see to it they weren't disturbed. But they visited frequently and this did Sally more good than anything. Her face would light up at the sight of her children and these were the only times she smiled and laughed and seemed to forget what had transpired between her and her husband. The children were delighted with the change in their pet horse, who had begun to fill out quite nicely and now stood tall and strong and had a healthy, shiny coat. Sally told me they had named the mare Angel because of her soulful eyes, and as the children would ride bareback across our yard, laughing with glee, it seemed to me the horse enjoyed it as much as they did. Afterward, they would feed her carrots and apples and run their little hands over her, planting many wet kisses on her muzzle. Fritz enjoyed their visits almost as much as the horse, chasing after them, barking with happiness, allowing them to pet and kiss and tug at him as if it were his due. When they left, Sally and the horse and Fritz would stand in the yard, watching mournfully as they made their way up the mountain. It near broke my heart, knowing that it could be Sally would never get the chance to live with her children again. I vowed to myself to do anything I could to ensure that didn't happen.

As it turned out, the Berryhills proved to be a good distraction for Sally, Hoyt entertaining her with tall tales and Maude fussing over her like a mother hen with her chick. Sally, not used to such care and consideration, soaked their attention up like a sponge and I thought it a blessing she finally had someone to dote on her and the childless Berryhills had found someone to nurture.

Since Sally didn't have the funds to hire a lawyer, Fletcher and I took it upon ourselves to collect money to help her in this endeavor. Fletcher approached Reverend Redmon about bringing up Sally's cause during his Sunday sermon, and at first our preacher was hesitant, saying he didn't want to put the church in the middle of what was shaping up to be a battle over poor Sally's soul. Fletcher reminded the reverend he often bemoaned the fact that he didn't have some cause to tout, a way of getting the congregation involved in church matters and passionate to do something about them. Reverend Redmon finally agreed to make an announcement about Sally's plight during Sunday's service but felt he could not conscientiously have the church itself involved in the matter since Sally had, after all, committed murder. "Even though the man had deserved it," he added with a pained expression. But if the congregants were willing to raise and/or contribute money toward Sally's cause, then the church would not object, it being the Christian thing to do.

Although I thought Reverend Redmon approached the subject quite tentatively to his pulpit, many supported this although Fletcher and Thorney Dalton, aided by Bull Elliott and Possum Gilliam, had to break up a fistfight between two men over whether Sally was innocent or guilty. But the majority of the church members eagerly took up the cause for Sally, holding potluck dinners and collecting money after Sunday Service until we had enough to pay the only lawyer in McDowell County, a young man named Amiel Gentry who looked as if he belonged in my schoolroom rather than standing before a judge.

I admit I had reservations about the defense Lawyer Gentry planned to present. Since Sally didn't remember killing her husband, Amiel told us he would plead temporary insanity under the McNaughton Rule. He explained to Sally, Fletcher and me that this rule, which deals with acts committed by the insane, was first used in the United Kingdom but later adopted by the United States court system in 1851. Precedence for temporary insanity began with the case of Daniel Sickles back in 1859 when Sickles, a US Senator who would later become a Congressman, killed his wife's lover, Phillip Barton Key II, son of Francis Scott Key, the author of "The Star Spangled Banner."

Amiel leaned back in his chair and hooked his thumb in his suspenders, a sign which I would soon learn meant he intended to impart knowledge to his audience. "Now Sickles was known as a ladies' man and had even been censured by the New York State Assembly for escorting a famous prostitute ..." he hesitated, a look of alarm on his face. "Excuse my language, ladies," he said with a slightly embarrassed glance, "by the name of Fanny White to the Assembly's chambers. I understand that when his wife was with child, he left her at home and took Miss White with him to England when he was Secretary of the United States legation in London." He leaned forward with a conspiratorial air. "His wife was but 15 when he married her and him 33. It's well-known her family had some serious objections about the union between Mr. Sickles and their beloved daughter but, as they say, love prevails." He waved his hand in the air in a dismissive gesture and I ducked my head to hide my smile. Amiel looked too young to even have contemplated the wonders of love. "In any event, Sickles proceeded to have numerous affairs during the marriage but when he learned of his wife's infidelity with Mr. Key from a letter she wrote on February 26, 1859, he confronted her and forced her to write a detailed description of the affair, which she did. The next day, he observed Mr. Key outside of their home, attempting to set up a liaison with his wife by waving a handkerchief at the house as he walked by. Sickles grabbed three guns and went after Mr. Key and caught up with him just across the street from the White House. There were 12 witnesses to the confrontation, all reporting that he shouted, 'Key, you scoundrel, you have dishonored my home; you must die,' and pulled a gun. The first shot missed, so Key, who wasn't armed, attempted to fight Sickles with his fists. But Sickles pulled a second gun as Key rushed toward him and when Key tried to run away, shot him, hitting him in the groin region and thigh. Key fell to the ground, saying, 'Don't shoot me,' and threw an object at Sickles which was later found to be opera glasses he used to see if Mrs. Sickles was signaling back from her second story window when he waved the handkerchief at her. Sickles pulled out the third gun and shot Key in the chest as he lay on the ground. This proved to be the fatal shot as Key died an hour later although Sickles stood over Key and tried to shoot him again, this time in the head, but the gun misfired.

"Well, with 12 witnesses, Sickles could do nothing but confess so he surrendered himself to the Attorney General who had no recourse but to put him in jail but so many people came to see him that he was given use of the head jailer's apartment. Many senators and congressmen paid him visits and wished him well and even President James Buchanan sent him a note. Unlike the other prisoners,

Sickles was given special treatment including being allowed to take possession of his personal weapon in jail. At his trial, Sickles' lawyer claimed that while Sickles was not insane, he had been driven temporarily insane by his wife's infidelity. The newspapers took it still further, claiming that Sickles was protecting other innocent women from the evil lustfulness of Key." He winked. "They seemed to have forgotten Sickles was a worse scoundrel than the man he killed."

I couldn't help but laugh at this observation.

"And being the despicable rogue he was, Sickles gave his wife's detailed confession to the press which turned the general public against her, and just like that, he became the victim. In any event, the jury acquitted him and since his alleged insanity was only temporary, Sickles got off scot-free." With a satisfied look, Amiel gave a curt nod.

"You think it will work?" Sally said, her eyes hopeful.

"If I can get the judge to agree to waive a trial by jury, I'm sure it will," Amiel said.

I squeezed Sally's hand, praying her lawyer was right and that Sally would be able to continue her life with her children.

Judge Hawkins returned to McDowell County a month after Sally's arrest and immediately ordered her trial to commence the following Monday. Since she had mostly recovered from her injuries, Sheriff Nanny told me he couldn't do anything to stall and Sally and her lawyer best be ready for what looked to be a trial ruled by passions. It was all I could do to keep poor Sally calm and focused on her testimony.

The Monday of Sally's trial dawned clear and hot, humidity lying over the mountain like a wet blanket. Sally rode in the wagon seat with Fletch and me as we made our way to Old Fort, the Berryhills sitting on quilt-covered hay bales behind us. I put my hand on Sally's and squeezed and she clutched it between both hands as if searching for an anchor. I smiled at her, thinking she looked awful young and pretty, and have to admit I was a bit glad the lingering effects of the beating she took still showed, her bruises now faded but still evident just beneath the pale skin of her cheeks and above the bodice of her dress. She had come to us wearing only a rough-spun gray one mended so many times it was a wonder the thing still held together. I suspected many of the rips were because of Nate and decided Sally would go to trial and begin her new life with a new outfit. Even though my skills with needle and thread were only fair at best, the navy-blue dress I had sewn for her complemented Sally's fair complexion and sunny hair and she was delighted by it.

On the outskirts of Old Fort, I heard a loud buzzing noise and wondered at its source but as we grew closer to the courthouse it became evident most of the people in our community were present for the trial about to commence. Some waved fists and shouted as we neared, while others reached for Sally and hollered encouragement as we drove by. Sheriff Nanny and two deputies stepped in front of the wagon, and after Fletcher braked to a stop, Sheriff Nanny told him they were there to escort Sally inside, fearing for her safety among the crowd. I kissed Sally's cheek and told her I would see her in a few moments. With a panicked look, Sally turned to the Berryhills and both leaned forward patting her consolingly, Hoyt saying, "It'll be all right, Sally." We watched as Sheriff Nanny helped her down, then sandwiched her between himself and a deputy with the third making a trail through the horde of people standing between us and the courthouse. I stayed where I was while Fletcher parked the wagon, my eyes never leaving Sally until I saw her safely inside. We all climbed down and made our way to the courthouse, trying not to hear the shouts and insults that followed us. I was thankful when several men from our congregation surrounded us, forming a barrier against anyone who might want to do us harm.

At the door, Holcomb Laughter stepped in front of us, stopping our progress. Like his son, he was a tall, gaunt man with a face stern and hard. I wondered to myself if the man had ever known pleasure in his life as I returned his malevolent stare. He moved closer and dropped his voice low. "You gonna pay for what you done, taking care of that girl, that, that murderer." He spat on the ground and wiped his mouth with the back of his hand. "After I take care of her,

I'll be a-seein you, you can count on it."

Sheriff Nanny appeared beside him and jerked him away. "I hear anymore threats like that, Laughter, I'm taking you to jail, and you can count on that," he said, taking my arm and guiding us inside.

Due to the controversy over this trial, Judge Hawkins had ruled that only witnesses and lawyers could remain in the courtroom but even so there was barely enough room for all of us to sit. Since the day was so hot, the door and windows were left open to let what little breeze there was into the rather small room, and people with no interest in the trial other than curiosity or to see justice done stood in the doorway and peeked in windows, much to Judge Hawkins' chagrin. I was bothered that Holcomb Laughter followed us inside, watching as he sat in the row of seats behind the prosecutor. I wondered what in the world he had to say and if he would bear true witness or false. I strongly suspected it would be the latter. A small, frail gray-headed woman sat beside him and I was curious what her relationship to Holcomb was. She seemed to huddle into herself, much as Sally had that day Nate brought her to our farm, as if she wished to become invisible, and I thought this must be Holcomb's wife.

Fletch and I, along with the Berryhills, took our seats behind Sally and Amiel and I was relieved when Sheriff Nanny joined us along with both deputies. Sally's ma and pa and oldest daughter silently sat in chairs in the row behind us. When the bailiff called the court to order, we all rose and watched Judge Hawkins sweep into the room wearing a voluminous black robe. He had more gray hair on his face than on top of his head and his nose reminded me of an eagle the way it hooked down. His green eyes were small and close together and his lips thin and set in a firm line. But I knew him to be a fair man and hoped he would understand the reasons behind Sally's actions.

After the judge banged his gavel to indicate court was in session, Amiel rose to his feet and requested a trial by judge instead of one by jury. An argument ensued between Amiel and the prosecutor, Ezra Kingston, who came over from our county seat of Marion, as Old Fort didn't have a prosecutor. Mr. Kingston was a stout man with a barrel chest and spindly legs who favored snapping his bright-blue suspenders against his shirt. His hair was a thing of envy, all snowy white and curling softly around his face and the nape of his neck. But his beard was something fierce, springy and wild, and covering his lower face and throat, tobacco juice staining a patch just beneath his mouth. I knew nothing of the man and prayed he would be fair in his dealings with the court. Amiel did most of the talking, pointing out that it would be nigh impossible to find an impartial jury, especially since it would be made up of men who would in all probability not be as sympathetic to Sally's plight as a woman might. He further pointed out that the town itself was divided over Sally's innocence or guilt and it seemed every citizen had chosen which side of the fence they would stand on before the trial even started.

After some deliberation, Judge Hawkins sustained Amiel's motion and I breathed a sigh of relief, thankful for this. Judge Hawkins was known for his justness and would not be prone to sentence Sally simply because she was a woman who had taken a man's life but would weigh the evidence and come to a just conclusion.

The judge allowed opening statements and it didn't take Mr. Kingston long to lay out his case, helped by the fact that Sally did not deny the charges against her.

When Amiel stood, I clutched Fletcher's hand, hoping the defense he had planned for her would work. It was a long shot but, as he explained, one that had some merit after all.

Amiel approached the judge, hesitated just long enough for me to fear he had frozen with anxiety, but then cleared his throat and said, "Judge, under the McNaughton Rule, we intend to claim temporary insanity. We do not deny these charges against us but embrace them and lay claim to them, our defense being Nate Laughter, Sally's late husband and father to her children, was a mean, vile, brutal man, a man who acted more like a rabid dog than caring Christian human being, a man who drove his wife temporarily insane by his treatment of her and her children. And I might add, a man who, like a rabid dog, needed to be put down." Gasps rang out in the courtroom and I shut my eyes. "Nate Laugher was a man who brought his fate on himself," Amiel continued in a raised voice.

A strangled cry behind me forced my eyes open and I turned around. Holcomb kicked his chair over and ran toward Amiel, shouting, "I'm a-gonna kill you for that." Sheriff Nanny was up in an instant and he and his deputies restrained Holcomb before he got to Amiel. He struggled and yelled and it took all three to drag him out of the courtroom, buzzing with excitement over the goings-on. Amiel's startled expression changed to one of relief as the throng of onlookers at the door parted then closed after Holcomb and his escorts passed through.

Judge Hawkins banged his gavel for silence, and when voices lowered to whispers then fizzled out altogether, he leaned over his podium and stared at Amiel long and hard. "Counselor, are you certain you want to proceed with this defense?" he asked as if he couldn't believe it.

"Yes, your Honor. We have several witnesses here to bear testament to Nate Laughter's evil disposition and the way he treated his wife and children and who have witnessed their bruises and contusions personally. Why, your Honor, if I didn't know better, I'd say the man was the devil himself."

A few titters escaped at that and Judge Hawkins glared around the courtroom till they died down. I glanced at the woman who had been sitting by Holcomb, feeling sorry that she had to hear these things about her son, but she now sat up straight with a defiant look.

Amiel cleared his voice and continued. "The Court will learn Nate Laughter's onerous ways and I have no doubt will come to understand why my client, this woman, did what she did. I'm certain, your Honor, if she had not gone temporarily insane and put a stop to it, the path her husband was on surely would have ended in him murdering one or all of his family." He bowed to the judge. "Thank you, your Honor."

With a resigned sigh, Judge Hawkins banged his gavel

and told the prosecutor to proceed.

I soon learned why Holcomb Laugher was in the courtroom. He was the first witness to testify and as we waited for Sheriff Nanny to collect him from jail and bring him into the courtroom, I prayed silently that he would be a Christian man who, sworn to tell the truth by laying his hand on the Bible, would do so. But that was not to be. Although Holcomb's manner of speech was crude and brusque, he managed to relay that Nathan was a good son, an honest Christian man who lived by God's rule and would never harm woman nor child. On cross-examination by Amiel, he denied knowing of any acts of domestic violence perpetrated by Nate against Sally or their children and claimed that Nate might have used his hand a time or two to straighten out his wayward wife and children but never in such a way that it caused any great harm. Amiel pressed hard but Holcomb would never yield and, with a disgusted sigh, he let him go.

Next was the woman who sat beside Holcomb who gave her name as Livia Holcomb. Deep lines etched her face, worn there, I was sure, by years of hardship. Her mouth turned downward in a perpetual frown and she sat hunched as if the weight of the world rested on her shoulders. She answered the prosecutor's questions in a shy, timid voice, basically saying the same thing her husband had. But on cross-examination, when Amiel reminded her she had sworn to tell the truth on the Bible, unlike her husband, who claimed veracity, she put her face in her hands and began to weep and became so hysterical, she had to be helped out of the courtroom. Amiel whispered to us that could go either way with the judge; he would think the hysteria came from the fact that she had been lying or that Amiel was bullying her too strongly. I prayed for the former.

Several more witnesses were called to testify about Nate's character and all basically confirmed Holcomb's claims. I found it interesting they were all related to the Laughters and felt they probably had been coached by Holcomb.

Mr. Kingston called Sheriff Nanny to relate Sally's confession that she had killed her husband and any evidence he had collected at the home. When Sheriff Nanny tried to describe Sally's injuries, the prosecutor cut him off by saying he had not been asked the question but Amiel explored this extensively on cross-examination and it was clear Sheriff Nanny felt much as Amiel had, that Nate did not deserve to live. Amiel had him describe the extensive injuries he had witnessed with Sally over the years, the times he had gone to their cabin and spoken to Nate, warning him about harming his wife and children, and the final beating Sally had endured. When Sheriff Nanny talked about Sally's statement that Nate had been at their oldest daughter, the courtroom erupted, with witnesses for the prosecution shouting in protest and those for the defense in rage. The judge had to bang his gavel several times before order was restored.

But on redirect, Mr. Kingston asked a damning question: if Nate was abusing Sally so severely, why had she not pressed charges against him? Sheriff Nanny could only say that he felt Sally was intimidated and afraid that Nate would hurt her even worse if she claimed he had beat her or their children.

The prosecutor rested his case and the judge broke for lunch. Fletcher and I chose to remain in the courtroom and shared a basket lunch with Sally, Amiel, the Berryhills and Sally's ma and pa and oldest daughter, Emily. She was such a pretty thing, small and thin for her age but with Sally's golden hair and big blue eyes. I tried to engage her in conversation but she was shy and seemed intimidated at her surroundings. I had never had any of Sally's children in my schoolroom and had questioned her as to the reason why back when I gave her the Queen Anne's lace seeds. Sally had replied that Nate didn't want them to attend school and when I asked why, she said, with an embarrassed look, "He needs 'em at home to help work the farm." I hoped that now, I would see little Emily in my schoolroom and that she would learn to read and write and come to understand that she could have a bright and happy future.

Amiel began his defense by calling me to the stand. Fletcher squeezed my hand before I rose and swore to tell the truth then took my seat. Amiel had me go through my confrontation with Nate when he brought Sally to our farm and the injuries I had witnessed at that time. He had me relay what Sally told me when I asked why she didn't stay with us, that she feared for her children if she did not return with her husband. He then moved on to the day Sheriff Nanny fetched me to care for Sally and had me list the injuries I had treated her for. He surprised me when he asked me if I agreed with what Sally had done to her husband. The prosecutor objected but Judge Hawkins allowed me to answer. I thought for a moment as I looked around the courtroom at friendly and hostile faces, and was glad Sheriff Nanny had taken Holcomb back to jail. My eyes locked with Holcomb's wife, who had returned to the courtroom after lunch, and I thought she gave me a curt nod of encouragement but told myself that could not be so. "I see that she had no other recourse. The man was evil, with no thought nor concern for any other human or animal. When Sally learned what he had done to her oldest daughter, I think she may have been so upset by this, she went out of her mind with grief and rage, and in that state of mind felt the only way to stop him was to kill him. I completely understand why she did it and I myself would probably do the same thing if I were in the same situation."

I left the stand to the sound of angry grumblings. Judge Hawkins once more banged his gavel.

Fletcher was called next and he relayed his confrontation with Nate that day at the farm and the threat Nate had made to me. He talked about Sally's injuries that day and when he brought her to our farm, and the love between her and her children.

A parade of witnesses followed, led by Sally's mother and father, each talking about the times they had seen Sally and the children with bruises and lacerations, Sally's broken arm, and the way Nate made the children work his small farm while he sat on his porch yelling at them. Several claimed to have tried talking to Nate to no avail.

When Amiel called for Livia Laughter to take the stand, startled gasps and grunts of despair echoed through the courtroom as Holcomb's wife slowly rose from her seat and approached the witness chair. Judge Hawkins reminded her she was still under oath and she quietly nodded and took her seat. Her eyes wide, she twisted a handkerchief in her hands as she watched Amiel approach. When he spoke, his tone was gentle and concerning.

"Mrs. Laughter, I apologize for upsetting you this morning while on the witness stand and will do my best not to do so again."

She glanced at Holcomb's empty seat then returned her gaze to Amiel and simply nodded.

"When I asked if you were telling the truth, you couldn't answer but I'm hoping you can do so now, if you'd be so kind."

Her voice was so low, we all leaned forward, trying to hear. "I reckon I got no choice," she said. "I placed my hand on that there Bible and swore to tell the truth afore God and this here courtroom."

"Yes, it is your duty to answer truthfully and I trust you will do the Christian thing. Let's return to my former question, Mrs. Laughter. Were you telling the truth about your son Nate Laughter this morning when you testified?"

She dabbed at her eyes, ignoring the grumbling throughout the courtroom, then seemed to find some inner strength as she straightened up and said, "It was all lies, not a word of what I spoke was the truth."

An angry buzz whipped around the courtroom and Judge Hawkins yelled for order.

Amiel waited for it to quiet before continuing. "Can you tell us the truth now?"

A defiant look crossed her face and she straightened with resolve. "If I don't, I'll burn in Hell so I got to. Nate was just like his pa, ain't no other way to put it. He could charm a snake if he a-wanted to but oncet he got his dander up, it was like the devil got ahold of him and he weren't satisfied till someone was broke and bleeding."

"And who bore the brunt of his anger, in your opinion?"

"Sally and those poor young'uns of hers."

"Did you ever witness Nate beating Sally and/or her

children?"

"Oh, many a time. Tried to stop him oncet, got a broken rib for it from him then his pa beat me when he found out I tried to help Sally." She sighed. "Give them young'uns a pup once, and they loved that dog somethin fierce. Nate was a-pounding away on little Emily and I reckon that pup, thinking he was protectin her, got between the two of 'em. Nate killed it in front of all of 'em. Made 'em all watch, told 'em that was gonna happen to them one day if they didn't straighten up."

Those poor, poor children, I thought.

"Did you actually witness this?"

"I shore did. Made me sick to my stomach." She chewed her lip for a moment. "He was pure evil, like you said, and I reckon I won't be alive come tomorrow for testifying here today but it's got to be said. He was my son and I loved him oncet afore his pa turned him, but the man that beat on his wife and young'uns, that weren't the son I knew. That was a demon."

Amiel paused while that sank in. I glanced at the witnesses behind the prosecutor and noticed they no longer seemed so angry or agitated. Some cast their eyes down, as if embarrassed, while others watched Livia with a sympathetic look.

"And because you've told the truth about Nate Laughter, you're afraid for your life?" Amiel repeated.

"Holcomb ain't gonna be none too pleased I didn't lie like he told me to. But that's all right. I got to do the right thing, the Christian thing, and tell the whole truth. I reckon the good Lord will protect me, and if'n He don't, I'm ready to go." She turned to the judge. "Sally don't deserve to be put in jail for what she done. Nate told me hisself if she ever run from him, he'd drag her back home and make her watch while he killed all his young'uns afore he killed her. I reckon she didn't have much choice in the matter if she wanted 'em all to survive. Life didn't mean nothin to him. He took it if he wanted. He's killed a whole passel of cats and dogs and I suspect he killed his brother, my sweet Ethan, although I never could prove it." Her voice broke at that and she sobbed into the handkerchief.

Amiel glanced at Sheriff Nanny. "I'm sure the sheriff will want to talk to you about your suspicions concerning your son."

I was glad Holcomb was in jail and prayed the sheriff kept him there while he investigated this.

Mrs. Laughter blew her nose before continuing. "Won't do no good. Holcomb helped him cover it up. They made sure no one would convict either one of 'em."

An audible gasp went up at that but she ignored it. "Nate didn't love Sally or her young'uns, not like a good man loves his family. All they was to him was workers for his farm and Sally a brood mare to produce more." She gave a curt nod. "And I reckon that's all I got to say on the matter." She looked at Sheriff Nanny. "Sheriff, if'n you need to talk to me, I reckon you better do it afore you let Holcomb out of jail. I don't expect to be here much longer but that's all right." And without being dismissed by the judge, she got up and walked out of the courtroom. Sheriff Nanny rose and followed her.

Judge Hawkins stared after Sheriff Nanny as he made his way through the people gathered in the doorway, looking to be deep in thought. When Amiel moved back to his seat, he glanced at him then said, "Call your next witness, counselor."

"I call Sally Laughter, Your Honor."

Sally gave me a fearful glance before rising to her feet and walking to the stand. Her hand visibly shook as she swore to tell the truth and she looked close to fainting when she sat down.

Amiel led her through the preliminaries, having her tell a bit about herself before she married Nate, then quickly got to the thick of things by asking, "When did Nate first beat you?"

"When he found out I was carrying our first."

"Was that before or after you married him?"

"Afore."

Amiel let that sink in, then said. "Yet you married him."

Sally gave a sad sigh. "I couldn't see no way out. I didn't want my baby to be no bastard, laughed at and scorned by the mountain folk. 'Sides, my ma and pa didn't have room or food for another mouth. I did what I thought was best."

"How was Nate when y'all were courting, was he abusive, treat you bad?"

Sally shook her head. "Oh, no, he was the sweetest man I ever knew. Treated me real good till he found out I was a-carrying his baby." She paused, wringing her hands. "It was like oncet he knew he had me good, he could be his true self, his real self, and treat me any way he liked."

I shook my head at that.

Amiel had Sally talk about their life together, go through all the wrongs she had endured by her husband, and it took quite some time to list them all. I stole glances at the prosecution side of the courtroom from time to time, noting the disgusted look on the prosecutor's face and the shocked and angry looks of Holcomb's witnesses. It seemed they had not known what was going on inside that little cabin Sally shared with Nate. Or if they did, chose to ignore it or turn a blind eye.

When Amiel turned to the night Sally killed Nate, it seemed everyone in the courtroom leaned forward so they could hear.

"Tell us what happened that night that was different from any other time Nate beat you," Amiel said, "different enough to cause you to lose your mind and commit murder."

Sally swiped at her eyes and took a deep breath. "I noticed my Emily..." she looked at the judge "... she's eight, Judge, was acting funny. Crying over nothin, jumpin at the least little noise, stayin right close to me all the time. I kept asking her if anything was a-botherin her but she wouldn't answer. Finally, I took her for a walk in the woods away from everybody and sat her down and told her to tell me what was a-goin on with her." Sally stopped, wiping at her eyes with her hands. Amiel quickly furnished a handkerchief for her. "Finally she told me her pa had been a-touchin her all over, tellin her he was a-gonna teach her how to be a woman."

Voices raised in horror at this but the judge quieted the room with a hard stare.

"I was right mad," Sally said. "That afternoon, when Nate was over at Thorney Dalton's buying some moonshine, I sent the young'uns with Tommy, my oldest, down to my ma and pa's place and told him to keep them there till I sent for 'em. When Nate got home, I could tell he'd been sampling Thorney's 'shine 'cause he was near to drunk. He got mad when he seen the young'uns weren't to home but I didn't let that stop me. I asked him what he'd been doing to Emily. He denied it at first, said he hadn't been doin nothing, and if she said he had, she wouldn't be able to walk for a month when he got through with her. But I kept at him." She looked at Judge Hawkins. "My Emily don't lie, Judge Hawkins. She's a good, Christian girl and I taught her to always tell the truth. Nate hit me for asking but I wouldn't stop and he beat me till I was just about passed out. But still I asked him and I reckon he'd had enough of the question 'cause he told me he'd been at her all right, planned to make her into a woman when she come of age, his woman, and once he did, he wouldn't need me no more. Emily could give him the young'uns he wanted to help on the farm." She shook her head. "I reckon I passed out 'cause next thing I remember, I was standin over him with my big ol' iron skillet in my hand with his blood and brains all over it."

The courtroom was so quiet, I could hear Fletcher breathing beside me. Amiel once more waited for this to be absorbed by the court then said in a quiet voice, "Thank you, Sally, for being so brave. That's all I have of this witness, Your Honor." Amiel helped Sally down from the stand. When she walked toward her seat, I gave her a smile of encouragement but I think the tears falling down Sally's face kept her from seeing me.

The judge asked the prosecutor if he wanted to cross-examine the witness and he simply shook his head.

Amiel stepped close to the podium and spoke in a low voice. "Your Honor, young Emily is in the courtroom today, and if it's your desire, I can call her to the stand to verify her mother's testimony."

Judge Hawkins shook his head. "I see no need, counselor, of putting that poor child through such a thing."

"Then that's all I have, Your Honor. Defense rests."

Judge Hawkins glanced at the darkening sky through the windows. "We'll save closing statements for tomorrow." He picked up his gavel to bang it against the podium for dismissal but Amiel stood abruptly.

"Your Honor, if it please the Court, I'd like to finish this case today. Sally's been through a hard time, being separated from her children, not knowing what's going to happen. My closing statement is very short, Your Honor. I think the facts speak for themselves."

The judge looked to Mr. Kingston who took a moment to spit tobacco juice into a cup on his table then said, "I have no objection, Your Honor, to continuing."

Judge Hawkins banged his gavel. "Proceed."

Mr. Kingston's closing statement was not as vigorous or passionate as his opening argument had been and it was evident he no longer considered Sally a murderer but simply a woman who was trying to deal with a dire situation.

When he finished, Amiel stood and simply said, "I think it's fairly obvious, Your Honor, that Sally loves her children and did her best to protect them from their abusive father but when she learned what he had done to their little girl, it was too much for her mind, especially when her husband made the comment about using Emily in such a horrendous way, and she simply went temporarily insane and in that state of mind did justice to the man who had committed such an atrocious act against her little girl."

Judge Hawkins seemed to consider for a long moment then said, "The evidence proves Mrs. Laughter was driven to an act of temporary insanity by her husband's confirmation of his assault upon their little girl." He banged his gavel. "The Court rules Sally Laughter is not guilty by reason of temporary insanity."

Pandemonium broke out over the courtroom. Some women cried into handkerchiefs, while a few of the men shouted outrage and anger, their clenched fists raised in the air. It seemed, though, that the majority now were not judging Sally so harshly. I hugged Fletcher, then Sally, who seemed stunned and unable to understand what had happened.

All through this, Judge Hawkins slammed his gavel against the podium, shouting for order. When voices finally died down, he glared until there was complete silence then said, his eyes raking the men who still grumbled in protest, "Those who disagree have that right but I won't brook any man or woman troubling Mrs. Laughter over this. In the eyes of the Court, she's innocent of any wrongdoing." He looked at Sally. "Mrs. Laughter, you're free to go." He banged the gavel one final time and swept off the bench.

Amiel clutched her hand and said, "You're free, Sally."

Sally was lost in a crowd of people shoving against one another, congratulating her and offering to help in any way they could with her farm or children. Emily clung to her mother, tears running down her face. The Berryhills hovered beside Sally, smiling and wiping their eyes. Mr. Davis and his wife stood stoically by, waiting for the chance to speak to their daughter. When the Courtroom finally cleared, I told Sally she and her children were welcome to stay with us until she decided what she wanted to do.

"I reckon I'll go on back to my farm," she said.

Mr. Davis grunted his approval. "I reckon your ma and me will stay with you for awhile just to make sure ol' Holcomb don't get it in his head to pay you a visit."

Sally glanced at the Berryhills and they smiled at each other. "Ain't no need for that, Pa. Hoyt and Maude offered to stay with us for a bit to watch out for Holcomb and help with the chores and such. And I'm thinkin of asking Ma Laughter if she wants to live with me and the young'uns. I'm sure Holcomb won't let her stay in their cabin after what she said."

As I watched Sally leave, I wondered if I would see a dark cloud around her but did not and took solace in that. Maybe she and her sweet family could now live a happier, better life. I prayed it would be so.

CHAPTER SEVEN

Late Spring 1916

He's so tall if he fell down he'd be halfway home.

The spring of 1916 proved to be as picture perfect as any I'd ever seen. Gentle breezes carried the smell of fresh-turned earth from our newly plowed garden plot. The birds flitted here and there; some courting, some busy building nests, and, at least in my imagination, some simply celebrating the beauty of the season. Wildflowers and herbs sprang up overnight in a riot of color and soft scent and competed with the delicate mint green of leaves unfurling on the trees. And above it all, the sun beamed out of cornflower blue skies, seeming to shower us with God's blessings.

School had just let out for the year, my garden was planted, and the morning chores tended to. I'd enjoyed the last of the coffee sitting on the front porch, idly pushing the swing with the toe of one foot, and humming some of my favorite hymns, including "Swing Low, Sweet Chariot" and Mama's favorite, "Rock of Ages."

With Sally no longer worrying me, my mind was in a happy place, remembering Green and Mama, and wondering what would have become of them if they had lived. I imagined Green with his lively sense of curiosity following in Papa's footsteps, working as a deputy in some small town until he rose up to sheriff or constable. And I thought Mama would be happy seeing her children grown and settled; me with Fletcher, Roy with Alice and three children, Loney with her husband and two little ones of her own, and Thee courting a young lady named Myrtle. I imagined Mama and Aunt Belle as matriarchs of Hot Springs watching over the social habits of the girls in town and shaking their heads over the antics of the boys.

And Papa, of course, would still be constable of Hot Springs and not doing carpentry work over in Knoxville where he didn't belong.

I shook my head, heaving a weary sigh, and told myself to quit spinning foolish dreams. Life was, or wasn't in the case of Mama and Green, what it was, and despite my imaginings I could do nothing to change the past.

Besides, I had a big day ahead of me with lots to do and at the end of it, I'd have myself a new organ—a dream long imagined and finally coming true.

Back in the winter, I had pored over the Sears Roebuck Catalog, debating between a piano or an organ for the parlor. I finally decided on the organ because in my eyes they were a prettier instrument than the pianos. They were also cheaper. Besides, if I wanted to play a piano, I could always play the one at church. An organ was more of a challenge and quite a bit more physical and that made me feel as if I were more involved in the music. Given all that, I also felt the organ suited me better somehow.

Fletcher had left early that morning to go to Old Fort to pick up my purchase from the train depot, where it was being held for me. I had paid a pretty penny for the organ but had no doubt it would be worth every cent. Just thinking of being able to sit down and play whenever I wanted brought a smile to my face. I imagined playing in the evenings while Fletch looked on, tapping his toe to the beat, or when we had company, perhaps the preacher on Sunday or the women's prayer group that rotated the location of its Wednesday night meetings between the members.

That thought, performing for company, naturally brought

on memories of banging out "Seven Drunken Nights" on Mama's piano for Avery Collins, the sissified and totally unsuitable, in my opinion, lawyer Papa had brought home one night in an attempt to draw my fancy away from Fletcher Elliott. I laughed at the thought of Mr. Collins' scandalized leave taking and Papa's flabbergasted, "Damn, Bess," before he followed the lawyer out the door.

Oh, Papa had not been at all pleased with me but I'd made my opinion clear, and after that, he had not attempted to interfere in my socializing anymore.

Laughing at the memory, I stood up and went inside to tend to my tinctures I'd started the week before. After gently stirring or shaking each of them, I planned to see to the cleaning of my jelly safes. I needed to make room for the wild strawberry jam I'd canned yesterday.

As I stepped through the door, I stopped and looked at the bare spot beside the window where my organ would stand when Fletcher brought it home. It would, to me, add the crowning touch to our parlor, making it into a home. I don't mean that it wasn't a home already, but when I was growing up, there had always been a piano in the parlor and the room seemed oddly bare without some sort of musical instrument.

"That will soon be rectified," I muttered to myself as I walked into the kitchen. As I did, I heard footsteps on the front porch and turned to see who it was. Bose Dalton stood there, a blood-soaked bandana wrapped around his hand. His Blue Tick hound dog stood beside him panting as if it had been running for hours.

Since everything that had happened with Sally Laughter, I found myself just a little bit leery of dealing with people I didn't really know, especially men. I knew Bose Dalton, a nephew of Thorney's, just enough to say "Good day" to him when I saw him but had never stopped and engaged him in conversation—not that he would have obliged me anyway. Bose Dalton kept to himself and then some, and his reputation on the mountain, shall we say, preceded him. He stood heads above most of the people on the mountain, well over six and a half feet, and was so skinny he'd have to stand up twice to cast a shadow. He had lovely warm blue eyes and a nose to match the rest of him, long and thin. He also, if the rumors held true, could gentle the wildest animal with his soft voice.

Still, I hesitated. Fletch wouldn't be home for hours but as I looked down at the man's injured hand a drop of blood dripped from his curled fingers to the floor of the porch. That was enough to get me moving. Shoving my uncertainty aside, I hurried over to the door and held it open. "Mr. Dalton, won't you come in? What have you done to your hand?"

The dog sat nicely with no more than a gesture from Mr. Dalton who then grinned sheepishly as he took off his hat and stepped through the door. "Well, Miss Bessie, I was up on Flinty Knob back behind your place yonder," he nodded toward the back of the house, "and I slipped on some wet moss and fell. Musta grazed a rock or a stick when I tried to catch myself." He shrugged. "Tain't near as bad as it looks, just bled a lot."

He held out his hand and I took it in mine. "You let me be the judge of that." I loosened the bandana to reveal a long gash running the length of his palm. Wrapping it back up, I said, "That isn't too bad. I don't think you need to have it stitched but I'll know more after I clean it and get the bleeding stopped." I looked back up at him. "Would you like me to take care of it or just bandage it well enough so you can get down the mountain to the doctor in Old Fort?"

"Folks say you're better than ol' Doc Widby any day and since it was bleeding pretty bad I figured I'd come to you instead of trying to make it into town. I got it slowed down some but every time I take the bandana off, it starts up again. I'd be much obliged if you can fix it, Miss Bessie. I don't cotton to that fancy doctor and his ways."

"All right, come with me and let's see what we can do. What were you doing when you fell?"

I'd heard the stories and knew already, or suspected I knew, what he had been doing but I wondered if he'd tell me. Bose Dalton spent most of his time roaming over the mountain searching for what folks had taken to calling

Bose's Booger, a large bear-like creature that he claimed stood as tall as two men stacked on top of each other, covered in dark, scraggly fur. And if Mr. Dalton could be believed, it often roared its displeasure with the world in general. He said the creature was as mean as a hungry grizzly bear just waking from hibernation and as ugly as a leathered old man's bare backside.

And just as Mr. Dalton had become a figure of ridicule on the mountain, his Booger had, at least with the mothers and children, gained a reputation similar to the Melungeon boogie-man of my youth used by mothers as a threat to their children in an attempt to make them behave.

"Well, I was just ramblin around looking for something I, uh, I lost t'other day. Charlie here..." he gestured to his dog "...was helping me. He found a scent and took off running and I didn't have no choice but to follow. He's my best huntin dog, ya' see. T'weren't looking where I was going, I guess, and when I hit that patch of moss, I went sprawling as—uh, backside over teakettle. My hand musta caught a sharp rock or stick when I went down." He shrugged and looked down at his dog. "I'm all right, a cut hand ain't gonna kill me or nothing, but I'd be much obliged, Miss Bessie, if you would give my dog some water. He liked to wore his self out following that scent."

I smiled and relaxed. To me, a man who saw to the care of his animals before himself was a man to be trusted.

I looked into those bluer than blue eyes and found myself feeling a little sorry for him. He'd obviously been made fun of so much he had stopped talking about his "Booger", but he still hunted for it which was another point in his favor with me. He believed and no matter what others thought or said, he stuck with his belief, hoping, mayhap, that he'd find it one day and prove all the naysayers wrong.

"Let Charlie in and bring him back to the kitchen with you. We'll get him a drink and one for you, too, and I'll take care of that hand."

He held the door open for Charlie and with a quiet command, the dog came inside then fell into step with his master who followed me into the kitchen. I gestured for Mr.

Dalton to sit at the table while I ladled water into an old pot for Charlie. "Would you like water, Mr. Dalton, or coffee? There isn't any left from breakfast but I could make a fresh pot if you'd like."

"Don't go to no trouble for me, Miss Bessie. Water's fine."

"All right. Sit down at the table and I'll be with you in a minute." Already planning what I would do to treat his wound, I almost missed him holding out his uninjured hand palm down in the dog's direction and moving it up and down twice. When the dog sprawled on the floor, placing his head neatly on his paws, I laughed. "He's very well trained, isn't he? I'd heard you could train any of God's creatures but I didn't realize you could do it without speaking commands to them. That's really quite something, Mr. Dalton."

His high cheekbones showed a touch of pink and he looked down at his hand, fidgeting with the bandana. "Tain't nothing. My pa taught me how to do it. He was a right good hunter and trainer in his time and he said sometimes when you're hunting it pays to be silent."

I turned to my jelly safe. "Well, it's quite a talent if you ask me." I riffled around in the cabinet until I found an unopened jar of honey. Turning back to Mr. Dalton, I saw his cheeks were a blazing red, making his cheekbones all that much more prominent, and I wondered idly if he was part Cherokee. Those high cheekbones, much like my own, and his dark hair, lightly salted with gray as Elisi's had been, seemed to indicate he had at least a little Cherokee blood. Or perhaps it was some other Indian blood, possibly Chickasaw or even Creek.

I smiled at him and considered the best way to put him at ease. I had no idea why he would be embarrassed at the skill but I'd learned over the years that a relaxed patient was easier to work with than one who was tense and anticipating pain. Perhaps talk of bloodlines would do the trick.

I set the honey on the table then turned and poured a glass of water from the pitcher beside the sink. "I need to go out to my herb garden for a minute, Mr. Dalton. I'll be right back. You just sit tight and enjoy your water."

He looked up and nodded. "Can I be of some help to you, Miss Bessie?"

"Thank you, but I only need to pick a few yarrow flowers. That's the best thing to stop the bleeding and they work best when they're fresh. After that, we'll deal with the cut itself, get it cleaned out and bandaged. You wait right here and drink your water. And keep that bandana wrapped tight until I get back."

"Yes, ma'am, I will."

I stepped out the back door, grabbing my trusty hoe in case I came across a snake, and went to my herb garden. Snipping several yarrow flowers, I put them in my apron pocket and then cut a few Pale Indian Plantain leaves, also better fresh and my trusted standby for preventing infection. I would use them when I got the bleeding stopped and the wound clean.

Mr. Dalton didn't know it but he'd picked the best time of the year to cut himself, at least as far as healing was concerned.

While I gathered what I would need, I considered the best way to talk to Mr. Dalton about his "Booger" and perhaps help him learn to accept, even take pride in, something most people would consider a burdensome mental affliction. By the time I returned to the kitchen, I knew exactly how I would do it; I would bring up the subject of bloodlines and perhaps put his mind at rest about the not-so-secret obsession he didn't want to talk about.

"Here we are, Mr. Dalton. That didn't take long, did it? I'm just going to wash these flowers and leaves and then my hands. After that, we'll get to work on that cut. You're not nervous or in pain, are you?"

He blushed and looked down at the bloody bandanna. "No, ma'am, I'm fine."

I smiled as I spread a clean rag on the table. Taking his hand in mine, I carefully removed his improvised bandage and studied the cut closely before placing his hand on the rag. I threw the bloody bandana in the sink.

"I'll wash that out for you when I'm finished with this. I'm going to prepare a poultice with these flowers and we'll let that set on the cut a while. After that I'll show you how to bandage it with the Pale Indian Plantain leaves—they'll help keep it from getting infected."

"All right, ma'am. There's really no need to wash that bandanna out, it's old and about ready for the rag bin anyway and I have plenty more at home."

I smiled as I stood at the counter and chopped the yarrow flowers then put in a bowl and poured boiling water from the tea pot over them. "We'll just let those steep a few minutes before we put them in the muslin. I'll wash out the cut while we wait."

I dipped some water out of the water bucket and picked up another bowl. Taking them to the table, I held Mr. Dalton's hand over the bowl and tipped the ladle over the cut. He winced so I started talking to take his mind off the pain.

Did you know my great-grandmother is..." I shook my head "...was full-blooded Cherokee, Mr. Dalton?" I looked up and smiled at him. "We lost her only a couple of years ago, back during that cold winter of 1914. You remember that, don't you?"

"Yes ma'am, I do. My feet like to froze to the ground every time I went out looking for...uh, I mean, I went out on one of my walks. Why, 'round about February, I was thinking about asking Ma if she could make Charlie some boots so his paws wouldn't get so cold. I heard tell them dogs up north where they had that gold rush sometime wear 'em." He hesitated. "I'm sorry about your great-grandmother, Miss Bessie."

"Thank you, Mr. Dalton. She had a long and happy life, the life she wanted, and I guess that's all anyone can ask for." I shook my head and laughed. "Boots on a dog? I would've liked to have seen that but I imagine Charlie wouldn't have been very happy to wear them."

"That's what I figured so I never asked Ma if she would make them. Why, I reckon 't'would've discomfited him something awful."

"Most likely." I dabbed at the cut. "There, that's clean. We'll wait a few more minutes for the yarrow flowers to steep and cool a bit. Do you have any Indian blood in you, Mr. Dalton?"

"Don't rightly know if I do, Miss Bessie, but I wouldn't be surprised. Most people around these parts do."

I nodded. "Well, my great-grandmother was full-blooded which would make me...a quarter Cherokee, I guess. She's the one who taught me most everything I know about healing. And she taught me a great deal about the Cherokee legends, too. We used to walk in the woods around our house up in Hot Springs and Elisi—that's what we called her, it's Cherokee for grandmother—would always have a story to tell." I sighed.

"You miss her, don't you, Miss Bessie?"

"Yes, I do, something terrible. Even though I didn't get to see her much since I moved here with Fletch, she was an important part of my life before my marriage." I shook my head and smiled at him. "She told me a story once about how the Cherokee healers could do a charm on a baby when it was first born and later in life, usually in times of strain or illness, the person would be able to leave his body and travel wherever he wanted to go. Now, I can't say I believed that one, but it's nice to think about, isn't it?"

He looked out the window. "I guess it is. Don't know as to where I'd go. I'm plenty happy right here on Stone Mountain."

I laughed. "Yes, our little corner of the world is enough for me, too. Elisi also told me that some Cherokee are able to assume the body of any creature they want. They call them skin-walkers. A skin-walker can turn into a mountain lion, wolf, fox, or any animal from a huge grizzly bear right down to a little frog or even a little bumble bee. Can you imagine?"

His cheeks flushed again but he kept his eyes on mine, his interest apparent.

"Now, if you ask me, Mr. Dalton, that would be a fine skill to have. Just imagine being able to transform into another creature whenever you felt like it. Say life has got you down or even when it hasn't, you can choose any animal and go walking around in its skin for a while." I winked at him. "I know quite a few ladies who would love to be able to do that. They could turn into a fly and light on a wall to get the latest gossip before any of their friends."

He raised his hand to his mouth but couldn't hold back the snicker. Lowering his hand, he said, "Well, I reckon I know a few like that, Miss Bessie. Got more than a couple in my own family." His eyes crinkled when he smiled and then he looked down at the table, his cheeks going as red as a pickled beet. "Uh, Miss Bessie, do you believe that, I mean about the people being able to turn into animals?"

Before I answered, I went to the counter, picked up the steeping yarrow flowers and poured them through a sieve, shaking it to get as much of the water off as possible, then I dumped them on the square of muslin I had waiting. Folding the corners in carefully, I picked it up and carried it to the table. "I'm going to put this poultice right on the cut, Mr. Dalton, and hold it there for a few minutes. That should stop the bleeding, or at least slow it down a bit. And yes, Mr. Dalton, I believe in the Cherokee skin-walkers, that some people are able to change into animals." I smiled. "Of course, some of them act like animals even when they're wearing their human skin. I've known or heard about a few of them in my life."

He lifted his eyes back to mine and nodded as the color slowly faded from his cheeks. "I reckon they are at that. I know my cousin, when he gets some of my Uncle Thorney's moonshine in him, can act like the dirtiest and meanest polecat you ever saw."

I nodded and removed the poultice, dabbing at the wound a couple of times. "Liquor can do that to some people and Thorney's is about as potent as it comes, or so I'm told." Looking down at his hand, I smiled. "There, the bleeding's stopped and I think it's safe to bandage it now."

As I started to stand up, he put his good hand over mine. "I appreciate you telling me the story, Miss Bessie."

"You're welcome, Mr. Dalton." I turned my hand and squeezed his. "Maybe it's the Cherokee blood in me or all those stories Elisi told me but I like to think a person with an open mind about things gets along a great deal better in life than one who has a closed and narrow mind." I pulled my hand from beneath his and stood up, shaking my head. "Mercy, Mr. Dalton, you have to believe in possibilities, else, what's the point in living?"

He surprised me by nodding and saying, "There are more things in Heaven and earth than are dreamt of by man. That ain't exactly right but I think you know what I mean." And then he winked at me and laughed, really laughed this time.

My heart warmed as I smiled down at him. "Yes, Mr. Dalton, I surely do."

Turning to the sink, I marveled at this mountain man who most thought was a little dotty at least and full-out crazy at most, paraphrasing William Shakespeare. You just never know what life will throw in your path.

I dressed the hand, showing him how to crush the Pale Indian Plantain leaves and use them when he changed the bandage. "Those should keep infection away but if the cut turns red or gets swollen I want you to come back and see me, Mr. Dalton."

"All right, Miss Bessie."

"Now, after a few days, if there are no signs of infection, you can switch to the honey. Just slather it on a bandage and wrap it up." I picked up the jar and handed it to him.

"I have honey at home, Miss Bessie, from my brother's hives. Can I use that?"

I nodded. "The most important thing is to keep the cut clean and bandaged until it scabs over. And try not to do it again, you hear? Be more careful when you're out tramping around the mountain looking for..." I waved my hand "...something."

He grinned. "I promise, Miss Bessie. What do I owe you?"

I waved that away, too. By this time I was wise in the way of the mountain people. I would be repaid in some manner or other at some point in time.

"I hope you don't mind me saying so, Miss Bessie, but I sure am glad I found my way to you today instead of heading down to the doc in town. I can't imagine I would've gotten half as good a treatment down there."

"Now why would I mind that? I hope that now you've been here, you'll find your way back to us every now and again—and not just when you're hurt."

He snapped his fingers and Charlie got up and went to him immediately. I watched them walk out the door and smiled when Mr. Dalton turned back and tipped his hat to me. I felt I'd made a new and interesting friend and hoped he would come back to visit.

Chapter Eight

Late Spring 1916

Good Lord willin' and the creek don't rise.

A strange thing happened later that day... well, maybe strange isn't the right word. Truth is, when you live with a gift such as mine, odd things happen quite often. So, perhaps I should say an unexpected thing happened. I reckon that works better.

After Mr. Dalton left, I decided to scrub the kitchen floor and was up to my elbows in hot water when I heard the clip-clop of the mules' hooves crossing our bridge. I didn't think anything of it at first, only that Fletch was home a little bit sooner than I expected him. I was backed up to the open back door, on my hands and knees, in a rather undignified position with my backside flapping in the breeze, you might say, and a small unwashed strip left to do. I hurriedly dipped my scrub brush into the bucket of soapy water sitting beside me and scrubbed furiously, anticipating seeing my new organ, then tossed the brush into the bucket and rose to my feet.

Since Fletcher had the organ with him, I assumed he would pull up to the front porch and bring it in the house that way but the hoof beats, now muffled, continued on around the house as if he were taking it to the barn.

I wondered what he could be thinking. It seemed it would be so much easier if he unloaded it at the front door which led directly into the parlor where we planned to put the organ.

I grabbed my shoes from where I'd left them on the back porch. Slipping them on, I looked to the right then to the left, expecting to see the wagon come around the corner of the house. Though I could still hear the mules, there was nothing there.

"What in tarnation?" I muttered to myself as I stepped off the porch, shaded my eyes with my hand and looked toward the barn.

Nothing. Not a soul or a mule or even a wagon in sight. In fact, there was no movement anywhere, no breeze to ruffle the branches of the trees, no barn cats slinking across the yard looking for a handout, nothing but the sound of a horse-drawn wagon moving beyond the house and on to the barn.

I thought of the slave ghosts and how I couldn't see them and wondered if this was another voice from the past. Had someone long ago driven a wagon around the house to the barn? Well, of course they had, but for what purpose? Perhaps it was simply a delivery to the long ago overseer of the Solomon Plantation? Or maybe it was a visitor calling on the overseer's wife? Or worse, the sheriff bringing back a runaway slave to face what I could only imagine was a dreadful and painful justice?

I kept my eyes on the dark opening of the barn door as the sounds of the wagon stopped, the brake creaking as it was engaged. I could hear it very plainly, just as I often heard the slave ghosts, and like them, I couldn't see what I was hearing.

Much as I had the first night I'd heard the rattling of invisible chains and the shuffle-thud of bare feet moving along the possum trot, I narrowed my eyes to a squint and shook my head, hoping to bring the sounds to life.

Still nothing but the blackness of the open barn door.

Wondering what it could mean, or if, in fact, it meant anything, I grabbed my hoe and stepped off the porch, intending to get a little weeding done. I soon forgot about ghosts as I inspected my garden. The cabbage was coming along nicely as were the green beans and tomatoes, though those had barely broken through the dirt since the seeds had only been put in the ground a little more than a week ago. The carrots, sowed in the early spring, waved their lacy tops as the wind gusted. The corn patch had yet to be planted and was more Fletcher's domain than mine anyway. I never had any luck with corn and had learned to leave the dealing of that to him.

I glanced over at the grape vines growing along the fence and was pleased to see the misty green of new growth emerging. I looked toward the ridge where Fletcher had started an apple orchard and smiled at the hint of pink from the blossoms. My mouth watered as I imagined picking the fruit and biting into the crispy, tart flesh. And later in the season, the jars of apple butter, apple jelly and spiced apples I would put by for the coming winter.

I entertained myself while I weeded the garden by singing the hymns I planned to play at that week's church service and before too long I heard the jingling and the clip-clop of hooves coming across our little bridge again. I held still and waited to see if the sounds would continue on around the house to the barn as they had before. When nothing appeared, I ran to the back door, set my hoe against the wall and raced through the house just as Fletcher yelled, "Whoa, my pretties," as he pulled the wagon to the front porch.

My organ had arrived!

And oh, was it a beauty. I stopped dead on the front porch and just looked. I could only see a sliver of the polished wood because Fletch had it covered with a tarp but that single shining streak had me smiling like a mule eating briars.

Fletch set the brake, draped the reins around it and hopped down from the wagon with a laugh. "You been standing there all day waiting for me, Bessie-girl? I recollect you were standing right there when I left this morning."

Forgoing the steps, I hiked up my skirts and leaped off

the porch then hurried around to the back of the wagon. "Of course, I haven't. I've been taking tea with the queen and visiting with Bose."

He put his hands on his hips, narrowed laughing eyes at me. "And just who might that be? Am I going to have to get my shotgun and hunt these new beaus down and set them straight about fooling with my wife?"

I laughed as I clasped my hands together over my heart and sighed. "I love it when you're manly, Fletcher Elliott. But no need for a shotgun—this time." I kissed his cheek. "It was only Bose Dalton looking for someone to tend his wounds. I didn't even have to tear a strip off my petticoat."

"Well, I suppose that's all right then. Bose doin all right?" he asked as he let the tailgate down then bounded into the wagon.

"Bose is fine, he fell and cut his hand while he was up on Flinty Knob."

"Still looking for his Booger, is he?"

I laughed. "That he is and with his faithful Charlie at his side." I was practically trembling by this time, wanting a look at my organ.

Fletch turned, held out his hand and hoisted me up in the wagon bed. "Hang on to your knickers, Bessie-girl, this beauty might blow 'em right off." Grabbing the bottom of the tarp, he whipped it away.

I put my hands on my cheeks and goggled at the organ. "Oh! Oh, mercy, Fletcher, that sure is a pretty thing, isn't it?"

The organ, encased in a carved walnut cabinet—a very elaborate carved Victorian-style walnut cabinet—polished to a high gloss with little shelves, curling posts, moldings and a mirror in the high back was gorgeous. I ran my hand lovingly over the keys.

"I reckon she is at that," Fletch said. "Here," he untied the stool and scooted it over to the organ. "Sit down and play us a tune while we wait for Tom. He was right behind me when I left Old Fort and headed for home to pick up Laura. They should be here in a bit. You and Laura can visit while Tom helps me unload the organ."

"I hope you asked them to supper."

"I did and Tom accepted." He patted the stool seat. "Play me a song, Bessie-girl."

"All right." I grinned as I sat down, placed my feet on the pedals and pumped, picking out a tune with one finger, just to hear the beautiful sound. Sighing, I squared my body and placed both hands on the keys, and continuing to pump my feet, played one of Fletch's favorite hymns, "When the Roll is Called Up Yonder." I sang, of course, and smiled in delight when Fletch joined in. I rarely heard him sing outside of church and he had a lovely baritone voice which I would have loved to hear more often.

Maybe now that we had an organ in the house I could convince him to sing in the evenings while I played.

Before we got to the last verse, Tom's horses clip-clopped their way over the bridge. I turned my head and smiled at Laura, sitting beside her husband and holding a basket. As they neared, they both raised their voices in harmony with Fletch and me in the final chorus.

I held the last note then jumped up and grinned as I clapped my hands. One thing about the Elliott men, they had fine voices, and though it was a rare thing to hear them together, when they harmonized, it was like listening to a choir of angels. "I swan, I don't know why we all don't get together and form us a quartet. We could sing at all the church gatherings and give the Stone Mountain Baptist Quartet some competition."

Stone Mountain Baptist Quartet was a group made up of John Ledbetter, his daughter Nina and son Clete, and Rube Laughter, kin to but not in the least like his cousin Nate Laughter. The group sang every Sunday and at all of the church functions.

Tom threw his head back and laughed as he pulled on the reins to stop his horse. "What about it, Fletch?" He winked. "We could bring Johnse in to sing those really high notes for us."

Johnson Elliott, or Johnse as the family called him, was a cousin of Fletcher's and Tom's who had a high singing voice. Very close to a soprano, he had been asked by the ladies of Stone Mountain Baptist Church not to sing during services because his voice was too high and he sang loud, drowning the women out. More accurately, what put them to shame was his voice was higher and clearer and he sang so much better than they did and that didn't sit right with them at all.

Fletcher snorted out a laugh. "The women folk would have themselves a collective dying duck fit if we did that— well, some of the women folk, Nettie Ledbetter in particular. You know she went to Preacher Redmon and asked him to ban Johnse from the church. Can't say if the preacher would've done it, but in the end, he didn't have to. Johnse left on his own and started going to Noah Vess's Holiness Church over on the other side of the mountain."

Tom took off his hat and scratched his head. "I think it was more jealousy because he has a better voice than any of them. That's not a very Christian way to act, if you ask me."

"Nope, it sure isn't. That's about as unchristian as it gets."

Fletcher held my hand and I jumped down from the wagon. "I miss seeing Johnse in church every Sunday. Nettie Ledbetter isn't a Christian on her best days but I believe there's a special corner in Hell for people like her. They proclaim their Christianity and believe they'll go to Heaven but I have faith that God has different plans for them." Tom helped Laura down and I held out my hand to her. "Laura, I'm happy to see you. Y'all will stay for supper won't you?"

She smiled. "Fletcher already asked us and since the children are having an afternoon with their granny and grandpap, we accepted." She held out the basket. "I baked sourdough bread this morning and brought a couple of loaves along."

I lifted the cloth covering the basket and sniffed. The loaves were perfectly baked, golden brown crusts with the customary cross cut on the top before baking. I had learned not long after I came to live on the mountain that the women did this as a precaution. They believed if they baked their bread without cutting the cross in the top, the devil would sit on it and ruin the loaf.

"Mercy, Laura, that smells wonderful. I love sourdough bread but can't seem to get the hang of it. My starter always goes bad."

Linking my arm with hers, I led the way inside as she offered to send Tom over the next day with a starter for me.

"That's a little like casting pearls before swine, Laura. Ma Elliott gave me a start more times than I can count and I never could keep it going. I think it's just not meant for me to bake sourdough bread but I'll put my biscuits up against any woman on the mountain." I grinned. "Would you like a cup of coffee?"

"No, thank you, I find it makes me nervous when I'm carrying." She put her finger up to her lips. "Don't say anything to Tom. I haven't told him yet but I wanted to ask you if there's anything you can give me to help with the morning sickness?"

Oh, how I envied her. She already had three children and so far I had none. But I wasn't giving up. I knew, deep in my heart, I would be a mother one day. I held onto that hope and put a smile on my face.

"Why, that's wonderful, Laura, congratulations to you and Tom. What are you hoping for?"

"All I care about is that the baby makes it through this pregnancy which is one reason I haven't told Tom yet. I miscarried twice since Stella, and since I'm only a couple of months along, I didn't want to get his hopes up. I swan, that man took those two miscarriages harder than I did."

"Is there anything different about this time? Are you feeling the same as you did when you miscarried or like you did when you had Dollie, Jessie, and Stella?"

After thinking about it for a moment, a smile bloomed on her face. "I hadn't thought about it that way, Bessie, but you're right, with the ones I delivered I was as sick as a dog in the first three months. The two I miscarried, I wasn't sick at all." She set the basket on the table and clasped my hands in hers ... and I knew.

I lowered my eyes, not wanting her to see the truth as I knew it; Laura would have her baby, but like Sadie's baby, it would be stillborn. I couldn't tell her that, of course. Not only was it not a sure thing but if I told her what I suspected, it might increase the chance that it would happen.

"How about some tea or does that bother you, too?"

She smiled and shook her head and in a flash, the premonition changed. I saw an older Laura holding a baby wrapped in a blue blanket and I interpreted that to mean she would conceive and carry another baby to term, only it wouldn't be right away.

"No, I mean, yes, I'd love some tea. Maybe something soothing would be best. I don't want to bother this little one." She rested her hand protectively over her stomach.

I patted her hand and smiled. "I have just the thing. You sit down at the table there and I'll put the kettle on. And while we drink, the men can bring in my organ and I'll tell you a few things you can do to help ensure that that little one gets born."

I gave her oat straw tea and talked to her of the Cherokee medicine Elisi had taught me; red raspberry leaf tea to be taken daily but only after the third month, slippery elm bark tea to help with the nausea, ginseng root tea for energy and general well-being, and buckeye bark tea to help with the pain of the delivery. I also snuck in a few treatments that would ensure she would get pregnant again and, more importantly, I ended with a caution not to give up.

"No matter what happens, Laura, promise me you won't give up hope. If something happens to this baby and I'm not saying it will, but just in case, keep believing that God will give you what you want."

"Oh, oh, Bessie, I'm sorry. This is probably the last thing you want to talk about since ... well, I know you and Fletch have been trying and here I am with three healthy children, asking you for help. I should just be grateful for the ones I have and..."

I squeezed her hand. "No, Laura, I'm glad you came to me and I'll do everything I can to ensure you deliver this baby. I'm happy to and my situation doesn't change that at all. You see, I know I will have a child in time. I have every faith that God will give me that."

"A child but not a child of your own, you mean?"

"Doesn't matter to me one way or the other. I only know that I'll have a child in time. Mayhap it will be my own but I'll take the child even if I don't carry it inside me because when I find him, he'll be delivered to me by God and he will need me." I smiled. "He'll need me and I will be there for him."

"A boy, you know it will be a boy?"

"No, I don't and there's no way of telling until it happens but I'm sure it will happen … in time. My mother had three children, me, Roy, and Loney, and then she miscarried twice and didn't get pregnant again for a long time, eight years, but she never gave up hope. She had faith God would give her another child and he did, three more, in fact." I squeezed her hand again. "So, what I'm saying is trust in God no matter what.

I patted her hand and got up from the table. "I'm going to give you a tin of slippery elm bark and another of ginseng root for now. Just remember to drink a cup of slippery elm bark tea in the morning to help with the morning sickness and have a cup of ginseng tea in the afternoon to boost your energy."

"Slippery elm in the morning and ginseng in the afternoon."

I nodded. "When the time comes, say in another month, I'll bring you a tin of red raspberry leaves and you can start drinking that in the morning and give up the slippery elm—if the morning sickness has subsided. I'll also give you a tin of buckeye bark for the delivery." I smiled. "Could be you won't even need that but you'll have it on hand if the labor goes on for too long. Elisi swore by that for easing the pain of delivery."

I vowed, no matter what happened, I would tell her of the other plants that would help her conceive again; red raspberry leaf, red clover, black cohosh, nettle leaf, wild yam, and oat straw.

"Thank you, Bessie. I wonder if I might ask you a favor?"

"Of course."

"I'm … well, to tell the truth and shame the devil, I'm really nervous about this birth and that's a first for me. I always had quick deliveries before and the pain wasn't too bad, well, not as bad as I thought it would be, but this time, I'm a bit fretful. I always used Miss Ellie before but she's getting awful old and I'd like to ask you if when it comes time for Tom to run the granny race, could he run to you?"

The mountain people had distinct sayings about having babies. "They lost their notch stick" meant they'd already notched nine months on a stick and still the baby hadn't come. "Running the granny race" referred to the husband's job when his wife went into labor, meaning he would run to get his mother, mother-in-law or the midwife to help with the birth.

I smiled at her and took her hand. "Yes, Laura, send him to get me. Good Lord willin' and the creek don't rise, I'd be honored to act as your midwife."

CHAPTER NINE

Summer 1916

Hang in there like a hair in a biscuit.

My new organ and Laura's news kicked off a summer filled with wide-reaching events, not only on Stone Mountain but throughout the entire state, the nation, and the rest of the world.

In truth, the second half of the second decade of the 20th century, though it would later be known as the Progressive Era, proved to be an evolving—and deadly—time to be alive. While it could be said that mankind did grow and even improve, it seemed we still had a lot to learn in some areas.

The war in Europe had escalated, with most of the European nations joining in the battle, and the weapons and methods used proved more lethal than ever before. With U-boats and airplanes, machine guns, poison gas, landmines and trench warfare, my old friend Death was in Its heyday. The newspapers were full of horrific goings-on from the sinking of the British ocean liner RMS Lusitania by a German U-boat, killing 1,198 people, to the first use of poison gas in the Second Battle of Ypres to the introduction of the tank at the Battle of the Somme.

The United States thus far had managed to stay out of the whole mess but we weren't to be denied our own battles.

Earlier that summer at the Democratic National Convention in St. Louis, President Wilson campaigned with the slogan, "He kept us out of the war." And while it may have been true as far as the growing conflict in Europe was concerned, we were currently engaged in a Border War with our neighbor to the south, Mexico. Though I guess that didn't count to President Wilson and those who voted for him, it wouldn't be long before he went against his own slogan and our nation entered into the fray across the ocean.

A lesser revered battle was being fought here at the same time, the fight for women's rights. Suffragists were forming groups all across the country, even here in North Carolina where they were led by Gertrude Weil of Goldsboro. Those women were determined to win equal rights, not only for women but all of human kind. As it turned out, it would be a long, hard-fought battle, mostly but not always bloodless.

It was a most progressive time of increasing technology with telephones, electricity, and automobiles becoming ever more popular and available to businesses and homes in the bigger cities. With the advent of moving pictures, radios and mail delivered right to your doorstep, it seemed to me the world was moving at a break-neck pace and getting more and more crowded every day.

With all that was happening around us, I relished the serenity of my mountain home, grateful for long summer days filled with chores in the morning, gardening with the heat of the sun on my shoulders in the afternoon, and peaceful evenings sitting on my front porch with Fletch or inside playing my organ if it was raining.

And then in July, one of my worst fears returned, dragging me back into the horror and anger that had consumed my life in the spring of 1899. It didn't help that I was 15 years older, married, a seasoned teacher, and living in my own home. Or that the cause of the flooding on Stone Mountain was completely different than the flash flood that had taken my little brother Green's life so cruelly when I was 18.

I didn't think much about it at first. After all, though July was usually a dry month on the mountain, a drenching rain wasn't completely unknown. And it was usually welcome, bringing much needed water to the crops, cooling the air a bit, and giving the farmers a day off from their hard work in the fields. Plus, after it was over, those fields would be a bit easier to work for a day or two. A little messier, true, but the wet ground and cooler temperatures combined to make the hoeing and weeding a mite less taxing on the farmers.

But this storm, oh, this storm was a different matter altogether. It started with a typical summer shower that lasted for over a day at the beginning of July, saturating the ground. What happened next took place so many miles away from us that we barely even noticed except for the newspaper headlines. On July 5th, a hurricane tore onto the Gulf Coast of Alabama. Three days later, the same storm would reach us, and while it was a good deal weaker than it had been down there, it poured heavy rain on the mountains of western North Carolina, swelling the French Broad and Catawba Rivers.

A few days after those torrential rains, another hurricane came ashore on South Carolina's coast, passing over the Charleston area and heading north. On July 15th, it was downgraded to a tropical storm and by the time it made its way to us it was a good deal weaker. But not weak enough, dropping record levels of rainfall on the already waterlogged grounds, raising the river and stream levels even more. With the ground already soaked, most of that rainfall became run-off, flowing to the already full waterways causing the rivers and creeks to rise rapidly. I swan, it rained so hard the animals were starting to pair off. When it was all over, the newspapers reported that the French Broad River crested at an estimated 21 feet, some 17 feet above flood stage. The average width of the French Broad where it ran near Asheville was 381 feet, but on those days in July of 1916, it widened to almost 1300 feet across.

The Catawba River which flows southeasterly into South Carolina from our mountains, experienced the same flooding, rising in some places almost 23 feet above previous high-water marks, 47 feet above flood level. Every bridge on the Catawba was washed away with the exception of one near Marion but the approaches to it in both directions were destroyed, severing telegraph and telephone connections.

Other rivers and streams flooded too, of course, and when it was all over, some 15 days later, the destruction was massive. Numerous people lost their lives; farms, homes, churches, bridges and factories were destroyed. In some places, the railroad tracks were completely washed away, in others merely covered with water but there was a section outside Old Fort where the tracks survived even after the ground underneath crumbled away. The Old Fort Sentinel ran a picture of a group of men standing on those tracks with nothing supporting them from beneath. I never could decide if those men were incredibly brave or simply stupid.

On Stone Mountain, the blacksmith shop owned by the Gilbert family and the saw mill at the Elliott homestead were demolished. Even our little branch of Cedar Creek rose high enough to flood our front yard but, thankfully, not enough to touch our house or the shacks across from it. As a precaution, Fletch and I slept in the loft of our cantilevered barn for two nights. The first was harrowing, bringing nightmares of Green drowning in Spring Creek every time I dozed off. In each one, I'd reach for the scrap of blue floating in that muddy water, screaming at Green to hang on, only to wake and find my hands empty.

When Fletcher shook me awake the next morning, I told him about the dreams as he stroked his hand up and down my back in an effort to stop the trembling. After I finished, he hugged me and held on for the longest time, and while he didn't actually say it, I knew it was a sign for me to just hang on, the storm would eventually be over.

The second night we spent in the barn loft proved him right as it turned out to be the final night of the storm.

Even though we hadn't slept well the night before—the hard wooden floor of the loft wasn't exactly a comfortable mattress and so we didn't really sleep, only drowsed—it felt as though I had just shut my eyes when the drops of rain on the tin roof of the barn lessened and, no more than fifteen minutes after that, stopped completely.

We'd lived with the ping-ping of raindrops so long that the silence was a little shocking. But the cessation of sound didn't last long as the crickets, frogs, and katydids all chimed in, serenading the storm on its way.

They were joined by a few tentative birds, and when we heard our two roosters crow outside, we rose, climbed down from the loft and threw open the barn doors. Still in my nightgown and barefoot, I started to step out into the wonderfully fresh air but Fletch, who had taken the time to pull on pants over his nightshirt and stuff his feet into his boots before climbing down the ladder, stopped me with a hand on my arm.

"Let me put down some boards first, Bess..." he nodded toward the yard "...or you'll be in mud up to your ankles."

"All right, but can you hurry, please? I have a powerful need for the outhouse and I really don't want to use that bucket again."

Fletch grinned and patted my back. "Won't take but a minute or two. I'll lay a path to the outhouse first and then I'll put some boards from there to the kitchen door. After the night we had, I could drink about a gallon of coffee."

"That does sound good but first the outhouse."

He went back into the barn and grabbed a few boards and in no time at all I was able to make my way to the outhouse and then to the kitchen without wading through ankle-deep mud.

I put on a pot of coffee then put on my shoes and went out to the back porch. Fletcher was standing on the steps, looking at the pig sty and grinning. He glanced at me and pointed to the pigs. "Happy as a dead pig in sunshine."

The pigs, from the fat sow and the temperamental boar to the piglets birthed only a few months before, were rolling around in the mud in what, indeed, could only be their idea of Heaven.

I shook my head. "I never understood that saying. How can anything be happy if it's dead?"

Fletch shrugged. "If a dead pig lies in the sunshine long enough, the heat from the sun will dry its skin and pull the lips back, making it look like its smiling." He nodded at the pig sty. "All that mud looks like pig Heaven to me."

"Are you reading my mind now, Fletch?"

"Don't think so. Why?"

"Because I was just thinking those pigs look like they're in Heaven."

He grinned and squeezed my hand. "Well, we've been married what, 15 years now?"

"Yes, and six months."

"I recollect Ma always said people who've been married long enough start to look alike. Could be we're starting to think alike instead."

I nodded. "Could be. Did the chickens come through all right? I see the roosters are fine but what about my laying hens?"

"They're all in the coop. Them ladies are too dainty to get their feet muddy. I imagine they'll come out later when you pitch some corn out for them."

I set my hands on my hips and breathed in deep. The air that morning was strangely sweet and somehow lighter than usual. "Mercy sakes alive, it's almost worth the wet and worry of the storm to have air like this after. Wish we could bottle some of that up and save it for the dog days."

Fletcher nodded. "And look there, Bessie-girl, that's about the prettiest sunrise I've ever seen."

Over to the east, the morning sky was a brilliant kaleidoscope of color; delicate pinks, sassy reds, golden yellows framed by the deep blue of the sky above and the bright green of the mountains below. This was one of the rare days on the mountain when the morning mist was absent.

I smiled and took another deep breath. "It appears God's in his Heaven and all's right with the world."

"Yep, and I'd say that's reason enough to get this day started. I'm going to grab me a cup of coffee and then I'm going to head up to the upper pasture and bring the cows down." He whistled for Fritz. "Where in tarnation did that dog get to?"

An almost nonexistent shiver ran down my spine. I

folded my arms in an effort to warm myself. "I haven't seen him since we went up into the loft last night."

"Probably found him a dry, soft bed somewhere." He whistled again. "Darn lazy hound dog…"

My heart sank when Fletcher whistled once more and Fritz still didn't appear. Another delicate shiver and then a flash of red drew my eyes to the graveyard where we'd buried George and his and Sadie's stillborn son. The mountain people believed cardinals signified death. And I knew. "Oh, mercy, mercy, Fletch," I whispered, clutching his arm.

"What is it, Bess?"

I didn't want to tell him but as soon as he walked around to the front he'd find Fritz's body. "He's dead, Fritz is dead. He's around on the porch, lying underneath one of the rocking chairs."

Fletch frowned then took off his hat and bowed his head. "All right, I'll take care of it but, Bessie, don't go out there until I do. I'll call you when I've got his grave dug and we can put him in the ground together."

I nodded. I'll get breakfast started." When he turned, I took his arm. "Dig the grave up yonder where we buried George and the baby. Fritz was part of our family, too. I'm so sorry, Fletcher."

"Me too. Fritz was a good dog, the best I ever had. I guess we should've been expecting this, he was old and having trouble gettin around. Mayhap now he's free of pain and with Ma and Pa in Heaven."

"I'm sure he is, Fletch, I'm sure he is. He was such a sweet boy, I can't imagine God not wanting him with Him up there." Turning, I walked into the kitchen, wiping the tears from my cheeks as I went.

We buried Fritz that afternoon right at the edge of the woods beside George and the baby. I sang the first and second verse of "God Be with You Till We Meet Again" and Fletcher led us in a prayer.

What would come to be known as the Western North Carolina Flood of 1916 had claimed many souls. And while it didn't take Fritz and his death would not be recorded on any of the many official lists of fatalities, it was a loss of great measure to us.

Two weeks later, after the excitement was past and life had settled back into its normal routine, Bose Dalton showed up at our place carrying something wrapped loosely in a quilt. When he came closer, I heard the little yips and saw the furry snout of a puppy.

Bose stepped up on the porch where Fletch and I sat on the swing, tipped his hat and held out the bundle to us. "Mr. Fletch, Miss Bessie, I heard tell you lost your dog." Shuffling his feet, he looked down at the puppy and went on in a rush, the words practically falling from his mouth like the rain during the worst of the storm with pauses at points where the rainfall would lessen only to begin again at a more furious velocity. "I'm right sorry for your loss ... you wouldn't let me pay you for doctoring my hand, Miss Bessie, and I wanted to do something nice for you in return ... for saving me a trip to the doc in town and all. One of my hounds had a litter a few weeks back and ... well, I thought y'all might like to have one of the pups, not to replace your dog, or anything like that ... well, this here's the runt of the litter but he's a pretty little thing and he'll grow to be a good dog."

He shoved the puppy, still in the quilt, into my arms. The pup wiggled and got his head clear enough to lap at my face. It was, of course, love at first lick.

Fletcher stood up and offered his hand. "I thank you, Bose. That's a right nice thing to do." He grinned down at me dodging the puppy's busy tongue. "I do believe that's the best payment my wife ever received for her doctoring."

I stood up, snuggling the puppy to my breast as I smiled at Bose. "I'll add my thanks to Fletcher's, Bose. He's right when he says this has to be the best fee I ever received and probably ever will receive. Your hand looks to have healed up right well. Has it given you any trouble?"

He dipped his head and aimed his answer at his feet. "Oh, no, Miss Bessie. No trouble 't'all."

I held out my hand. "Mind if I take a look?"

He placed his hand palm up in mine and I received what

I'd come to know was a rare gift from this shy man when he looked up at me with a full-fledged smile on his face.

I tried to convince Bose to stay for dinner but he said he needed to get back to home. As soon as he'd made it far enough away that he couldn't hear, Fletch started laughing. He put his arm around my shoulders and squeezed. "I reckon I'd better keep my eye on that one," he said.

"Whatever for?"

"I do believe he's got a little case of puppy love for you, Bessie-girl. Gotta protect my woman."

I laughed and shook my head. "He's a married man, Fletcher, with five young'uns and another one on the way. His only interest is in my healing powers. That's all it is." To be honest, I was more than a little pleased. What woman with 15 years of marriage behind her wouldn't be?

He took the puppy from my arms and held him up at face level to get a better look. "What are we going to name him?"

"I have no idea. Papa always named our animals and since this little one will spend most of his time with you I'll leave the name up to you."

"Huh, maybe we should wait until we get to know him a little better." He set the dog down on the porch, and in typical puppy frenzy, he immediately jumped up and put his paws on Fletcher's legs. Tongue lolling out, he whined in a bid to be picked up again.

"Sure does have some big paws. If he grows into those things, he's going to be bigger than Fritz," I said.

Fletcher picked him back up again and tucked him under his arm. "Pa always said that's a sign of a good huntin dog. I'll take him out with me tomorrow and see how he does."

The dog was to be the second of many dogs in our time together, and like the first one and all to follow, Fletcher called him Fritz. He said it was a perfect name for a dog and besides he would probably end up calling the dog that half the time anyway. I likened it to myself at the beginning of a new school year when I often got the names of my students wrong. Or the way Fletch called every flower he ever saw a calendula whether it be a hollyhock, Joe Pye weed, or a rose. Ma Elliott had calendulas growing all around her place and it was the first flower name he learned and so for the rest of his life his name for any flower.

Contrary to July, August proved to be uneventful and when I returned to school that fall, I decided to add some lessons on poetry since Papa had sent me a lovely collection of poems. I had never taught poetry before and was pleasantly surprised at the interest shown by my students. We studied various poets, primarily American, Dickinson, Longfellow, Thoreau, and Emerson. The children particularly enjoyed the rhyming words and I would often catch them speaking in rhymes during their recess.

Since my students seemed most taken with the works about nature, I gave the older ones an assignment for the fall harvest break; write a poem about something in nature, at least four lines long and it could be either free-style or rhyming. It was a simple assignment really and I looked forward to reading and sharing their work on the first day back at school.

My students surprised me when even the most recalcitrant of them completed the assignment. Instead of reading them myself, I decided to have them read their poems to the other students.

The poems, for the most part, were well written, if a little immature, but that was to be expected since many of the students had never heard or seen poetry before.

One poem in particular delighted me though it didn't technically fulfill the assignment. Jimmy Dalton was the last to recite.

When I called on him, he came the front of the room, cleared his throat loudly, then started: "The River by James Dalton." He cleared his throat again. "I went to the river to take a swim, I threw my shirt upon a limb, I dropped my pants into the grass." A few students put their hands to their mouths in an effort to staunch their titters. Jimmy took a moment to beam a smile at them before he went on. "And jumped in the river up to my knees."

The whole class erupted in laughter and Jimmy's cheeks flushed. He executed a sweeping bow then looked expectantly at me. I shushed the giggles and when they were quiet, said, "Very good, Jimmy, but the last line doesn't rhyme."

Looking down at his feet, he said, "I know, Miss Bessie, but it would've if the river'd been deeper."

The class erupted again and I knew there would be no calming them down this time. I nodded to Jimmy as I clamped down my lips and ordered myself not to laugh. "Yes, Jimmy, but maybe you..." And I couldn't contain my amusement anymore. I walked quickly to my budding Longfellow and put my arm around his shoulders, giving him a warm hug. "Thank you, Jimmy, you did very well."

He grinned. "If Ma had let me write it the way I wanted to, it would've rhymed but she said I couldn't say that word in front of ladies so I changed it."

When I arrived home from school that afternoon, I found an old woman sitting in one of the rockers on the front porch waiting for me. She smiled shyly and rose from the rocker as I came up the steps. She held a walking cane in front of her, and her shoulders were so hunched, she practically leaned right over it. Her hands were gnarled and swollen, the veins rising from the brown-mottled skin like snakes in a river. Her gray hair had been pulled into a bun, framing a face creased and wrinkled. I thought to myself she had a rather interesting visage as I stared into eyes as dark green as moss on a river rock. Puzzled, I offered a somewhat hesitant smile in return as I greeted her.

"Hello, can I help you with something?"

She kept her eyes down as she spoke softly. "I'm Bose Dalton's great-granny. Are you the one he calls Miss Bessie, the one who healed his hand?"

"Yes, I am. I'm pleased to meet you, Missus—is it Dalton?"

"Yep, Tancy Dalton."

I smiled. "That's a beautiful name. I hope Bose is all right?"

"Oh, yep, he's fine. I come to hear you play your organ if'n you don't mind. Bose and all t'other folks say it's the prettiest thing they ever heared and I wanted to hear it before I die."

My smile widened at the compliment. "Isn't that a nice thing to say? Won't you come in and sit while I put my school things down? We can have some supper and then I'll play for you."

"Oh, no. Don't go troublin yourself none, Miss Bessie." She bent down and picked up a milk pail sitting by the chair. "I brought my own supper and I done et it while I was waitin for you to come home."

"All right. Won't you come in then? I can get you some water or a cup of tea."

She waved that away and sat back down in the rocker. "If'n you don't mind, I'll just sit out here. It's a nice evening and all."

I nodded. "Do you have any songs you'd particularly like to hear?"

"You just play whatever your heart tells you to play. I ain't 'ticular."

I smiled and went inside, placing my school things on the kitchen table before going to my organ. I had been working on songs for the annual Christmas Eve Midnight Service at the church and the music I was considering for that program was stacked on my organ so I played those. After six or seven Christmas carols, I ended the impromptu recital with Papa's favorite hymn "The Old Rugged Cross".

When I went back outside to the porch, the old woman was sitting there with tears running down her face. I rushed over and knelt beside her chair, taking her hand in mine.

"Are you all right, Missus Dalton?"

She looked up at me and smiled through the tears. "If Heaven is as beautiful as that, I can't wait to die."

It was the finest compliment I ever received for my music.

CHAPTER TEN

Early Fall 1918

As lonely as the last pea at pea time.

The first day of school was always a chaotic affair, filled with greeting returning students and meeting new ones, deciding where to place each one, and evaluating their strengths and weaknesses so that I could make individual lesson plans. The day had been warm with just the hint of autumn first making its presence known in the pale golden drifts of sunlight piercing the trees' foliage, the breeze hinting at the promise of the changing season with a soothing cool touch as it played across my face, and the spicy aroma of leaves beginning their tragic albeit beautiful passage to death.

I walked to school that morning, feeling the need to be alone with my thoughts, and as I strolled toward home late afternoon, my mind turned to the nagging sensation that had plagued me throughout the day that something terrible waited just around the corner, biding its time, ready to jump out and pull me into its ominous grip.

What in the world could it be, I wondered, as I traipsed along, wishing now I had ridden Pet to school if only for the company. I glanced up and spied a woman ahead of me, standing in the middle of the path, hands folded together, as if patiently waiting for me to reach her. She was too far away to make out her features but I felt certain I knew her in the way she held her body and the tilt of her head.

As I drew nearer, the high, wide cheekbones which dominated that lovely face held my gaze and I focused on the eyes which I knew would be dark to match the heavy, thick hair tied back into a bun. Mama! I started to shout as I quickened my step but the woman smiled and I knew this was not my mother but her sister Belle. My lips turned up with joy and I laughed with delight. "Aunt Belle," I said as I drew nearer, "I have missed you so..." My words faded and my smile disappeared, realizing I could see the path and trees behind her as though she were transparent. Oh, God, please, no, I thought as I fell to my knees. She gave me the most beatific smile as she raised her fingers to her lips, kissed them, then waved them toward me; Aunt Belle's way of saying goodbye. "Please, don't go," I called, watching as she seemed to drift away from me then disappear altogether.

I sat there for the longest time, watching the place I had last seen her, willing her to come back, if only for just a moment so I could tell her how much I loved her and how much I would miss her. Although as a youngster I had found Aunt Belle to be a pompous, opinionated woman, I had grown to understand her and love her for the dedicated, loving woman she was, the person who been my mother's best friend and had loved her with a fierceness that had comforted me after Mama passed. A woman who had taken Mama's place.

I have no one else in Hot Springs, I thought to myself with dismay. Papa, Loney, and Thee lived in Knoxville now, along with Roy and his wife Alice. Jack had married a railroad man by the name of Ed Tillery and was living in Asheville with him. The last I heard, she was pregnant with her first child. Aunt Belle's husband Uncle Ned had passed the year before from a sudden heart attack. I had at that time tried to persuade Aunt Belle to join me on Stone Mountain but she had gently refused, telling me she had lived in the house Ned and Papa built for her her entire adult life and didn't intend to leave it while alive. "Besides," she said, "who would be left to tend to Lucinda's and little Greenie's graves?" I put my fist against my mouth, stifling a sob. I had lost so many family members and the grief still lingered, raw and bitter. Would it ever ease, would I ever be able to accept the loss of each one? I truly doubted it.

At last I rose to my feet to resume my journey toward home, trying to distract my grief by keeping my mind busy with plans to make the trip to Hot Springs to bid my aunt goodbye. Unless a temporary teacher could be found, school would have to be delayed by a week or so. Mayhap I could speak to Nettie Ledbetter about taking over for me. Although her words could be harsh and biased, she had a college education and I had noticed she seemed to take a gentler approach with the younger ones. If I could find some subtle way of suggesting she handle them with great care, she would be a good candidate for substitute teacher.

Fletch met me on the path leading up to our house, a piece of paper clutched in his hand. He took one look at my face and nodded. "We got a telegram but it looks like you already know."

"I saw her, Fletch." I clutched his hand. "On the path coming home. She stood there, watching me, then kissed her fingers like she used to when she'd tell me goodbye and just ... left."

My dear husband, usually so pragmatic and logical, didn't question this but simply pulled me closer and hugged me. "I reckon you'll be wanting to go home," he said against my hair.

"This is my home," I answered, my voice muffled. "But yes, I do want to go back, to say goodbye and to visit the graves of my family."

"I'll send a telegram telling 'em we're coming." He held my hand and we began the walk toward our farm. "Tonight's prayer meeting and it's our turn, Bess. You want me to ask the others to have it somewhere else?"

I wiped my eyes. "No, it's good it's here, Fletch. I figured I'd talk to Nettie Ledbetter and ask her to take over my classroom until I get back." I looked at him. "How long should I tell her we'll be gone?"

"The rest of the week, I reckon. We can come back

Sunday if that'll give you enough time."

I nodded. "And if not, I'll tell Nettie if she doesn't see me at church Sunday evening to tend to my students on Monday."

It was a bit discomforting the speed at which news traveled across our mountain. Friends and neighbors came by with food, offering their condolences and to take care of chores while we were away. Most stayed for the prayer meeting, after which I asked Nettie if I could speak with her. To my relief she seemed happy I chose her to teach while I was away. I told her where I kept the lesson plans and the seat chart, explained the ones who may be troublesome but confided they were all special children in need of encouragement and support which worked much better than negative words or actions.

She nodded with a sage look. "I know you find my disposition trying at times, Bessie. Lord knows, my husband does." A brief smile touched her lips. "I'm afraid I have never quite mastered the art of holding my tongue. But I will do my best by these children and mind what I say to them."

I clutched her hand. "Thank you, Nettie. It means so much that you're willing to do this for me."

"Why, I don't reckon there's anything I wouldn't do for you," she said, and surprised me by hugging me tight. Nettie was not a person prone to show affection either physically or verbally. She released me, stepping back and saying, as if to clarify her former statement, "After all, it is the Christian thing to do." I sighed inwardly.

Fletcher and I left on the train the next morning, and as I traveled through the seven tunnels between Old Fort and Asheville, I thought of all the trips I had made back to Hot Springs and then home to Stone Mountain and knew in my heart this would be my last trip to that small charming town where I had grown up. It bothered me no one in our family was left to tend to the family graves and then it occurred to me Miss Cordy might be so willing. She lived nearby and I thought of her as a family member. I looked forward to seeing her and hoped her dog Little Bit was still alive although I knew he most probably wouldn't be, as he would be well over 20 years old now. The two had been inseparable and I was glad I had saved the mutt from death. In the end, he had saved Miss Cordy, distraught over losing her pet hen.

Hot Springs, usually a quiet town, was a bustle of activity when our train pulled into the depot. With a base population of 650, Aunt Belle had written that the town had more than tripled when it became home to a German concentration camp, housed at the elegant Mountain Park Hotel where Fletch and I had spent our wedding night as guests of Aunt Belle and Uncle Ned.

Fletcher and I made our way to Aunt Belle's home, greeting friends as we walked along Bridge Street and accepting their words of sympathy. When we reached Aunt Belle's house, we were not surprised to find her kitchen table filled with food brought by neighbors and friends. I brushed away tears, thinking how much I had missed this small town and its citizens.

Aunt Belle had been laid out in her parlor in her finest dress of golden silk, her hands folded upon her chest, her eyes weighted with coins. I went to my knees beside her and briefly touched her hands, so cold and inhuman now, and told her I hoped she was with Uncle Ned, Mama, Elisi and Greenie and that I looked forward to seeing them again one day. I rose to my feet, noticing the changes death had inflicted upon her, thinking our bodies are only shells housing our souls; nothing could attest to that better than a corpse. Movement behind drew my attention and I turned to see Tommy Bearing standing near the window, hat in hand.

"Tommy," I said, smiling at him. "It's so nice to see you."

"I reckon it's right nice to see you too, Bessie," he said.

"Where are your sisters, Tommy?" In the past, where you found Tommy, you found one or all sisters hovering nearby, ready to protect him at a moment's notice.

"They're around, I reckon."

I nodded. "Who took care of her, Tommy?" I asked in a low voice. After all, like me, Aunt Belle had no family left in Hot Springs.

"I did," he said with a proud look. "I come ever mornin to see if she needed anything, her being alone and all, and I was the one what found her." He swallowed and blinked his eyes several times. "Miss Belle was awful kind to me," he continued, "always asking how I was, how my sisters was a-doin, wantin to know if we were wantin for anything." He hesitated and his eyes met mine with defiance. "She saw me, saw who I was, as a man with worth, a man full-growed, not somebody to be laughed at."

I nodded. I knew that some of the townspeople found Tommy and his sisters an oddity and shunned them for this reason, a few even laughing at them, especially after Tommy shot his neighbor's white mule, thinking it was a ghost. But I had not realized Tommy was aware of this as well. And I too had avoided them, in my pride thinking Tommy had feelings for me. My face reddened at this and I felt small and petty. But Aunt Belle, acting the way a true Christian should, had seen past the overprotective sisters and pampered brother to the people beneath.

I crossed over to him and took his hands, pressing them with my own. "She was right to do so, Tommy. I'm glad she got to know you and your sweet sisters. I should have done the same."

He gave me a curt nod.

Aunt Belle and Uncle Ned had not been blessed with children and I found the thought of her dying alone agonizing. "Do you know what happened, Tommy? Did she suffer? I can't stand the thought of her being alone when she died."

"Doc thinks it was a heart attack. Looked to me like it came on sudden-like. I found her sittin at her dining room table, a cup of coffee afore her. She had her head down on the table and looked to be sleepin." Tears came to his eyes. "'Bout killed me when I realized she weren't here no more." He bit his lip and turned his face to the window.

"Thank you for taking care of her. It helps me to know that someone who cared was there for her."

He turned back to me. "I mean to see to her grave after she's buried. Don't worry about the rest of your family neither, Miss Bess. I'll see that their graves are taken care of. I'll tend 'em like they was my own family."

I threw my arms around him and hugged him tight, tears streaming down my face. "Thank you, Tommy. That means the world to me."

He grunted in response before leaving me to my grief.

Aunt Belle's funeral drew most of the township of Hot Springs. All pews in Dorland Presbyterian Church's chapel were filled and those who could not find a place to sit lined the walls or stood outside. Papa and my brothers and sisters had not been able to make the trip back for the funeral and Fletch and I were the only family Aunt Belle had to bid her goodbye. Her surviving brothers and sisters and host of nieces and nephews, grand and otherwise, were scattered all over America.

I had asked Doc Nanny to play his violin and he stood proudly at the pulpit, his eyes closed in concentration as he drew the bow across the strings, giving the congregation a beautiful rendition of "The Old Rugged Cross." As I sat there, listening to Doc play, I prayed she had not been too lonely since Uncle Ned's death but in looking about the church decided she must not have been with so many people here today to pay her homage. This was borne out after Pastor Gentry spoke, when many felt the need to speak of her and the things she had done for them. It was lovely hearing all the wonderful deeds by Aunt Belle and realizing the love these people had for her.

After the service, we followed the casket, borne by Fletcher, Tommy and four other men, to the graveyard, and after the casket was lowered into the ground, I threw a white rose into the grave on top of the coffin, followed by others doing the same and soon it was covered with her favorite flower. The preacher asked me to sing "Amazing Grace," and as I did, my voice began to falter but others quickly joined in and by the end of the song, all those gathered around the grave were singing, tears falling down their faces.

As per tradition, we retired to Aunt Belle's house for food and remembrance and although it was a sad affair I was also comforted by the testimonials which continued of Aunt Belle and the ways she had helped this small community. There was much talk about her generosity, even in death, willing her home and fortune to the church. Doc Nanny was there with his fiddle and I accompanied him on the piano to some church hymns then surprised him by borrowing his fiddle and playing it while he pounded on the piano. Many saw Doc as a simpleton, but to me, there was no greater musician than Doc and it pleased me tremendously when he complimented me on my skills.

Seeing Miss Cordy cheered me up some, although she had aged considerably. I looked around for Little Bit but didn't see her faithful dog anywhere. Noticing this, she said, "He died last year." Tears filmed her eyes and she blinked them away. "He lived a long and happy life and I shore do miss my Little Bit. I'll never be able to thank you enough for bringing him to me, Bessie. He was truly a special gift and I cherished that little soul every day he was with me."

"As he did you," I said.

She smiled at this. "But he didn't leave me alone. 'Bout a month afore he passed, he disappeared for a bit and when he come home, had a small pup with him." She stared into my eyes. "Like he knew he was gonna be a-leavin me and wanted to make sure I had a companion and wouldn't get lonely."

"I don't doubt that's what he was thinking," I said.

When she smiled this time, there was pure joy on her face. "I've named this one Little Bit Junior but call him Junior."

I looked around, thrilled for her. "Is he here?"

She shook her head. "Left him at home, inside where he can't get lost or nothin. I'd've brought him but he's still a pup and likes to chew on anything he can find. Plus he's not rightly broke to the house yet. But I do want you to meet him afore you leave."

"I can't wait, Miss Cordy. I'll be sure to drop by."

She patted my hand. "I reckon I'll head on home now. I miss the little fella when I'm away from him."

I walked her outside so I could get some fresh air and

smiled at Harry Hill, smoking a cigar under the big oak in Aunt Belle's front yard. Harry came from a well-known family, being the son of the town's first mayor and nephew of Colonel J.Edwin Rumbough, owner of the Mountain Park Hotel.

"I hear the Mountain Park underwent some pretty severe changes," I said to him.

He nodded as he puffed on his cigar.

"I'm surprised your uncle agreed to such a thing."

He shrugged. "To be honest, he'd rather be traveling or at his mansion in Asheville than here seeing to the hotel. When the government offered to lease the property, he jumped at the chance."

"I find that sad. Fletcher and I spent our wedding night there. It was such a beautiful place."

He blew smoke into the air. "And will be again if the government keeps its word. They're in the process as we speak of shutting the prison camp down."

"I hadn't heard that, Harry, but it will be nice to see the Mountain Park back in business again, don't you think?"

"To be honest, Bess, I hate to see the prison camp go. It's been a real boon to the town's economy. Not to mention the internment camp put a good many men and women to work, me included." He puffed with pride. "I was a guard there."

"I hope most of the employees were from Hot Springs," I said somewhat drily.

"For the most part. Of course, they hired some from outside the town, but most were from here. In addition to that, the camp helped the town out in other ways, buying some materials from the local merchants such as ice, butter, and what vegetables they needed that weren't grown on the hotel grounds. Also paid the county for electrical and telephone service." He took time to puff more on the cigar. "They used seven acres of the hotel garden to grow produce and sub-leased six more to local farmers. All in all, a most profitable venue, wouldn't you say?"

I didn't answer.

He studied me a moment and I suppose saw that I was

not convinced. "We're awful proud the government chose us for their internment camp. After all, they considered seven counties in Western North Carolina. I understand the two deciding factors in choosing Hot Springs were its proximity to the railroad and the hotel itself, situated as it is between the railway tracks and the French Broad River."

"A shame it had to be the hotel," I said.

"It weren't all for naught, Bess. Listen, why don't you let me show you around while you're here so you can see for yourself?"

"They would allow that?"

He shrugged. "I'll have to clear it with the Inspector." He cocked an eyebrow my way. "Thomas Kirk, he was the camp head, from over Stanly County. You know him?"

I shook my head.

"He'll be around till it's completely shut down. I don't reckon it'll be a problem. We used to have people in all the time touring the compound."

"Really?"

"It was well-guarded and we didn't have any violent internees. You'll see why we had so many visitors if you come for a tour."

"All right, I'd like that," I said after considering for a moment. "After all, this is a part of history involving our small town, isn't it? I'd like to be able to tell my children and grandchildren about it."

We arranged to meet early the next morning at the entrance to the drive of the hotel and he left with the promise that I'd change my mind about the internment camp once I saw the good that had been done there.

I didn't say it but I honestly doubted I would.

CHAPTER ELEVEN

Early Fall 1918

As ugly as a mud fence.

The next morning, I found Harry waiting for me at the end of the long drive leading up to the hotel. Fletcher had stayed behind at the behest of Tommy Bearing, who needed his aid in carrying Aunt Belle's tombstone and placing it on her grave. After the usual amenities, Harry took my arm and steered me across the street to what was called the upper lawn of the Mountain Park. As we walked along, he said, "We'll head on up to where the golf course used to be." He arched his eyebrows at me. "I reckon Old Fort suffered from the Great Flood of 1916."

"I'm afraid we did," I replied.

"Well, it didn't spare Hot Springs. The French Broad overflowed and the waters tore straight through the town. Destroyed the Wana Luna Golf Club, washed it right into the hotel and knocked out the Mountain Park's lower corner walls. Also damaged the bath house and filled the swimming pool with mud. My uncle made the necessary repairs, and when the government offered to lease the property for an internment camp, I reckon he was ready to give it up for a bit so signed the lease."

"How long ago was that?"

"Well, let's see. He asked the guests of the hotel to leave in May of '17 and weren't too long after that the government came in and started building." By this time, we had reached the upper lawn over the golf course.

"We have two camps here, Bess, Camp A and B where the internees were housed. Of course, the German officers stayed at the hotel. Had a right nice life there too, living in a place that was steam-heated and had electric lighting. Got to play tennis, billiards, bowl in the hotel's bowling alley. It was a bit more primitive for the rest of them as you'll soon see. Since we're close, we'll start with Camp A."

He pointed out the eleven barracks, rows of single-story structures covered in tarpaper and raw planks, their accompanying lavatory buildings, the long mess hall and cook house, a smaller wash house, and a fifty-foot high water tank which he proudly stated had a 30,000 gallon capacity. I stared in amazement at the transformation that had taken place on the lawn of the Mountain Park Hotel. The beautiful grounds had been torn up in order to add water lines and sewer pipes and now appeared rutted and covered more with dirt than grass. Electric and telephone wires marred the sky overhead. As if that were not ugly enough, a board fence which Harry proudly pointed out was eight feet tall by 2,251 feet long, topped with two feet of barbed wire, ran along Bridge Street and down the railroad side. A barbed wire fence ten feet high completed the perimeter.

"It's all so unattractive," I said.

"I don't reckon you'll find any internment camp you'd consider pretty, Bess, and of course, it'll all be gone soon. Why, I reckon this place will look just like it used to but it's not all this industrial. You'll see as we go along."

We crossed the street to Camp B, on the lower lawn to the back and side of the hotel, where five more barracks and lavatories, a dining hall and an office building had been erected. As we strolled farther along, Harry pointed out smaller structures. "We got us a warehouse, jail, two post offices, workshop, blacksmith, electric meter plant, boiler house, pump house, store house, five wells, and two coal bunkers. Not to mention the dormitory for personnel and the inspector's office. Around the perimeter are 24 guard houses, which are, ah, about four-square feet each." Harry gestured toward Hampton Cottage which he told me was used as a hospital before a new one was built in November of 1917 and showed me the railroad siding constructed on the west boundary across from the Southern Railway depot.

"How many did the camp employ?" I asked.

"Well, let's see. I reckon we had anywhere from seventy-five to a hundred guards, all civilian. They worked eight-hour shifts, patrolling what we call beats—meaning certain areas of the encampment. Pay was pretty good, thirty-five dollars every two weeks. Our foremen made eighty-five dollars a month, and we even paid some of the Germans for building their own barracks, same wage the American soldier made." With a wink, he added, "Can't accuse Uncle Sam of unfair treatment. We also had messengers, matrons, mechanics, a watchman, commissary clerk, five inspectors and six clerks. All in all, it was a right busy little place, wouldn't you say?"

"It's like a small city," I said, staring in amazement at all the buildings around us.

"'Twas that," he said with a proud look.

"Did you have any problem with the prisoners?"

"Just so you know, the Department of Immigration didn't classify them as prisoners of war, Bess, 'cause most of these men were civilians, officers and crew of German and Austrian commercial ships that took cover in American ports when Great Britain declared war on Germany back in '14 for fear of being attacked crossing back over the ocean. After we declared war on Germany, those ships were seized on April 6th. So they were officially called enemy aliens or just aliens. I like the word internees myself. But for the most part, they didn't give us any problems. Fact is, they seemed to like it here. Some even had their families living in Hot Springs. Course, we did have one escapee. Man named Siegfried Sonneck, escaped with his wife and another German woman with a dog. Never did find him. Some think he swam the river over to Paint Rock where he met his wife and they escaped from that point. Others think they were aided by imperial agents." He shook his head as if unable to understand why the man would do such a thing. "I reckon he'll surface at some point."

"How many Germans were within the encampment?"

Harry studied the sky, thinking for a moment. "Let's see. The first internees arrived June 8th, 1917, eighteen men, I think. Five days later, we got fifty-eight more and they kept coming in from time to time. The camp was built to hold 2200 prisoners but I suspect we may have ended up with more than that 'cause by the end we were a bit crowded."

We had circled around to the bath house and back to what he called Camp A and Harry led me beyond, saying, as we walked along a decorative wooden fence, "I reckon most being sailors and all, they must have had some idle time on their hands 'cause a lot were good at making things out of wood. We even had an artist here name of Edwin Kussner. You ever heard of him?"

I thought then shook my head.

"Me either but I reckon he'll make a name for himself. He's an awful talented artist." He looked around, smiling. "I think what you're about to see will change your mind, Bessie. It's not all ugly." With a look of pride, he pointed to what appeared to be a small village with intricately detailed cottages. "Some of us refer to these as garden houses."

I smiled with pleasure, admiring the small chalets, each different from its neighbor and made, Harry explained, of driftwood from the French Broad River and debris from the Great Flood. Some had window boxes and bark baskets on the front walls filled with blooming flowers. Each had a matching fence, gate and walkway. Most looked to be single-roomed and Harry told me the Germans used berries and plants for paint.

"It may be rustic but I can't believe how charming and delightful it is," I said.

Harry nodded. "I reckon they looked at these as their own personal sanctuaries for letter writing, reading, playing chess or what-not."

I stopped when we came upon a two-story log chalet with curtained windows and a patterned balcony on all sides. The former occupant had planted a small garden around the house and withered corn stalks blew in the breeze. Another larger house had an octagon-shaped, two-story tower with eight gothic windows accenting the front along with diagonal latticework and a miniature widow's walk. I admired the spindles of one hut's porch railing only to be told by Harry they were made from empty thread spools.

"They heated 'em with little furnaces they built from cast-off bricks and stones," Harry confided.

We came upon a church which rested on a foundation of rock masonry with a looming steeple, gothic windows, and cross-centered rose window over the entry. The roofing and siding were made from flattened Prince Albert tin cans, Harry told me, which reflected the sun's bright rays giving the building a bit of a haloed effect.

I turned and smiled at Harry. "It's just beautiful, isn't it?"

He returned my smile, saying, "There's a pulpit and pews inside but it can't hold more than twenty men."

Beyond the church, we crossed an arched, dry foot bridge which led to a well and an interesting feature, a life-sized alligator with sharp teeth and claws, carved into a tree trunk at the river's edge. I stepped back, thinking it real.

Harry laughed. "Like I told you, we had some right good carvers here."

I looked around, noting a circular patio floored with flagstones and walled with river rocks, dotted here and there with hand-made tables which Harry said were for playing cards. Tiny vegetable and flower gardens dotted the landscape in circular, square or rectangular beds. I clasped my hands to my mouth, staring in awe at a carousel that had been erected nearby. It was beautiful, with a pretty octagonal base, standing twelve feet tall and ten feet through, with chain-suspended chairs made to swing outward from a twenty-foot high circular canopy. It had eight oval-arched windows trimmed with bright borders of hand-painted flowers.

"We had a lot of visitors wanted passes just to see this," Harry said, watching me. "Played music as it turned. Can you believe that?"

"I can see why it would draw so much attention," I said.

"Camp B sailors also had their own village," Harry confided, "and a chapel, but it's not as big as this side. The government didn't contribute one cent to any of these buildings so the only material they had to use was scraps from the hotel itself and driftwood and debris. I reckon you got to give credit to the skill of the German sailors who built these things."

"They're not only craftsmen but artisans as well."

"I would agree to that, Bess. And these buildings served a purpose other than fraternizing. Groups got together to do woodworking, one was an artists' studio, some men even wove in one. And those that didn't want to do things of that nature occupied themselves in other ways, such as digging out the Mountain Park swimming pool which the flood filled in. Some were cobblers and barbers, others ran a clothing shop and laundry. They even had a canteen that sold tobacco, jam, honey, cakes and such other luxuries as the government didn't provide. Some even raised rabbits to sell, I believe they were them large Belgian hares. Had a 35-member Imperial brass band of German Red Cross workers who were also soldiers that gave concerts for townspeople every Sunday afternoon. And it wasn't just people from Hot Springs come to hear them, either. We'd all gather at the depot's loading shed where we could look right over the fence and watch them play." He shook his head. "They were right nice to listen to."

As we turned to go, Harry continued to talk about the camp. "Of course, there was some discord between the citizens of Hot Springs and the camp. I don't reckon there was a family around these parts who didn't have somebody fighting in the war so naturally at first people were skittish about the idea of Germans living here. But for the most part we realized soon enough that there wasn't nothing to fear from these men. I reckon the biggest issue to come up was that some felt the aliens received special treatment 'cause they got meat two times a day while we Americans had to honor meatless and wheatless days. Somehow word reached the Labor Department 'cause they sent down word that the aliens would have to observe the meatless and wheatless days too but that it wasn't necessary to sign Food Administrator Hoover's pledge cards like we all did. But all in all, things were pretty lax for an internment camp. Why, before Sonneck escaped, some of the guards even took aliens home with them for dinner and let the officers visit with their families in Hot Springs." Harry took my arm once more and turned me back to the small patio. "Let's sit for a bit, Bess, all this walkin's got me out of breath."

I noted with some alarm that Harry's face was beet-red and his breathing had become labored. "Are you all right?"

"I reckon I'm well enough," he grunted. "Smoke too many cigars and eat too much of that good food my wife fixes for me is all."

I gave him a look.

He sighed with resignation. "Doc says my heart ain't as strong as it used to be. Told me to try to take life a bit easier." A grimace passed across his face. "Which ain't hard now that the camp's closed."

"Have your wife make a decoction of dogbane," I suggested. "It helps with heart and circulatory problems."

A smile flitted across his lips. "I heard you were a healer, Bess. Learned it from your Cherokee kin, they say."

"Yes, my great-grandmother Elisi."

"I reckon that's good enough for me. I'll be sure to tell the missus, I sure will."

"If she needs my help fixing it, tell her to come by and see me. I'll be more than happy to teach her how to make it."

"I thank you, Bess."

We retired to a small table with two chairs and I sat, admiring a bed of bright red geraniums, saddened at the thought that with the advent of cooler weather, they would be wilted and dying soon.

When Harry look to be recovered, I said, "When did the camp close, Harry?"

"Just last month. Government decided to transfer our seamen to the custody of the War Department instead of the Department of Labor 'cause the War Department holds all other classes of prisoners of war and interned aliens. In May of this year, they sent some of ours to Arkansas, Georgia,

Texas and Oklahoma. Some even received paroles to live here in America if they had a job and a sponsor to secure their bond. Most were slated to go to the War Prison Barracks at Fort Oglethorpe, Georgia but they wanted to stay right here. I suspect because there, they would be put to work doing hard labor building roads and such side by side with true prisoners of war, those who committed real crimes against the Allies. One alien even escaped 'cause he didn't want to leave. They found him 'bout 15 miles away near Sandy Bottom and he ended up at Fort Oglethorpe anyway. The others got a reprieve till August 1st 'cause Fort Oglethorpe wasn't equipped to handle over 2000 additional prisoners. But then they started getting sick and when one even died, rumors started flying around that they poisoned their own drinking water so they could stay here but misjudged the amount so got sicker than they meant to. Another rumor was that they tried to commit suicide by deliberately drinking filthy water. The Surgeon General later issued a report saying it was due to an insufficient supply of good water and that the illness came from the service wells which were intended for toilets and bathing but from which the internees had been drinking. He didn't think it was a suicide attempt, simply a matter of too many internees in an overcrowded condition without enough good drinking water.

"Anyway, we ended up with 110 suspected of having typhoid so all available buildings were converted into temporary hospitals and we used Hampton College as a special ward." He shook his head. "Seems nearly every day we'd have a wagon loaded with coffins carrying the dead to Oddfellows Cemetary right outside of town. They sent 159 sick internees to a hospital at Biltmore. Loaded them in five baggage cars and it took all morning to do it. Most of the rest were transferred August 22nd and by the 31st only 26 remained, those judged too sick to travel but they soon left for the Biltmore Hospital."

I leaned back and looked around. "What's going to happen to all of this, Harry?"

He shrugged. "I imagine it will be destroyed. For now, the camp will act as a hospital for recuperating soldiers."

"And when the war is over?"

"It all goes back to my uncle, supposedly the way the government found it."

I stared at the carousel, envisioning it turning, music tinkling in the air, riders laughing as they swung; people sitting at the tables around us, enjoying the fresh mountain air, each other's company, and the beauty of the small village behind us. I sighed. "It's a real shame."

Harry smiled. "Told you you'd change your mind about it, Bess."

I nodded. "I reckon I have, Harry. Thank you for showing me all this. I'll never forget it."

"I don't suspect the town will either, Bess."

After I left Harry, I made the long walk to Sandy Gap Cemetery. It bothered me that Aunt Belle had been buried at Oddfellows Cemetery next to her husband and would not be sharing the same hallowed ground as Mama, Greenie and Druanna, the young Melungeon runaway I tried to save, but I told myself their souls were together, it did not matter where their bodies were. I sat on the grass at the foot of their graves and talked to them about my life on Stone Mountain with Fletcher. I told them about our church and friends and that I was happy there. After I had relayed all of my news, I simply sat and enjoyed the day, which was not too warm and not too cool, one of those ideal days where you were glad to be alive and the world felt to be in perfect harmony. "Thank you, God," I said, my face toward the sky. I smiled when I noticed three birds on a limb above, each watching me.

"I wish you all were here," I said as I rose to go. I glanced at the three birds, perched silently side by side, their eyes following me. "Perhaps you are," I said to them and smiled. I left the cemetery, tears streaming down my face, not knowing if I would visit again. At least Tommy had promised to look after their graves so they would not be forgotten.

The next day, I borrowed one of Uncle Ned's horses which, along with all the livestock, had been bequeathed to the Dorland Presbyterian Church, and rode to Elisi's small house. It pained me to see how overgrown her yard was, green vines running up the side of the house and onto the porch and weeds dominating the flowerbeds and lawn. Elisi had been proud of her little cabin and kept it neat and tidy with flowers blooming in wooden boxes and along the front of the porch. I opened the door and stepped inside, ignoring its loud creak. Nothing had changed inside her home except that a heavy layer of dust coated the floor and furniture, all hand-made by Elisi's husband.

I stepped to the hearth and knelt down, staring at the bricks which had been removed and then replaced so that Elisi could be buried beneath. I placed my hands on them, startled that they seemed so very warm. I closed my eyes, feeling for her. Elisi had told me death was not the end of life but the beginning of another journey and I knew in my heart this to be true but wished I could have her here with me just one more time. "I love you, Elisi," I finally said, bending down to kiss the bricks then walking away without looking back.

On the way home, I decided to stop by Miss Cordy's to meet her new pup, Junior. This seemed a time for saying goodbyes, I reflected, as I rode the overgrown path to her cabin. Miss Cordy was what my great-grandmother called a whistling woman and what I aspired to be. She lived life by her own terms, not as dictated by others, and willingly embraced her talent for healing and soothsaying. Some in town called her a witch but that word was too primitive for the person she was. Like me, she had the gift of prophecy and her world was ruled more by intuition than logic and law. The only time I had known her to adhere to tradition had resulted in the death of her pet hen, by Miss Cordy herself, in order to feed the preacher who was coming for Sunday dinner when she had nothing else to feed him. After I learned this, I made it a point to take baskets of food to Miss Cordy each week and Loney had promised to continue this when I married and moved to Stone Mountain as Miss Cordy had no one to help her. When Loney moved with Papa to Knoxville, I wrote my concern to Aunt Belle and she assured me she would see to it that Miss Cordy did not want even though Aunt Belle considered her a witch.

I found Miss Cordy outside with her small puppy, dipping her hand into her folded-up apron, scattering feed for her chickens, the pup chasing the fowl around, all fleeing with wings flapping and squawks of alarm when he charged. I laughed as I got off the horse and tied her to a nearby tree, giving her enough room to graze the grass around her.

Miss Cordy laughed with me, and we stood together a moment watching Junior charge the hens, playfully nipping at their running feet. I noted with some amusement that he was smart enough to stay away from the rooster who would in all likelihood attack with sharp talons and beak. The pup looked to be just under a year old, a mongrel with paws that foretold the large dog he would grow into. His fur was a golden brown and his ears flopped as he ran, his feathery tail brushing at the air. "He's beautiful, Miss Cordy."

She nodded with a look of pride. "He's gonna be a might bigger than his pa, look at them paws."

I smiled. "I noticed."

She brushed the rest of the feed off her hands and called to the dog. "Come on over here and meet Bessie."

Junior skidded to a halt with what looked to be a wide grin and trotted over to join us. I knelt down to run my hands over his fur. "You're a pretty boy," I told him. I did not fail to notice the way he placed his body between his mistress and me. "He's protective," I said.

"He is that," she said with a proud look. "Won't let no stranger get near me."

"I'm glad for that."

"Come on in the house and I'll fix us some tea," she said, ruffling the dog's fur.

We had a lovely visit, catching up on each other's lives. Before I left, I asked if she needed anything and Miss Cordy assured me that things were much better for her since that awful day I found her weeping over the death of her beloved pet chicken. "Your Aunt Belle got the whole church involved in seeing to it that I don't go hungry or want for nothin," Miss Cordy assured me. "For the most part, I can see to Junior and myself, what with gardening and a bit of hunting, but if things ain't goin well or I ain't feelin up to par, they take care of me good and proper." She put her hand on mine. "Don't you worry about me, Bess. I've got good people lookin after me and this wonderful dog to keep me company. Why I reckon I'm a blessed woman."

I kissed her cheek. "I'm glad, Miss Cordy. You deserve to be."

She cupped my cheek in her hand. "I'll be fine." She stared into my eyes. "You're goin to have a good life, Bess. A lot of people are goin to love you and you'll love them. You got a child comin to you. He'll mean the world to you and you to him."

Tears stung my eyes. "Thank you for telling me, Miss Cordy. I'm so happy to hear it."

I noticed shadows creeping into the room and knew if I didn't leave now, I would be riding home in the dark. With great reluctance, I bid her goodbye. "I'll write," I promised. "Let you know how things are. You be sure and do the same if you don't mind."

"My eyesight ain't so good any more but I'll find someone who can read it to me and help me put the words to paper."

I kissed her goodbye, told Junior to take good care of her and took my leave, tears streaming down my face but a small warm spot boiling in my chest. A child!

Before we returned to Stone Mountain, I toured the grounds of the Mountain Park Hotel once again, this time with Fletcher in tow, another witness to the good this little town had done and the people who had visited for a short time, who, although enemies, had come to love Hot Springs as much as its citizens and had during their brief stay added a bit of their own beauty and culture.

CHAPTER TWELVE

Fall 1918

They lived so far back in the sticks they had to pump in sunshine.

Each day when I passed out biscuits and ham to those children who didn't bring lunch to school, I noticed little Timmy Nevins watching my progress with a forlorn look. He would then try to trade his meal with the other students but none of them were willing to do so and with a dramatic sigh of resignation he'd pull cornbread from his lunch pail and with what seemed great reluctance take a bite.

After several days of this, I asked him why he wanted to trade his cornbread for a biscuit.

He shrugged his little shoulders. "I reckon 'cause I don't like the taste of it."

"Have you asked your ma to make you a biscuit instead?"

He shook his head. "I can't do that, Miss Bessie."

"Why is that, Timmy?"

A worried crease crossed his forehead. "My ma's been sick so my Pa's having to take care of us young'uns and the only things he knows how to cook are beans and cornbread."

I thought of his mother, Molly. I'd taught her as well and found her to be an intelligent young woman who shared my love for reading. But when Molly met Timothy Nevins, nothing else seemed to matter and she quit school to marry the young man. "What's wrong with your ma, Timmy?"

"She's got a bad cold, I reckon. Got a fever and coughs a lot. She's so weak she can hardly get out of bed."

I reached in my basket and pulled out a ham and biscuit. "Here, I'll trade you for your cornbread."

His face brightened at that and he eagerly made the barter.

I ruffled his copper-colored hair. "Why don't I come by tonight and fix dinner for you and your family? And I promise I won't make cornbread."

His bright smile lifted my heart.

I hurried home after school, my mind on Molly and her family. I cut up a chicken, dusted it in flour and placed it in the frying pan then fetched a ham from the smokehouse. While the chicken cooked, I rolled out enough biscuits for dinner and breakfast and placed them in the oven then began packing a picnic basket with the ham, jellies and jams, eggs, fresh vegetables and canned squirrel, adding the biscuits and chicken when they were cool enough. Fletcher came home just as I was getting herbs together for my medical bag.

He eyed the picnic basket on the table. "You planning a picnic this evening, Bess? Looks like it's gonna be a right good night for one."

I kissed his cheek. "Sorry but I'm going to Molly Nevins' house. Her son Timmy told me today she's been sick and his pa's having to take care of them. Seems like the only things Molly's husband knows how to cook are beans and cornbread so I thought I'd go help with dinner then see to Molly."

He nodded. "You need me to go with you?"

"I reckon I can get there and back all right. I may end up staying overnight if Molly's as sick as Timmy says she is. Your supper's in the warmer whenever you're ready."

"You're a fine woman, Bess." He put his hat on his head. "I'll go saddle up ol' Pet for you."

Fletcher helped me up in the saddle, then lashed the hamper on behind me and looped my bag of herbs around the saddle horn. "I sure hope Molly's not got that Spanish flu old Doc Widby's been telling us about," he said with concern in his eyes.

Doc had been keeping me updated on a world-wide influenza pandemic which was quickly spreading across the world and our country. He said it started in our state in the small coastal city of Wilmington and was spreading west, following the rail lines, leading straight to Old Fort. It was a fearsome disease, and unlike the more common influenza which was most damaging to the weak and elderly, preyed on the young and healthy, often proving to be fatal.

"I'm praying it's not that, Fletch. I don't think there's much I can do for her if it is. It's a fast-moving virus and Timmy said she's been sick awhile so hopefully it's only a bad case of influenza."

"Well, you do what you can to keep from getting it," he said, a worried look in his eyes.

"Don't worry, I'll take precautions." I leaned down to kiss him and with a wave turned Pet toward the road and we went on our way.

Timothy Nevins had built their cabin in a heavily wooded area, with the intention of clearing his acreage for farming, and although he worked constantly at this, it looked as if Mother Nature was winning the race, surrounding their small cabin with clusters of scrub bushes and foliage that seemed to spring up overnight. It took me awhile to get there simply because I kept Pet to a slow pace, maneuvering down a path strewn with broken tree limbs and pitted with shallow holes from wild boar rutting for food.

Molly's husband Timothy stepped outside as soon as I rode into their small yard. His face was haggard and there were dark circles around his eyes. As he helped me down, he said with a look of relief, "I shore do thank you for coming out and seeing about Molly."

"I'd have been here sooner if someone had told me, Timothy."

"Well, you know Molly, she's as stubborn as a mule and

don't want no one tending to her. She kept telling me she'd get better soon enough but it's been going on too long."

I nodded. "That's our Molly." I had found her to be an independent girl and I'd always liked that about her but sometimes that could prove to be an obstacle. "I brought some food for you and your young'uns. It's in the basket there." I took my medicine bag off the saddle horn. "Can you bring it in? I'm going to see to Molly."

"She's in the bedroom," he called to me as I stepped inside.

Timmy and his little brother Nash and sister Mavis were playing with toy soldiers in front of the fireplace. I smiled at them and told them I'd be right back before going into the bedroom.

I had to stifle a gasp when I saw Molly, who had always looked so clean and neat. She lay on the bed in a stained gown, her copper hair a tangled mass around her flushed cheeks. Her face burned with fever but I could see she would be as pale as watered milk otherwise. But more concerning to me was the rattling sound in her chest when she breathed. I was relieved her skin didn't have a blue cast to it, one of the signs of the Spanish flu, and prayed this was simply a bad case of influenza. She looked at me through slitted eyes and struggled to sit up but didn't have the strength.

I crossed over to her and gently eased her back down. "I'm here to help you, Molly. Can you tell me what's wrong?"

She coughed into a stained rag, and as she did so, I turned my head against any germ spray.

"I got the worst cold I reckon I've ever had," she finally said, breathing raggedly. "Cough keeps me up most nights and this fever doesn't seem to want to break."

I nodded. "I've got something to help with that." I patted her hand. "I'll be right back." I closed the bedroom door behind me, crossed over to the small kitchen, and pulled out tins of feverwort and sage leaves from my medicine bag. "Does Molly have a teapot?" I asked Timothy.

He nodded and gestured toward the wood stove.

I picked it up, shook it, and handed it to him. "Fill it with water, please."

While he was outside at the well, I found a small pot and placed feverwort inside then added kindling to the wood stove to get it hot. When Timothy returned, I poured water over the herb and set the pot on the stove to boil, placing the tea kettle on another eye. "We're going to need cold water to bring her fever down, either from your well or the creek, whichever's coldest."

"I'll go fetch you a bucket full," he said, going outside again.

I noticed Timmy watching me with a worried look and smiled at him. "Can you watch your brother and sister while we tend to your ma, Timmy? We won't be long."

"I reckon I can," he said, lines furrowing his brow.

While the herbs brewed, I returned to the bedroom. Molly's lethargy was a concern to me and it took all my strength to strip the stained gown off of her. "I'm going to cool your body with cold water, Molly. We need to get that fever down." I placed two pillows behind her and propped her up as best I could to help with the congestion in her lungs.

Timothy returned with the bucket, his eyes widening at his wife's naked body.

I glanced at him. "Does she have another gown? And I'll need pieces of clean material."

He gave me a blank look. "Material?"

"We're going to lay cold cloths on her body, try to cool her down some. Does Molly keep cut-up pieces for rags or quilting?"

Without a word, he went back into the kitchen and returned with a pile of soft rags. "Her gown's in the chest over there. I'll fetch it."

I dipped one in the cold water, wrung it out, and placed it on her chest, proceeding to do likewise with all the rags, laying them over her body. When she broke out in goose bumps. Timothy said, "Maybe we ought to take 'em off of there, she's getting cold."

"She's just chilling from the fever, Timothy." I lifted the first one I'd placed off her chest and said, "Feel how hot it is.

That's from the fever." I dipped it in the bucket of cold water and wrung it out then replaced it on her chest. "I need you to keep doing this with the other rags until her body's not so hot."

"Yes, ma'am." He bent to the task, his eyes filled with concern for his wife.

I returned to the kitchen and found the tea kettle whistling. I poured the boiling water into a mug and added sage leaves. While it steeped, I took the boiling pot off the stove and strained the feverwort decoction into a bowl then set it aside to cool. I carried the mug with me back to the bedroom where Molly was shivering but seemed more alert. I put the back of my hand on her arm, then forehead, relieved her skin felt somewhat cooler. "I think it's working, Timothy. Let's continue doing this for a few minutes more while the tea steeps."

Once the tea was ready, I took the mug over to Molly. "Help her sit all the way up, Timothy. Let's try to get this sage leaf tea down her. It should help with her lung congestion."

Molly obediently sipped at the tea and it took awhile but I finally got her to drink the entire cup. "Keep those pillows behind her, we don't want her lying down," I said.

"Wouldn't she be more comfortable 'ataway?" Timothy asked.

"Not with her lungs filling up with fluid. She needs to stay upright as best she can."

I felt her skin again, which was markedly cooler. I had Timothy remove the rest of the rags and help me slip the gown over her head and down her body. Molly lay back with a sigh. "I thank you, Miss Bessie, it's easier to breathe now."

"You be sure to sit up till this congestion's gone, all right?"

"Yes, ma'am." She closed her eyes and drifted off.

I gathered up the damp rags. "Let's let her rest a few minutes while I fix dinner for y'all."

Timothy picked up the bucket, his hand lingering on his wife's. He lowered his voice to a whisper. "Is she gonna be all right, Miss Bess? She shore is sick."

"If we can keep her fever down and get that congestion under control, I think she'll be fine, Timothy."

He nodded but didn't look too convinced.

In the kitchen, I unpacked the picnic basket and slid the biscuits in the cook-stove warmer. "Y'all go wash your hands," I said.

As they scrambled to the wash bucket, I said to Timothy, "That means you, too, Timothy. All of you should make a habit of washing your hands before each meal. And don't let them near Molly until she's symptom-free."

"Symptom-free?"

"She's not running a fever and no longer coughing. She's contagious right now, and any one of you could get what she's got if she coughs near you or sneezes. You have to be careful."

"Yes, ma'am, I will, although I got to tell you I'm probably already infected since I been tending to her."

"Maybe your body's stronger and you won't get it," I said. "Just be sure to be careful, especially with your children."

"I will. I shore don't want none of them to get sick like poor Molly."

Timothy made his children stand back while I set the table and they all watched patiently as I set the food out, although I could see the hunger in their eyes as they stared at the fried chicken, fried corn, sliced tomatoes and cucumbers I placed on the table. Only when I was finished would Timothy allow his children to sit. As one, they bowed their heads as Timothy said grace and immediately began grabbing for food when he finished.

While they ate, I took the decoction of feverwort into the bedroom and helped Molly drink it. She made a face. "What's this, Miss Bessie?"

"Feverwort. It will help your fever."

She lay back exhausted. "I sure am sorry to trouble you like this. I know how busy you are what with teaching and helping take care of a farm."

I pushed damp hair off her face. "It so happens I'm doing one of the things I love best, using the Cherokee medicine my great-grandmother taught me to help someone who's ailing."

She smiled at that. "We're blessed to have you, Miss Bessie. I can't thank you enough for coming."

"Thank Timmy. He told me you were sick."

"I'll be sure to do that," she said before drifting off to sleep.

While Molly slept, I ate dinner with the family, then cleared away the table with the help of Timothy and little Timmy. I showed Timothy the ham I'd brought and extra biscuits along with more tomatoes and cucumbers, ears of corn, the canned squirrel and jams. "This should hold you a few days," I told him, "and hopefully by then Molly will be feeling a bit stronger. Of course, she'll be mighty weak for a week or two, so you and your children will need to help her but I reckon she can at least supervise your cooking."

He gave me an embarrassed grin. "I reckon I got a bit of learning to do when it comes to cooking."

"Most men do, Timothy."

I heard Molly coughing and hurried to the bedroom. The rag she used as a hankie was old and cracked with mucous. I took it from her and handed it to Timothy. "Burn this then wash your hands." I took a clean rag from the pile he'd brought me and handed it to her. "Use this, Molly." I thumped her back while she coughed, not sure if it would loosen congestion but the poor soul sounded so miserable, anything that might help was worth doing in my thoughts. When she lay back, her breathing seemed quieter. I put my hand against her forehead. "Your fever's down, Molly. Tells us the feverwort is working."

She gave me a weak smile then closed her eyes. "Will you stay with me tonight, Miss Bess? I don't reckon I've ever felt so miserable and it sure would comfort me to know you're here."

"Of course I will, Molly. Your man Timothy looks like he hasn't had much rest so I'll watch over you while he sleeps. You just lay back and close your eyes. I'll wake you when it's time for more medicine."

And so the night was spent brewing teas and decoctions for Molly, and having her chew garlic which she objected to at first until I told her it should help kill whatever germs plagued her. Each time she had a coughing fit, I pounded her on the back, giving her a clean rag and burning the old one.

Close to dawn, I looked up and noticed her watching me. I stroked her hair. "How are you feeling?"

"A mite better." She gave me a weak smile. "I was just remembering my school days. I loved going to school, Miss Bessie, more than anything. Why, during the summer I'd long for school to start just so I could hear you tell us one of your great-grandmother's Cherokee legends."

I smiled as I fluffed pillows behind her then eased her back. "And I love telling them."

"Do you think you could tell me one now?"

"I can. Do you have a favorite?"

"The one about the little water spider. Ever since you told us that story, I haven't been afraid of spiders as much."

"Me too. Of course, snakes are a different matter. I reckon the Creator created each being with a purpose in mind but I wonder what harm it would have done to leave off the poisonous snakes, especially those old rattlers that like my barn so much." She smiled as I sat on the bed beside her and held her hand, which now seemed much cooler than when I first arrived. "In the beginning, the world was cold because there was no fire."

With a sigh, she settled back and closed her eyes, a small smile on her face.

"So the Red Thunder Beings in the Above World sent lightning down and put a fire in the bottom of a hollow sycamore tree growing on a small island. All the animals could see the smoke and feel a little bit of its warmth so knew the fire was there. They wanted to be close so they could warm themselves but couldn't because the island with the sycamore tree could not be easily reached. So the animals held council to decide what to do about the situation. All were there including Raven, Screech Owl, Hooting Owl, Horned Owl, Racersnake, Blacksnake and Water Spider, and all of the animals who could fly or swim were eager to go fetch the fire.

"The first one to volunteer was Raven and all the others thought he would be the best to go since he was big and strong. Raven flew high and far over the water and landed on the sycamore tree. While he was wondering what to do, the heat from the fire scorched all his feathers black and frightened him so much he went squawking back without the fire. And to this day, Raven is black from being scorched by the fire.

"The next animal to offer to go was little Screech Owl. He flew high and far over the water and landed on the tree. While he was looking down into the hollow of the tree, a blast of hot air came up and almost burned out his eyes. So he flew back without the fire and it was a long time before he could see well again. And to this day, his eyes are red.

"Horned Owl and Hooting Owl both said they would go after the fire. They flew high and far and landed on the sycamore tree. But by the time they got there, the fire was burning fiercely and the smoke nearly blinded them. The ashes from the fire, carried up by the wind, made white rings around their eyes. Horned Owl and Hooting Owl returned without the fire, but no matter how much they rubbed their eyes, they could not get rid of the white rings. To this day, both have white rings around their eyes.

"After this, none of the other birds would go after the fire so the little Racersnake spoke up and said he would go and everyone thought he might have a good chance because he was small and quick. So little Racersnake swam quickly across the water and when he reached the island crawled through the grass to the sycamore tree and then into the tree through a hole at the bottom. The heat and smoke were unbearable and he dodged over the hot ashes until he almost caught fire. When he finally managed to get out through the same hole he entered, his whole body was scorched black. And since then, little Black Racersnake darts and doubles back on his track as if he is still trying to escape the fire.

"By this time all the animals were starting to worry because they had no fire. A great big snake, the Climber, volunteered to go after the fire and off he went, swimming across the water to the island. He climbed up the tree from the outside the way snakes like him always do but when he put his head into the hole, the smoke choked him and he fell into the burning stump. When he finally got free, his whole body was as black as charcoal. So he too returned without fire and to this day is called Blacksnake.

"The animals were very worried because it was cold and they had no fire so they held another council. But the other animals were afraid that if they went near the sycamore tree they would get burned so they thought up reasons not to go. Except for little Water Spider who had black downy hair and red stripes on her body and could run on top of the water or dive to the bottom. She listened patiently as the animals talked about their situation with great dismay and when it was time for her to speak said she would bring back the fire for all of them. The animals wondered how she could do that and some even began to laugh at the very thought that she, being so small and not strong, could bring back the fire. 'I'll find a way,' she said and began to weave a bowl from spun thread then fastened it on her back. She crossed the water and went through the grass where the fire was still burning, then put one small coal into her bowl and brought it back for all the animals. They all rejoiced and the animals built a sacred fire from the coal around which they danced in celebration for many days. And since that time, we have had fire, and to this day the little Water Spider keeps her bowl. And so, it is good."

Molly squeezed my hand and said in a drowsy voice, "I miss you, Miss Bessie."

"And I miss you as well, Molly. But now I have Timmy and later Nash and Mavis so in a way I still have you with me."

"I tell them your stories," she mumbled. "I reckon they love them as much as I do."

"I'm glad. Now go to sleep," I whispered, smoothing the hair off her face.

By the time the sun peaked over the mountain to our East, Molly's breathing had evened into a more regular rhythm and her face was no longer flushed from fever. She was even alert enough to request a breakfast of biscuit and ham and managed to eat most of it. By mid-morning I felt confident enough that this was not that vile Spanish flu but the more common influenza and left after instructing Timothy on how to brew the sage tea for congestion and make the feverwort decoction for fever, eliciting the promise from him that he would send for me if Molly got worse.

Although I'd had a sleepless night, I felt calm and at peace as I rode sweet Pet toward home, happy Molly would be all right and that out town would not be plagued by a virulent virus that was sweeping across the world, not knowing that at that moment, it loomed close, carrying with it death and heartache.

CHAPTER THIRTEEN

Spring 1919

He's so bad off, his eyes look like two piss-holes in a snow bank.

Life on our mountain continued even as the Great War overseas drew to a close and finally ended in 1918 when the commander in chief of all Allied forces, Ferdinand Foch, sent a telegram to all his commanders: "Hostilities will cease on the entire front November 11 at 11 a.m. French time." Altogether, some 9 million soldiers were killed and another 20 million wounded, some on the morning of November 11 when the commanders ordered their troops to continue to fight even though they knew peace would be declared at 11 a.m. At a peace conference in Paris, France in June of 1919, the Treaty of Versailles was signed, the Allied leaders hoping the treaty would safeguard against another devastating war in the future.

Even as the killing ended overseas, there was disturbing news from Doc Widby about the Spanish flu which now ravaged our own country, marching its deadly way through cities large and small, leaving heartbreak and devastation behind. I found myself prickly with apprehension, waiting for this deadly virus to make its presence known, and prayed constantly that it would die out before reaching our small town where so many young and healthy people lived, not knowing they would be the ones who would be targeted.

And when it came, it took as its first victim a small female child who had not even been given the chance to live.

While playing the organ at Stone Mountain Church one midsummer morning, I noticed Timothy Nevins standing just inside the doorway, wringing his hat in his hands, a look of great agitation on his face. I glanced at him then away then back, aware now that he was staring at me as if he needed to speak to me of something of great import.

When the parishioners seated themselves after singing the Doxology, I quietly got up and walked down the outside aisle. Fletcher lifted his eyebrows as I passed and I tilted my head toward the door. He quickly rose to his feet and followed me. When I reached Timothy, he stepped outside and we waited in silence for Fletch to join us after closing the door to the church.

Timothy's face was deathly pale and his eyes seemed to bulge from his head. Tears pooled in his eyes and he worked his mouth as if afraid to say what he had come to tell me.

I put my hand on his arm. "Is it Molly? Did the influenza come back?"

He shook his head, putting the back of his hand up to his mouth, then ripped it away and said in a rough voice, "It's little Mavis. She's sicker'n a dog. Can't hardly breathe and her skin's turning blue."

I looked at Fletcher and did not miss the alarm in his eyes. I'm sure we were both thinking the same thing: Spanish flu.

"Did you get Doc Widby to take a look at her?"

"No, Miss Bess. Molly wants you to come, she said she trusts you more'n him. She said you'd know what to do. She's crazy with fear, won't leave little Mavis's side for more'n a minute."

I nodded. "I'll need to go home, get some herbs together, Timothy, then I'll be on over. You go back, tell Molly I'm coming, but maybe it'd be just as well if you try to find Doc

Widby first."

Fletcher said, "I'll find the doc, Bess, I reckon Timothy don't want to be gone from home too long with his little girl that sick."

I kissed his cheek. "Thank you, Fletch."

He squeezed my hand and stared into my eyes. "You be careful. If it's what we think it is, you could be in danger too."

With a curt nod, Timothy stuffed his hat on his head and hurried off while Fletcher and I climbed in the wagon. He kept darting glances at me as we rode toward home at a clipped pace.

"What is it?" I asked.

"I'm afraid for you, Bess. According to Doc, this virus is deadly, especially to the young, healthy ones. You'll be exposed if that's what little Mavis has and I'm scared you'll get it. Doc says near half the ones who do die from it."

I leaned against him. "Fletch, I'll wear a hanky over my face, wash my hands, do everything I can to keep from getting exposed but I have to help that little girl."

He grimaced but nodded. "I reckon you do. Wouldn't be you if you didn't. Just be careful."

"I'll be as careful as I can," I said in a distracted voice, my mind already on the herbs I would need to take with me.

Fletcher saddled Pet for me while I put herbs into my medicine bag. Before helping me mount, he pulled me to him and kissed me with a fierceness that surprised me. "Take care," he said as I settled in the saddle.

"I promise," I told him, then turned Pet toward our pathway and galloped away.

Timothy stood on the front porch of their small cabin, once more wringing his hat in his hands. The deep furrows in his forehead eased noticeably when he saw me. He hurried to help me down from the horse, his hands shaking. "I'll take care of your horse for you, Miss Bess, you go on inside."

I pulled my medical bag off the saddle horn and rushed through the doorway. Little Timmy and his brother Nash sat solemnly at the kitchen table, their faces creased with worry. I forced myself to slow down and ruffled Timmy's hair. "Where's your ma?"

"In the bedroom with Mavis. She's awful sick, Miss Bessie."

"I'm here to help her, Timmy. You think you can take care of your little brother for us while I do?"

He nodded, biting his lip, and slipped his hand into his small brother's. As I made my way to the bedroom, I heard him say in a timid voice, "Don't worry none, Nash, Miss Bess will fix her up just like she did Ma when she was sick."

I opened the door to the bedroom and stepped quickly inside, taking a moment to tie my hanky over my nose and mouth.

Molly sat on the bed beside her small daughter, holding her hand, tears rolling down her face. She looked around and sobbed when she saw me. "Oh, Miss Bess, she's so sick and I'm so scared," she said.

I squeezed her shoulder. "You should wear a cloth over your face, Molly, to keep from getting this." I glanced at little Mavis, trying not to let the concern show on my face. She did not resemble the little girl I remembered, the blue cast battling for dominance over the fiery red fever scorching her skin, her sunken eyes so bloodshot they appeared to be bleeding. She opened and closed her mouth, gasping for breath like a fish out of water. "Molly," I said in a firmer tone. "I need you to go find Timothy and get him to show you how I made the feverwort and sage when you were sick. We'll try that on little Mavis, see if we can get her more comfortable. I'm also going to need a bucket of cold water and some rags to put on her body to cool her down just like we did with you."

She put her hand to her daughter's face, stroking it.

"Now, Molly, we need to do it now." I put my medical bag into her hand and urged her to stand.

She rose from the bed and hurried out of the room.

I sat beside Mavis, pushed hair off her sweet little face. Her skin was so hot, my palms burned where they touched her. I quickly peeled her dress off of her, worried that she was so apathetic and didn't seem aware of my actions. "I promise I'll do my best for you, sweet girl," I told her in a low tone. "You got too much living to do and I mean to see you do it."

Molly returned with a bucket filled with cold water and rags. "Timothy's getting the sage tea going," she said.

I nodded. "First put a rag over your nose and mouth, Molly, we don't want you getting sick."

She quickly masked her face, and as we placed rags dipped into the cold water over Mavis, whispered, "Why is she so blue, Miss Bess? I've never seen anything like it."

"I think Mavis has the Spanish flu, Molly." I glanced at her. Her expression was curious so I surmised she hadn't heard of it. "It's a form of influenza that has now become a pandemic."

"You mean it's spreading across the country?"

"Across the world."

She drew in her breath. "Is it ... is it fatal?"

I nodded. "It can be. I mean to see it isn't." I drew her away from Mavis. "Do you know how she got sick? Has she been around anyone who's been coughing or running a fever?"

Molly chewed her bottom lip, wringing her hands, glancing at her daughter then away as she thought. "Not right offhand..." Her eyes widened. "Oh, wait, we took Timothy's ma to the train station a couple of days ago. She was going to Asheville to visit her sister. A man got off the train, coughing into a hanky, and come to think of it, he did look a bit poorly. He stopped us to ask directions to the geyser, said he wanted to see it while the train made a stop if it was close enough. He reached down and patted Mavis on the cheek, told her what a pretty little girl she was."

Mavis began coughing, a deep rumbling sound that would be more natural coming from a grown man than small girl. We sat her up and I patted her back, alarmed when foamy blood blew out of her nose and mouth.

"Oh," Molly cried, stepping back.

"If you got any on you, go wash now," I said.

Molly rushed out of the room only to return a moment later with a tin cup of the sage tea. We both looked at little Mavis, her eyes slitted, her mouth open. "Do you think we can get her to drink it, Miss Bess?" Molly asked.

"We'll have to, Molly. Has Timothy started the feverwort decoction?"

She nodded. "He said it's almost ready."

"All right, lift her up and I'll try to pour a little down her throat." It took a good while to coax Mavis, who was so weak she could barely swallow, to drink the tea but we eventually got it down her. "That tea should help her congestion," I said as we began placing the cold rags over her once more, which quickly grew warm from her body's heat. The blue cast to her skin was so deep and widespread that it was impossible to tell what color her skin had been before she got sick.

Timothy came into the room a short while later with the decoction of feverwort and we once more went through the process of getting the liquid down Mavis's throat. For the first time in my life, I found myself wishing I had a hypodermic syringe and medicines that might cure her at a faster rate if there were any although I had not heard that there were.

And so the night advanced: placing cold cloths on Mavis's small body, switching to beech bark tea for her lung congestion and cedar bark tea for her fever and flu-like symptoms when the sage tea and feverwort didn't work. At times, I would find myself talking to Elisi in my mind, asking her what we should do now, arguing the merits of this or that herb. Molly and Timothy stayed by their daughter's side, helping tend to her, and we all despaired that she grew progressively worse as dark turned to day.

Doc Widby showed up at dawn, carrying his medical bag, a grim expression on his face. When he saw her blue skin, he glanced at me and I could not help but notice the look of resignation in his eyes. "When'd she first get sick?" he asked Molly.

"She woke us up coughing night afore this past one." She grabbed his hand. "Doc, Miss Bessie thinks it might be that Spanish flu. You reckon it is?"

"Looks to be, Molly." He squeezed her hand. "I'm awful sorry."

Molly snatched her hand from his, her eyes narrowing. "What? Are you saying she ain't gonna live? Are you giving up?" She turned to me. "Please, Miss Bessie, she's my girl, my baby. Please don't let my baby die."

"Molly, I promise you I'll do everything in my power to keep that from happening. For now, let's concentrate on getting this fever down, help her fight this flu."

Molly nodded and she and Timothy went back to placing cold rags on their little girl's body.

Doc Widby gestured for me to join him at the door. "What herbs are you using?" he said sotto voce then nodded his approval when I told him.

"But they're not helping, she keeps getting bluer and brings up blood when she coughs. Is there anything you have, any medicine you can give her?" I asked, unable to keep the desperate plea out of my voice.

He shook his head. "I read they're working on a vaccine but it hasn't been developed yet that I know of. It may not work anyway, if this is caused from a virus and not bacteria." He glanced at little Mavis. "I'm afraid, Bess, that blue color means she won't live, least according to the information I've read. I prayed this wouldn't happen to our small town but looks like it's here and from what I've read it's gonna hang around awhile. I'll need your help 'cause if it's as contagious as I'm told, it's going to affect a lot of people." He ran his hand over his face, his fingers rasping against his whiskers. "Little Mavis isn't the only one sick. I've been out at the Weaver place all night tending to their boy Anson, sick with the same thing."

Alarm skittered up my spine. "Oh, no. How is he?"

"Got the fever down and he was a bit better when I left, but most times, if it doesn't kill you the first time, it comes right back and does the job the second time. Family's all tore up with worry, he's their only child, you know."

Tears welled up in my eyes. Anson was my student, a fun-loving, inquisitive boy who helped fetch wood for the wood stove and looked after the younger students.

Molly shrieked behind us and when we turned back to them, I noticed little Mavis's chest was still, her eyes rolled back in her head, her mouth open. Molly clutched her daughter to her while Timothy collapsed on his knees, his hands over his eyes, bellowing his grief. Tears rolled down my cheeks and I thought, Molly has just exposed herself to this flu, but could not bring myself to pull her away from her daughter. After all, would I not be doing the same thing? I stared at that sweet little girl, thinking I would never experience the joy of having her in my classroom, see her eyes light up with excitement over solving a math problem or reading a book, hear her sweet laughter and watch her as I told one of my great-grandmother's Cherokee legends. A sob escaped my throat, and I excused myself and left them to their grief, thinking I needed to now tend to the living.

When I stepped out of the bedroom, little Timmy and Nash, both sitting at the table, glanced up. The expectant looks on their faces vanished as their faces scrunched up and they began to cry. I cursed myself for not having my emotions under better control. Movement behind me pushed me into the room and I turned to see Molly and Timothy at the threshold, clutching one another, tears streaming down their faces. Timmy and Nash ran to them and they enfolded their little boys in their arms, and the grief in that room was so powerful and raw, I knew I could not bear witness to this. I rushed to the door and ran outside, stopping when I reached the well. I turned the handle furiously and when the bucket came into view, grabbed it and set it on the well lip, plunging my hands into the cold water, my mind quickly riffling through things I might have done differently, ways I might have saved that precious little girl. When Doc Widby spoke, I jumped, splashing water onto my bodice and face.

"Wasn't nothing you could have done," he said, putting his hand on my shoulder and squeezing. "Her die was cast the moment she got sick."

"I've never seen anything like it," I said, feeling sick to my stomach. "That blue color, the blood foam coming out of her mouth and nose." My eyes met his. "Please, tell me that's not going to be the case each time. Please."

He shook his head. "I'm sorry, Bess, but from what I've learned, it will happen quite a bit. Not all the time but most."

"What are we going to do?"

"Our very best. That's all we can do."

I leaned against the well. "The family's been exposed. What do you think? Should we quarantine them until we know they're not sick? Is there a protocol, any sort of procedure to this?"

"I think quarantine will be a good idea for now. Molly know how she got exposed?"

When I told him what Molly had said, he became alarmed. "No telling how many people that man came in contact with." He thought for a moment. "I think we need to find a place to set up a temporary hospital, Bess. From the statistics I've read, this will spread fast and I reckon a lot are going to be sick. Asheville's next on the railroad line if it ain't there already, and they'll be busy with their own so I don't see that it will do any good to send our sick there."

"As fast as it kills, I doubt they could get there in time for treatment." I looked at the small log cabin, once filled with happiness and laughter and now heavy with grief and despair. "What about Stone Mountain Baptist Church as a hospital? We could bring in pallets, pillows, blankets. It's on top of the mountain, away from most. A good place to keep the sick separated from the healthy."

Doc nodded. "I'll go speak to Reverend Redmon now." He glanced at the house. "I'll let the neighbors know but warn them not to go into the house. Maybe the more people we can keep away from the sick ones, the better we can control it."

I watched him mount his horse and leave before returning to the house. Molly and Timothy had calmed down somewhat and the two small boys looked to have cried themselves out. Nash lay in his mother's lap, his eyes drooping, and little Timmy leaned against his pa, rubbing at his cheeks.

Molly handed Nash off to Timothy and approached me. "What do we do now?" she asked, dabbing at her eyes with her apron.

"We bury her."

She put her fist to her mouth. "I don't know if I can put my sweet little girl in the ground, Miss Bessie. I don't know if I can do that."

I put my hand on her arm. "Molly, this is probably going to be the hardest thing you'll ever do but you have to let her go. You have two small boys who need you and a husband who is grieving just as much as you are. She was precious and sweet and did not deserve to die but she's in God's hands now and on another journey. All you can do at this point is tell her goodbye and hold her dear in your heart until you meet up again."

She nodded and I could see her struggle to hold herself strong and not succumb to the grief that threatened to overwhelm her.

"Molly, this is important. I know they'll want to say goodbye but we can't let the boys touch little Mavis. She may still be contagious. We don't want them getting sick so we need to keep them away from her."

Her hand flew to her mouth. "Oh, Miss Bessie, please tell me my boys won't get this awful thing," she wailed. Nash opened his eyes and cried out in horror, hearing his mother's pain. "Please tell me God ain't so hateful as to take my two boys away from me after taking my little girl."

"I mean to see to it that they stay well. That's why we need to keep them away from her. Why don't you and I prepare her little body and Timothy can tend to the boys while we do that, all right? That might help, taking care of her one last time."

And so while Timothy and the boys tried to distract themselves from their grief by cutting down a tree for the coffin, Molly and I, after covering our faces, washed Mavis's small body and then dressed her in her finest dress, a pretty pink one Molly had made for her, covered her eyes with coins, and held her mouth closed with a pink ribbon to match the dress. She looked like an angel, and as I stared at her, I thought what a beautiful young woman she would have grown into and why did the young and innocent always seem to suffer so much more than the old and corrupt. At times, it did not help to tell myself it was God's will. Since my little brother Green's death, I had struggled with this question about death and suspect I always will.

By the time we finished, family and friends had begun to

appear, bearing food and comfort. I had asked Timothy to keep them outside and he did so, although Molly's father caused an uproar when he was not allowed to see his granddaughter upon arrival. Molly told me little Mavis had been his favorite and so I stepped outside and requested that he do his precious granddaughter one last deed by overseeing the making of her casket and the digging of her grave and this seemed to appease him. I have found that most men, given a job to do when they feel so helpless against something they cannot fix, will grab onto it, no matter how large or small, as if an anchor. I told those gathered on the porch that they would see Mavis before her burial although should not touch her and this seemed to appease most. Some could not grasp the concept of contagion but others seemed fearful enough of it that they did as requested without objection.

Fletcher arrived in time to help with the casket and we stood side by side, holding hands, as Timothy carried Mavis to the casket beside the freshly-dug grave and placed her inside. He and Molly and the boys knelt beside the tiny wooden box, tears streaming down their faces. The women openly wept as did most of the men as they said their goodbyes to a small child who would never lay claim to a well-lived life, and when Molly covered Mavis with her favorite quilt made just for her, I had to bite my fist to keep from crying out in grief and anger. Fletcher put his arm around me and squeezed tight, and I could see his jaws clenched and knew he was trying hard to keep his emotions in check.

After the funeral, Doc Widby, who had returned by then, made an announcement about the Spanish flu and warned everyone there to be aware of the symptoms and to immediately go to the Stone Mountain Baptist Church at the first signs. He also told them it would be better if Molly and Timothy, Timmy and Nash would remain in their home and have no contact with others until we were sure they had not caught the Spanish flu. I noticed alarmed looks being passed among some of the mountaineers while others seemed to pay it no mind. I told Molly I would visit her family daily to make sure they stayed well, and when I left, I prayed the flu would remain in check but feared greatly it would not.

As promised, I looked in on Molly and her family each morning before going to Stone Mountain Baptist Church. At first, people with colds and aches and pains would visit daily, and as I ruled each case out, I would breathe a sigh of relief for one more person not sick. Doc Widby continued to care for Anson who seemed to be improving. I was personally glad his parents were well into middle age and hoped this would save them from the flu.

Before the week was up, Noah Vess appeared in the threshold, leaning on his cane, his dog Moss panting by his side. I took one look at Noah and knew he was gravely ill. I rushed to him and took his arm. "Come inside, Mr. Vess, and tell me what's ailing you."

He turned his face to me, his eyes cloudy and vacant. "Moonfixer?" he said in a weak voice.

"Yes, it's me."

He stumbled and I placed my shoulder beneath his arm to support him better.

"I heared you and Doc was tending the sick. I'm afeared I'm mighty ill. Can't breathe good and I'm as weak as a newborn kitten. Wouldn't have never got here without the help of my good friend." He waved his hand at his dog and began coughing. I didn't think he'd ever be able to stop.

I led him to the first pallet and helped him to lie down. I placed pillows beneath his head, elevating him, alarmed at the red spittle flying out of his mouth as he coughed. Moss paced around the pallet, whining as he watched his master. When the coughing spell passed, I held a tin cup of water to Noah's mouth and he drank greedily.

"I thank you kindly," he said after he drained the cup.

"You just rest," I said, pulling a blanket over him. "We'll take good care of you."

"Can Moss stay?" he asked. "Please, Moonfixer, I'm lost without him."

I stroked the dog's back as he lay beside Noah. "Moss can stay here as long as you do, Mr. Vess."

As I encouraged Noah to drink some sage tea, I studied this elderly man who looked so fragile, and thought about the sadness that had come into his life in the past few years. His hands, wrapped around the tin mug, were large, speckled with liver spots, the veins raised, knotted and blue. His palms and finger tips were rough with calluses, and I marveled that these very hands had been used by this blind man to build and destroy a church. Although Stone Mountain Baptist Church was the only place of worship on Stone Mountain, that had not always been so. At one time, there had been one called the Holiness Church, which Noah built with the aid of his many children and grandchildren. The mountain people had called those who attended Noah's church the Holy Rollers and I wondered as I took the cup of tea from him if he had been aware of this. I had seen the church once and it was a beautiful thing to behold. But during a revival Noah held at his church, Noah's wife and daughter disappeared, having run off with two men there to preach, and Noah had gone out one night by himself, blind and filled with anger, and torn down the church. I had through the years wondered if Noah ever regretted it.

"Does anyone in your family know you're here, Mr. Vess?" I asked, noting the blue color of his skin, intuiting that this man did not have long to live.

He shook his head and began coughing again. Afterward, he grabbed my arm. "Moonfixer, I need you to do something for me."

"Certainly," I said, squeezing his hand.

"After I'm gone—"

"Mr. Vess—"

"No, ain't no use denying I'm dying. I ain't been right with God since my wife and daughter run off with them no-count preachers and I tore down His house of worship, but I reckon He ain't so mad at me as I thought. I had a visit from Him last night and He said I'd be most welcome in Heaven." He sighed with such sadness, tears welled in my eyes in answer. "I'm ready to go, Moonfixer, I've had a long life and it's time. But I'm worried about my dog. Can you find a good home for him? We been together nigh on fourteen years and he's getting on in age but he's still a good fella." He reached out and Moss scooted forward and nudged his hand. Noah began petting the dog, who lay down beside him. "Why, I don't reckon I'd still be here if not for Moss. He's saved me from poisonous snakes, falling down into ravines, all kinds of dangers. He's the best friend I've ever had and I want to see him taken care of afore I go."

I touched his cheek, cleared my throat and said, "I promise you, Moss will have a good home. If I can't find anyone who wants him, why, he'll come home with me."

Noah's shoulders eased and I realized how much this had meant to him as he seemed to melt onto the pallet. "Thankee, Moonfixer. I knew you'd be so kind."

I ruffled Moss's fur. "He's a good boy for certain, Mr. Vess, and he deserves a good home till he's ready to join you in Heaven."

Noah sighed. "I tell you one thing, Moonfixer, if I get up there and there ain't no dogs, why I reckon I'll turn right around and go somewheres else. Can't imagine a world without dogs."

I smiled at this. "I agree with you on that point."

He closed his eyes and drifted off to sleep.

Moss alerted me to his owner's death that night, howling with such sadness and agony, I feared I'd cry out right along with him. Fletcher and Doc wrapped Noah's body in a sheet and buried him in the cemetery by moonlight, poor Moss watching all this and constantly howling or whining. After we said prayers over the grave, I brought Moss inside with me and lay down with him, fearful he might run off or try to unbury Noah.

When I woke the next morning, I could not find the dog. I went outside, saw a furry mound lying next to Noah's grave and walked that way, calling for Moss. And when I got there, found the dog frozen and stiff. I sat beside him and stroked his rigid body and told him I prayed he was with his friend in Heaven. Flecher found me there and without saying a word fetched the shovel and dug up the grave and we placed the body of Moss beside Noah. I could not think of a better place for him to be as I said goodbye to both.

But I did not have time to grieve these sad deaths, as the church had begun filling with young men and women and children sick with fevers and coughs, and every waking moment was dedicated to brewing and giving teas and decoctions, trying to control fevers, the constant state of alarm at seeing bluish skin and reddish eyes. We were so overwhelmed that Fletch began to stay at the church with me and help, much to my grave concern. I loved my husband dearly and could not imagine life without him and feared more for him than anyone. When I expressed my concern, he only said, "I feel the same for you, Bess, and that don't stop you." What could I say to this?

Doc and I made constant pleas for volunteers to help us but only Sheriff Nanny's wife Melanie and Reverend Redmon along with Nettie Ledbetter were willing to expose themselves to the flu and who could blame those who were not willing to? I lived in a constant state of exhaustion and stress and slept in four-hour shifts and despaired that no matter what I did, no matter what tincture or decoction or tea I tried, nothing seemed to help. It seemed daily, Fletcher and Doc Widby were digging a grave behind the church.

And the day Timothy brought Molly to us, with a high fever and deep cough, I began to withdraw and became more a machine than human, trying not to see each person before me as a friend or family member or acquaintance but a patient that needed to be saved, a cough that needed to be treated, a fever that needed to be cooled. The days passed in a haze of treating symptoms, debating which herbs to use, allowing myself pangs of grief when someone passed, then moving on to the next one, always, always, keeping an eye out for my husband, searching his face for any signs of fever, becoming alarmed if he coughed or sneezed or blew his nose, touching him, always touching him, ascertaining he was still here, strong and healthy and alive.

Throughout my life, I have been at odds with my God but no more so than this period of time. I prayed constantly for patients to survive only to curse God when they passed. I saw small children die terrible deaths, watched as husbands clung to their dead wives' hands, wives screamed their agony over their husband's bodies, parents bayed their grief while clutching their child to their bosom. Watched women and men and children crying, always crying, and knew there was nothing I could do for them except tell them how sorry I was and move on to the next patient.

But always thinking, this could be me one day. Oh, Fletch, I would beg in my heart, please, please, do not leave me here. I bargained with God for my husband's health and life, knowing this was wrong, but there was nothing else I could do.

But slowly, so slowly as to be almost indiscernible, fewer and fewer cases were diagnosed, and our pallets began to empty. The day Molly awoke without a fever and congestion was the best day in a very long while and I rejoiced that she had been spared and could rejoin her family.

And when we finally closed the hospital, I put my hand in my husband's and we returned to our home, and I was thankful and praised God for allowing me more time with this beautiful man and gladly vowed to myself to keep my bargain with God.

Not knowing that this flu was not done with the world but would sweep through twice more, the third time more deadly than the first.

CHAPTER FOURTEEN

Fall 1919

It's about as hard as trying to steer a herd of cats.

Although the battle against the Spanish flu pandemic and the end of World War I continued to dominate the news, another, more personal battle was being fought close to home, one that had been raging for almost 80 years. Women's quest for the right to vote had been a long and arduous journey, as proven by the mindset of 1919, when the female gender, although encouraged to vociferously support the troops and the president during the war, were otherwise expected to remain silent and accepting of their fate. But women like Susan B. Anthony, Alice Paul, Lucy Burns and North Carolina's own Gertrude Weil were blazing a trail for the rights of women that I ardently followed through newspapers. Living in a small community in the mountains of North Carolina tended to be a bit confining as there wasn't much I could do to support the suffrage movement other than write letters to the President, our Congressmen and the newspaper, all of which were ignored. When I read in The *Old Fort Sentinel* that Alice Paul would be making a speech in Asheville, I told Fletcher I intended to go and began saving money for a train ticket. My sweet husband said he'd come along if I didn't mind. Before we returned, we intended to visit my sister Jack who had married the year before and had recently moved with her husband and baby to Asheville. I was anxious to see my sister and meet her infant son.

The trip by train was not a long one and we arrived in Asheville early in the afternoon. I was impressed by how clean the streets were, unlike Old Fort, where the dirt roads quickly turned to mud when it rained. These were paved and uncluttered with clumps of soil or droppings from horses. And unlike Old Fort, where most traveled by horse or horse and wagon, streetcars and automobiles interspersed occasionally by boys on bicycles, whom we learned were delivery boys, occupied the roadways, industriously going about their business. Fletcher and I sat at a small outdoor café watching with some amazement all the activity on the street along with the busy march of people on the sidewalks around us. I noticed a rather large automobile with what looked to be a wooden wagon attached to the rear lumber to a stop nearby. Two men dressed in some sort of uniform jumped from the back of the vehicle, picked up large trash bins and deposited the contents into the rail-slatted back. Our waitress, noticing my interest, said, "Them's Model T one-ton trucks invented by Henry Ford. We call 'em garbage trucks."

"They're designed to pick up refuse?" I asked.

"Sure are. The city provides them. But those aren't the only trucks the city uses. They got some with pressure hoses to wash off the streets." With a wink, she added, "Sure makes things look nicer now, don't it?" before going back inside the restaurant.

As we were preparing to leave, she asked us where we were headed. I told her to the Battery Park Hotel to hear Alice Paul speak that evening. With a grin, she said, "Even though it's been dry here since 1908, you can get some fine whiskey at the Battery."

I smiled, thinking it was most likely provided by Thorney Dalton, whose business was booming.

Since we had time, we decided to go see George Vanderbilt's massive mansion, the Biltmore House. After making inquiries, we acquired the correct street car and enjoyed the ride out to Biltmore Village, which we learned had been devastated by the Flood of 1916 but saw, as we were told when we arrived, that the Biltmore House had remained untouched.

On the way back, Fletch remarked to me that he didn't think it was healthy breathing in all the smoke hanging in the air from various industries and automobiles. I had to agree I missed the clean mountain air.

A lady sitting behind us leaned forward to confide that a businessman by the name of Thomas Wadley Raoul had been named head of a smoke committee and had hired an engineer to come up with a way to make furnaces smokeless. "But all in all, it's a right clean city," she said. "Why they've even got a law against spitting in public now," and went on to tell us the boardinghouses in the city would put people out on the streets if they thought they carried germs, after which the city would come along and disinfect the place. "It isn't legal for livestock to roam free within city limits anymore. We got us a dog catcher and he'll nab your dog if he's not muzzled. One time, he nabbed Buster, the city's official rat catcher, and nearly got mobbed for it so now Buster's been granted dispensation from the muzzle law." Fletcher and I couldn't help but laugh at that image. As we traveled down Patton Avenue, which she said was called the Great White Way, she pointed out the Sondley Building. "That's where O. Henry had an office when he came here with his wife Sara Coleman back in '09. They say he couldn't write and kept crumbling up the pages and throwing them out. He's buried at the Riverside Cemetery here in Asheville."

I was excited to learn this bit of history. "He and his wife honeymooned in Hot Springs, my home town," I told her. "At the Mountain Park Hotel. They say he told his wife those were the happiest days he'd had in years."

She smiled at me. "I can see why. My husband and I visited there once. It's a right pretty place." I wondered what she would think of the Mountain Park Hotel now after the grounds had been so severely changed by the German internment camp and hoped that it would be as Harry Hill claimed the government had promised and put back to the way it used to be. She waved her arm at the city whizzing by, bringing my attention back to her and said, with a proud look, "They call this the Paris of the South. Isn't like it used to be but it's a booming town."

The streetcar braked to a stop and with a wave Fletcher and I stepped off, noting the afternoon had gotten away from us and we needed to make haste for the Battery.

Shortly before the appointed hour, we made our way inside the hotel and to the large room set aside for Miss Paul's speech. Although the room was filling up quickly, we managed to find two seats near the front and settled in. I looked at the podium where two older women were seated, talking quietly to one another. I had never seen a picture of Alice Paul but had imagined a younger woman. I wondered which one would turn out to be our guest speaker as an elderly woman rose and approached the podium. Although she was well past middle age, she must have been impressive in her youth as she stood tall and stately and held herself in a regal way. She introduced herself as Helen Morris Lewis, the great-great granddaughter of Lewis Morris, a signer of the Declaration of Independence, and organizer of the first woman's rights association in our fair state. She proceeded to apologize for Miss Paul, who had been taken by illness and would not be with us tonight. Several people made disappointed noises at this but soon quieted as Miss Lewis began to speak. She was an eloquent spokesperson and quickly captured the audience, talking at length about the long battle to gain suffrage for women that began with Lucretia Mott and Elizabeth Cady Stanton, who, being barred from the World Anti-Slavery Convention in London, held a Women's Convention in America in 1840 followed by the first Women's Rights Convention in Seneca Falls, New York in 1849 at which renowned abolitionist Frederick Douglass spoke for the rights of women, leading to a strong alliance with the Abolitionist movement in 1850.

In 1857, a big step granting women more independence was reached when Congress passed the Married Woman's

Property Bill, allowing women to sue, be sued, make contracts and inherit and bequeath property. However, this did not address the disenfranchisement of women.

The suffrage movement came to a halt during the Civil War as women committed their energies toward the war effort but picked up momentum in 1868 with the formation of the American Equal Rights Association by Elizabeth Cady Stanton and Susan B Anthony which was dedicated to suffrage for all regardless of gender or race. This was a busy year, with Senator S.C. Pomeroy of Kansas introducing the federal woman's suffrage amendment in Congress which was defeated by the ratification of the 14th Amendment defining citizens and voters exclusively as male. A rift followed within the American Equal Rights Association regarding whether to support the proposed 15th Amendment which would enfranchise Negro American males while ignoring women altogether, bringing forth the National Woman Suffrage Association formed by Elizabeth Cady Stanton and Susan B. Anthony. When the 15th Amendment was passed in 1870, the National Woman Suffrage Association advocated for a 16th Amendment dictating universal suffrage, followed by the formation of the Anti-Suffrage Party in 1871.

1872 was a contentious year in which Susan B. Anthony was arrested and tried in Rochester, New York for casting her ballot for Ulysses S. Grant in the presidential election. She was fined $100 which she refused to pay and the government never tried to collect. The Women's Christian Temperance Union joined the fight in 1874, bringing about strong opposition for women's enfranchisement by the liquor lobby, fearful that women would use their vote to prohibit the sale of liquor.

Finally a Woman Suffrage Amendment was proposed and defeated in Congress in 1887, which led to the formation of the National Council of Women in 1888. 1890 was a big year, when Wyoming was admitted to the Union with a state constitution granting women the right to vote and the American Federation of Labor declared its support for woman suffrage. Colorado joined Wyoming in 1893 in adopting women's right to vote with Utah doing the same in 1896 and Washington State in 1910.

"The women's suffrage movement in North Carolina began in 1894 with the formation of the Equal Suffrage Association right here in Asheville," Miss Lewis said with a proud look. She told how in 1896 she had been surprised to learn she received five votes for the office of representative of the United States Congress, although she had not been a candidate, and all five votes were from men. In 1896, she became the first woman in North Carolina to seek an elective office when she ran for position of superintendent of waterworks for the city of Asheville. As a disenfranchised woman, she could not even vote for herself and, of course, did not win.

"As president, of the Equal Suffrage Association," she said, "I sought a state amendment which was supported by Senator J.L. Hyatt who introduced a bill in the 1897 legislative session. This bill, however, was referred to the Committee on Insane Asylums, of all places, where it died." There was a burst of ironic laughter at this.

She went on to say the movement lay dormant for several years until a federal amendment in 1911 was opposed by the organization of the National Association Opposed to Woman Suffrage. This group included wealthy, influential women, distillers and brewers, urban politicians, Southern congressmen, corporate capitalists and even some Catholic clergymen. She paused while there was much laughter at this then smiled and went on, saying that the California suffrage campaign did succeed followed by Theodore Roosevelt's Bull Moose Party announcing its support for women's suffrage in 1912.

In 1913, Gertrude Weil formed the North Carolina Equal Suffrage League in Charlotte which helped develop local groups while lobbying legislators and distributing pamphlets and giving speeches. In 1915, Lilian Exum Clement of Asheville started a branch of the Congressional Union which was later renamed the National Woman's Party, of which Alice Paul was the founder. This more militant organization sought to obtain suffrage through a federal amendment but all attempts to enfranchise women were voted down by the legislature, much of the controversy being that anti-suffragists feared allowing women to vote would increase pressure to reverse laws that prevented Negros from voting.

At this point, she said that since Miss Paul was not there to speak, Gertrude Weil would do so for her and introduced Miss Weil to much applause.

I sat forward, mesmerized, and was glad she began by telling us Miss Paul's background as I knew of her but did not know much about her. The newspapers were quick enough to report what she did but not why or what brought her to it. When she told us Miss Paul was born into a Quaker family on January 11, 1885, I thought, why, she's younger than me, and admit to feeling a bit forlorn I had not made my mark upon the world as she had. Unlike me, she had studied at a real university, the Swarthmore College in New Jersey, and went on to do graduate work in New York City and England. While in London, she joined the women's suffrage movement where she was arrested and jailed on several occasions for protesting.

Miss Paul returned to America in 1910, and spurred by her efforts in England, joined the National American Women's Suffrage Association where she was quickly appointed head of the Congressional Committee in charge of working for a federal suffrage amendment. She went to Washington D.C. in 1912 to manage this movement and there organized, along with Lucy Burns, a massive march by women during Woodrow Wilson's presidential inauguration on March 3, 1913. The two women, along with Inez Milholland, led the procession wearing Greek robes and sitting astride white horses, but were not well-received. Men threw insults and obscenities at them and some even attacked them while the police stood passively by and watched. However, this was not all for naught. The following day, this group made headlines across the nation and the disenfranchisement of women became a much-discussed topic among politicians and the general public.

Although Miss Paul shared the goal of universal suffrage with the National American Women's Suffrage Association president, their political strategies were not compatible. NAWSA wanted to focus the majority of its efforts on state campaigns while Miss Paul's goal was for a national amendment and to hold President Wilson and his party responsible for not giving women the right to vote. So Miss Paul severed all ties to the NAWSA and in 1916 formed the National Woman's Party, organizing "Silent Sentinels" to stand outside the White House holding banners directed toward the President. Wilson's attitude toward them was initially condescending but changed when America entered World War I after they began calling him "Kaiser Wilson". He and many others saw their protests as unpatriotic and the demonstrators were often attacked by angry mobs because of this.

Miss Weil described Alice Paul and her Silent Sentinels demonstrating in front of the White House in January after President Wilson took office. They held round-the-clock vigils demanding the vote for women, hoping to humiliate the president and expose the hypocrisy of his statement to make the world safe for democracy when there was none for women in America. They held banners stating, "Mr. President, how long must women wait for liberty?" and even went so far as to hang him in effigy and burn copies of his speeches.

In June, the arrests began wherein the protestors were charged with obstructing traffic and called traitors. They were placed in the Occoquan Workhouse in Virginia where they were given rotten food to eat, refused visitors and not allowed medical care. They applied for political prisoner status but were denied. But this did not deter them in their efforts. Once released, the women returned to the White House gates where their numbers swelled. By November, an investigation had been launched into the conditions at the prison and the activities of the warden, W.H. Whitaker, who was known for his cruelty. But this did not stop his involvement in the Night of Terror.

The room grew quiet when she mentioned these three words. As one, we all seemed to hold our breath and lean closer to hear the facts of this horrible night. On November

14, 1917, Whitaker and 44 of his club-wielding guards met Alice Paul and 32 other demonstrators in front of the White House, where they beat, kicked, dragged and choked them. Some were lifted into the air and flung to the ground. One was stabbed between the eyes with the broken staff of her banner. Guards twisted women's arms as they dragged them and hurled them into concrete punishment cells. Lucy Burns was handcuffed to the bars of her cell in a position of torture. When thrown into a cell, Dora Lewis hit her head against an iron bed and was knocked out cold. By the end of the night, some women were barely alive.

Warden Whitaker ordered the guards to teach the suffragists a lesson and for two weeks the women's only water came from an open pail and their food was infested with worms.

Alice Paul, in protest, began a hunger strike so they moved her to a sanitarium where they tied her to a chair, forced a tube down her throat and poured liquid into her mouth until she vomited. She was tortured like this for weeks until word was smuggled to the press of her treatment.

During this, President Wilson and his advisors tried to persuade a psychiatrist to declare Alice Paul insane so she could be permanently institutionalized. But the doctor refused, saying Miss Paul was strong and brave and that didn't make her insane. He went on to say, "Courage in women is often mistaken for insanity."

A burst of applause went up at this. I clapped loudly, thankful this man had the strength to stand up to a powerful president and his cohorts.

She continued, saying that this night, however, turned the tide in favor of giving women the right to vote. A court-ordered hearing two weeks later exposed these beaten women to the world and the judge agreed they had been brutally abused for nothing more than exercising their constitutional right to protest. Voices raised in agreement at this, mine among them. President Wilson, in response to a public outcry over the atrocious treatment of the suffragists, reversed his position and announced his support for a suffrage amendment, calling it a "war measure". I shook my head, thinking this was probably done for nothing other than to save face.

Louder applause resounded around the room at this and Miss Weil smiled and went on with much spirit to encourage each woman and man there to do what they could to help the suffrage movement, telling us that no effort was too small. She left the stage to thunderous applause and shouts and whistles of encouragement and I vowed to Fletcher I intended to do any and everything I could to help make the enfranchisement of women an amendment to our Constitution.

Fletcher rose to his feet, saying, "I reckon I'll do whatever it takes too, Bess." He eyed me, a smile playing along his lips. "Although I'd probably be killing my vote every time. Knowing you, you'll choose your pa's party and vote Democrat."

I laughed and kissed him on the cheek, thankful for a husband who saw women as equal to men and not as chattel or a slave to do their bidding.

Jack's home being close to the hotel, Fletcher and I chose to walk there, jumping at loud noises as young men sped by in their automobiles, blowing their horns and waving bottles of liquor in the air. We could hear music playing from the Asheville Opera House and admired the electric street lights that lit up Patton Avenue. "I can see why they call it the Great White Way," I said.

Jack greeted us at the door, her face lit by a smile and bearing a blanket-wrapped baby in her arms. I smiled at my sister, wondering how in the world she could be so short and petite while I was so tall and gangly. The only similarities between the two of us were our dark hair and eyes. Jack hugged Fletcher and me and urged us to come inside. I looked around but didn't see her husband, Ed Tillery.

Jack, noticing this said, "Ed's working."

I nodded.

"His job with the railroad's a good one but he has to work nights." She shrugged. "It gets lonely but I've got my baby."

I peeled back the blanket and smiled with delight. "Oh,

Jack, he looks just like a miniature Papa. Or you when you were born." The memory of Mama holding a just born Jack and smiling up at Papa flashed into my mind and I felt a twinge of sadness.

The baby opened his eyes and looked at me and I knew in that instant that this boy would be an important part of my life. I thought back to the vision I had had when Liza and Ruth left our farm and knew without a doubt this was the child I saw. And I remembered Elisi's words in the dream: "In time, the path will lead you to a child, and when it does, you must stand up and do what you know is right for him."

Could this be the child Elisi had spoken about? But how could that be? This little one belonged to my sister and I could see she loved him. I couldn't imagine any circumstance in which I would need to stand up and do the right thing where this child was concerned. I forced the memory away and made an effort to listen to what Jack was saying.

"I named him Raymond Earl but Papa took one look and said he's going to be called John."

I shook my head. "Named after Papa, I suppose." I took a closer look at the baby, who stared at us, his eyes bright and alert. "He's got Papa's brown eyes, his dark hair, light coloring. Just like a tiny Papa."

She smiled. "I do hope you'll stay the night, Bess. We have an extra bedroom and I made up the bed for you and Fletch."

I glanced at Fletcher, who nodded. "We're happy to stay, Jack. Thank you for having us."

We took turns holding the baby and making comments about who he favored and wondering what he would be like and the man he would grow up to be. Fletch began yawning and Jack offered to show him to the bedroom. I told him I wanted to visit for a bit with my sister. With a nod, he kissed me on the cheek and went off to bed.

Jack and I stayed up most of the night catching up on our lives and family. Although my little sister was 20 years younger than me and I had married Fletch when she was just a baby, I still felt a strong connection to her. I have to admit that at times, it hurt to see her because I always associated her with Mama's death, Mama having died shortly after Jack was born. But I loved her dearly and wished for her a happy life. We finally retired long after midnight and had little time to visit the next morning as Fletch and I had to catch our train early. Ed hadn't returned home yet and we were disappointed we didn't get the chance to meet him. With teary eyes, Jack and I kissed and hugged each other and promised to write and visit more often. Before leaving, I put my hand on that precious little baby and told him in my mind I looked forward to whatever life had in store for us, knowing that it would be a good and happy thing. As I kissed the top of his head, I prayed I would know what to do when the time came ... if it ever did. There were no guarantees, I knew that, but, oh, my heart told me different. I asked God to take care of him until then, to keep him safe and unharmed, and to give me the courage to act when needed.

I returned to Stone Mountain determined to rally our mountain women to aid in attaining the right to vote. The next Wednesday, after our Bible study meeting, I told the ladies about our trip to Asheville and Miss Lewis's and Miss Weil's speeches. I said I intended to write weekly letters to our representatives in Congress, encouraging them to support the suffrage movement, and asked if anyone would be interested in doing the same.

Sheriff Nanny's wife Melanie stood to be heard. "I've been looking for some way to help this cause and I certainly will write letters each week, Bess." She smiled at me. "I only wish I could do more."

I nodded in agreement.

Junior Hall's grandmother struggled to her feet, breathing heavily. She had once been a robust woman, proud of her strength and size, but her advanced years were beginning to burn away the extra flesh and height so that now she put me in mind of a snowman with her soft, white hair billowing about her face, her bosom making one roll and stomach the next, supported by legs which resembled two stout sticks. Her eyes were dark and piercing and had not yet succumbed to the aging process. I feared for her health as she never seemed to be able to get enough air into her lungs and suspected that came from years of smoking a corncob pipe. "I only got one thing to say," she wheezed. "I ain't never voted, ain't never seen the need to it anyways, seeing as how it all looks to be nothing more than a game to me among brainless men with too much money in their pockets and not enough sense nor compassion to think to spend all those funds on those in need rather than their own greedy lust for power and profit." She nodded her head curtly, holding up her hand, signaling us to wait while she caught her breath. "I reckon that's all I got to say on the matter but you can count me out of any kind of letter writing. I got better things to do." She lowered herself back into her seat with the aid of Melanie.

Sofie Hall, whom I had treated for depression after her husband left her when their baby was born, set her little girl on the floor at her feet. "I ain't much of a letter writer but if you'll help me with the words, I reckon I can do the same and I'm more'n happy to. That's a right good idea, Miss Bessie." She looked at the other women. "Can you imagine what that Miss Paul must a-felt when they beat all them demonstrators and put 'em in prison? But she kept a-going back and protesting." She shook her head. "Lawsy mercy, she's a strong woman and I'm sure glad we got somebody like her and all them other women trying to help us get the right to vote. Why, writing letters is the least I can do, I reckon, considering all she's been through."

Several of the other women nodded at that, talking excitedly to one another, but I noticed two women remained silent about the subject, their mouths downturned. Everyone quieted when Nettie Ledbetter stood and cleared her throat. I steeled myself for Nettie's response. She always seemed to find fault with something or someone and although we were constantly subjected to her prickly comments never could quite get used to them. I told myself this was just her nature but her tongue could be as sharp and venomous as a snake's fangs and at times it was all I could do to ignore her and not retaliate in kind.

"I must say, I find that Miss Paul's actions unladylike and militant," she began. "After all, I believe we can all agree she has brought much of her so-called brutal treatment upon herself." She sniffed with disdain, and I thought, she has her nose so high in the air, she could drown in a rain storm. "Hanging the president in effigy," she continued, "calling him Kaiser Wilson, and marching around in front of the White House with pejorative signs. Well, I never heard the likes. He's our president, the ruler of our country, and as such must be accorded respect and loyalty."

"Even though he had her tortured and tried to force a psychiatrist to declare her insane," I said, my voice strained.

"Well, he did reverse his opinion on the matter of giving women the right to vote."

"As an appeasement and nothing else. There was so much public outcry over this, I see that he had no choice."

Several of the other ladies murmured their agreement.

Nettie sighed as if dealing with a wayward child. "Regardless, Bess, we should not hold Miss Paul up as a role model. Why, if so, many young women might think it their right to march around, carrying signs for this or that cause, whatever strikes their fancy."

"And what is wrong with that? It's their right as Americans."

"They should be where they are needed, at home tending to their families, not flitting here and there protesting this or that."

I opened my mouth to object but she held up her hand. "However, I do agree the vote should be given to women and I will add my own letters to our Congress, asking they support this very important cause. Just don't speak to me of Miss Paul's aggressive efforts. We're women, and as such, we can do this in a very respectful, gentile manner."

I smiled at her. "Thank you, Nettie. My suggestion would be that those who wish to participate write these letters after our prayer meetings since that's a proven time we're all together." The women quickly agreed and I closed the meeting, happy that although I would not play a large part in the suffragette movement, the part I did play might nonetheless help bring it about.

CHAPTER FIFTEEN

Summer 1924

The room was so crowded you couldn't cuss the cat without getting fur in your mouth.

As it turned out, on October 2, 1919, President Woodrow Wilson suffered a massive stroke. Paralyzed and unable to carry out the duties of his office, his wife, Edith, with Wilson's personal physician's help, concealed the severity of his disability from the cabinet, press and public. Calling herself his steward, she decided who would be allowed to see him, screened the papers and issues that would be brought to his attention, and reported his decisions to government officials. It was, to me, a fitting comeuppance that a man who at one time did not see women as his equal now trusted one to run the country.

God does, indeed, work in mysterious ways.

The year 1920 finally ended the long battle for the enfranchisement of women. On August 18th, the 19th amendment was ratified, giving women the right to vote. Although I had not played a large role in this fight, I felt a proud sense of victory that I had at least been a part of it.

In 1922, Reverend Redmon finally decided it was time to retire and, with a sad voice tinged with a bit of relief, announced his decision at service one Sunday. The congregation was understandably upset; after all, he'd served as our preacher for years, longer than some of us had been attending services at Stone Mountain Baptist Church. When Nettie Ledbetter stood up and asked him why, he answered, "I'm too old to be traveling around to three churches every Sunday so I've decided to follow the Lord's example. I'm going to rest on the Sabbath."

Even Nettie couldn't argue with that.

We were sad to see him go and after a month of Sundays with fill-ins were more than happy to greet our new minister, Preacher Franklin Justice. He was about ten years younger than Reverend Redmon, very personable, and well-liked in our congregation. He wasn't a tall man, in fact, an inch or two shorter than me, with narrow shoulders and bowed legs which he claimed came from riding horses much of his life. His pewter-colored hair flowed past his collar and I imagined must be the man's one vanity as he favored combing his fingers through his curly locks. His face was as average as a face can be, and there was nothing about the man other than his hair to call attention to him. But he had a deep, booming, musical voice and listening to him would be, I thought, much like listening to the voice of God.

Like the good reverend, Preacher Justice lived in Old Fort though his home was much fancier. Unlike Reverend Redmon, who was a Presbyterian, Preacher Justice was Baptist and he didn't seem to have any problem with traveling around to three different churches every Sunday, probably because he was the first person on the mountain to own one of those newfangled automobiles.

Most of the men folk were fascinated by that strange machine, except Fletcher. He didn't cotton to anything that could go so fast and would only shake his head when asked what he had against them and mutter something about "useless contraptions" under his breath.

Useless to my Fletch anyway. The truth is, my husband didn't see the point of going so fast when he could walk anywhere he wanted. He claimed it didn't cost him a thing, except maybe a case of sore feet now and again, and as he walked he had the added benefit of actually seeing the world he lived in. He could look at the flowers and trees or the great expanse of mountains jutting up into the blue sky, listen to the birds sing or the soft burbling of a creek, smell the delicate scents of the wildflowers or the harsh tang of tobacco drying in a tobacco barn, and feel the softness of the air as it touched his cheeks or the sharp jabs of sleet falling on his coat and hat in the winter.

My husband, as I had always known, was a sensual man who took pleasure in the world around him and enjoyed nothing more than experiencing it fully. And in his eyes, walking wherever he needed to go was the best way to do that.

Unlike the other men in the congregation, he didn't gather round Preacher Justice's Model T, going over every detail with a fine-tooth comb and making admiring noises, speculating on how fast the thing could go. Fletcher just wasn't interested. Walking was good enough for him, and when he needed to go a little faster, there was always our mare, Pet, or our two red mules and the wagon.

But he smothered his objections a couple of years later when I needed to go to Knoxville to see Papa and Preacher Justice just happened to be traveling there in his Model T.

I dreamed about Papa one night in early summer and when I awoke the next morning knew without a doubt I needed to go to Knoxville but intuited there was no need to rush. Thus, following my usual routine, I fed the chickens, gathered the eggs, and milked Ginger and Belle. Then I went in to fix breakfast and waited patiently until Fletch came in to eat.

After he sat down I put his plate in front of him and handed him the butter dish. "I need to go to Knoxville to see about Papa. I dreamed about him last night and something's wrong over there."

Fletch picked up his cup of coffee and studied me over the rim, as if trying to gauge what was going on in my head. As usual, it didn't take him long. "Is your Papa sick, Bess?"

"No, I don't think so. That's not the feeling I'm getting anyway. There's no way I can know for sure, of course, but I don't think it's anything really bad. I think Papa's all right as far as his health's concerned." I shook my head. "It may have something to do with the rest of the family. All I really know is, I feel like I need to be there."

He nodded. "All right, Bess. How long you planning on being gone?"

I thought about it for a moment and then shrugged. "I hope a couple of days should do it."

"All right, I reckon we can ask Bose Dalton if he can look after the farm while we're gone."

I smiled with relief at not having to travel alone. I'd hoped Fletcher would offer to accompany me, even though I knew it was impractical—summer was the busiest time on the farm—but hoped I would have the support of my stoic husband if I needed it.

"You can go with me?"

"I reckon I can, we have enough friends and neighbors around to take care of things if Bose can't or if he needs some help."

I took his hand and smiled. "It's such a relief to have you going with me, Fletch."

He nodded. "All right, I'll head over to Old Fort and pick up our tickets. You get packed while I'm gone."

As it turned out, he ran into Preacher Justice while he was in Old Fort and mentioned that he was there to buy tickets to Knoxville. Preacher Justice told Fletch he had planned to head that way the next day and offered to give us a ride. His sister Muriel would be accompanying him but he assured Fletch there would be plenty of room for us.

Early the next morning, Fletch and I were sitting on the front porch swing when Preacher Justice's black Ford Model T chugged down our road and over our little bridge. To my surprise, his sister Muriel was driving. I smiled with delight, a fleeting dose of yearning passing over me, and wondered if Preacher Justice would let me try my hand at driving. I often drove the mules and wagon around the farm. Surely it wasn't that much harder to drive an automobile.

Fletch turned to me and smiled. "Don't go getting any far-fetched ideas, Bessie-girl."

I tried my best to look innocent but I'm sure the desire

was written all over my face so I gave up and laughed. "Do you think he'd let me drive? I bet I could sweet-talk him into it."

Fletch laughed too. "Yep, you probably could, but for my peace of mind, please promise you won't."

"Well, mercy, Fletch, it couldn't be that much different than driving the wagon, could it? I drive the wagon all the time."

"You do, but that's not a coupla' trained mules pulling that contraption. It's a machine, a powerful one, and there are a lot of curvy mountain roads between here and Knoxville."

I huffed out a breath, pretending to be resigned to the fate my husband had directed for me. Truthfully, the desire to drive that automobile was nothing more than a flash in the pan, a mere flicker of flame that grew ever dimmer the closer Preacher Justice got to the house. Then when Muriel braked to a stop and shut the engine off, kicking up such a ruckus it woke Fritz from his nap, sending him careening around the house to the barn, that little glimmer winked out entirely.

Fletch straightened, eying the automobile with a wary look. "That thing sure does make a commotion. I think I'd ruther the train or maybe a good swift horse."

My thoughts had turned to being trapped in the automobile as it plunged off the side of a mountain and burst into flames when it hit the ground. The train, definitely the train, I thought as I draped my scarf over my head, tying it securely under my chin.

Fletch hopped up and went down the stairs. As he approached the automobile, Preacher Justice climbed out and held out his hand. "Good mornin to you, Fletch," he said and nodded to me then pointed toward the worn valise at my feet. "Missus Bessie, that all you have?"

I reached down, curled my fingers around the handle of Mama's old satchel as I nodded. "Good morning, Preacher Justice. Where should I put this?"

"You just give it to me and I'll stash it in the back." He winked at Fletch. "Don't worry, Muriel won't be driving. She just wanted to practice for a bit. I'll take over now and we'll get to Knoxville in about six, seven hours, give or take."

"Safe and sound, I hope," Fletch said.

"Oh, I don't expect any trouble. We have good weather and my Lizzie girl is pretty reliable, even with a novice like Muriel driving." He patted the car. "These things are made tough and can handle just about anything. We have paved roads most of the way so she'll go just fine." He puffed out his chest. "My Tin Lizzie can handle the roads here on the mountain and that means she can handle just about anything."

Fletch took the valise and handed it to Preacher Justice as Muriel stepped out of the car. "Miss Muriel, how are you today?"

"I'm fine and dandy, Mr. Elliot. Yourself?"

"Can't complain."

She smiled at me. "Bessie, how are you? Not nervous, I hope. Franklin's a very good driver and he'll get us there without any trouble. Why, he's made this trip so many times I think he could do it in his sleep."

I decided not to mention my earlier spell of apprehension and shoved the thoughts of plummeting over the side of the mountain out of my brain. Heavens, I'd ridden the train to Hot Springs and back more times than I could count and had never worried about getting there safe but the train was a good deal bigger than this automobile. Still, I determined to put the nerves aside and look at this as an adventure.

I laughed. "Let's see if we can keep him awake, Muriel." I took her hand. "I'm doing just fine though I am anxious to get to Knoxville. I haven't seen my family in a coon's age."

Fritz came back around the house and immediately went to stand at Fletch's side. Fletch reached down and scratched him between the ears. "Bose'll be here soon. You be a good ol' boy and look after the farm. We'll see you when we get back."

The trip was uneventful as far as the automobile went. I enjoyed traveling at a slower pace and being able to see the towns I had only glimpsed from the train. We passed through Old Fort first then Black Mountain. After that it was the

Swannanoa Gap which I'll admit made my heart flutter a few times as Preacher Justice maneuvered around the sharp curves. We passed through the thriving little township of Swannanoa where Dr. E. W. Grove, the owner of the increasingly well-known Grove Park Inn in Asheville, had established the Grove Stone and Sand Company to obtain material for building his hotel.

Then it was on to the hustle and bustle of Asheville where we clearly saw the effects of this economic booming age that would come to be known as the Roaring Twenties. There were more automobiles than I could count, fancy, colorful street cars buzzing this way and that, women dressed in flimsy dresses that barely touched their knees with short hair worn in waves, service stations where they sold gasoline to fuel the ever more popular automobiles, theaters where they showed moving pictures, and a great many speakeasies. Though I didn't know what those were and had no way of recognizing one since they were generally plain buildings, Preacher Justice pointed out a few as we passed them. It was a little hard for me to imagine hidden places where people gathered to listen to jazz music and buy alcohol even though the sale of liquor was now prohibited nationwide. Of course, alcohol had been declared illegal in North Carolina way back in 1908 while the rest of the nation hadn't outlawed it until 1920 with the ratification of the 18th amendment. Most people blamed that on the Women's Suffrage movement and the 19th amendment, a revision that most states endorsed soon after it passed through Congress but which North Carolina wouldn't ratify during my lifetime.

We saw the new McCormick Field where the Asheville Skylanders played Roy's favored game of baseball, a sport that was becoming more popular every day. We even caught a glimpse of George Vanderbilt's palatial estate with its acres of groomed land and gardens of brilliant flowers that seemed to spill from every nook and corner of the grounds surrounding the house.

After Asheville came familiar territory, first Marshall and then Hot Springs. Marshall hadn't changed much that I could see nor had Hot Springs since I was there for Aunt Belle's funeral. I started to ask Preacher Justice if he would mind driving us up to Sandy Gap Cemetery so I could put some flowers on Mama's and Green's graves and maybe visit with Miss Cordy for a bit but decided not to. We were, after all, just passengers on this trip and nonpaying ones at that.

Not long after Hot Springs, we crossed the border into Tennessee where we stopped by the French Broad River to have a picnic lunch Muriel had packed for us. While we ate fried chicken and potato salad, I shared the story of the picnic Papa and I had on the banks of the French Broad outside of Paint Rock where I thought I saw the Melungeon boogie-man. I told them the same story Papa had told me that day about the Shelton Laurel massacre during the Civil War in an effort to soothe my fright of the imagined monster.

Muriel was horrified at the retelling of the massacre. It was a gruesome story, I admit, and was a little surprised she didn't grasp the true moral of the story that evil wasn't always easily recognized. Sometimes monsters came in uniforms or even normal clothes. Preacher Justice understood the meaning behind the story and nodded his head when I finished, saying, "Your papa's a wise man, Missus Bessie."

After that, we continued on our way, passing through Newport where we stopped at a service station for gas. Next came the tiny town of Sevierville and finally Knoxville.

I admit I was getting a little tired of sitting in such a confined space by then but my first glimpse of Knoxville had me sitting up straight and turning my head in order to see everything. I had thought Asheville was bustling and filled with people but Knoxville, oh, Knoxville was truly a big city. It had all of the newfangled amenities of Asheville with a lot more people and buildings, but it wasn't anywhere near as clean.

I missed my mountain almost from the minute we drove into the city limits and knew even before we pulled up to Papa's house I would be uncomfortable for the entire planned visit. I was used to open spaces and clean, fresh air and felt confined, surrounded by buildings set close to one another and people milling on porches or sidewalks, cars flashing by on the streets. And the noise! The clamor of automobile horns blaring and people shouting, children laughing and screaming, and the racket of buildings being erected assaulted my ears. I thought it a wonder anyone could hear anything at all, much less their own thoughts.

I wasn't sure what to expect when we got to Papa's house. Loney had fulfilled her dream of domesticity by marrying a man named Bob Day a few years after Papa moved the family to Knoxville. She had two children, a son named Gene and a daughter named Bessie, after me. I had never met Bob and doubted I would on this trip as Loney had written that he was living with his mother, taking care of her in her old age, while Loney had moved in with Papa. I didn't really understand why or what was going on in that marriage but I wouldn't ask. If Loney wanted me to know, she would tell me.

The house was a one-level dwelling off one of the main streets through the city, not far from downtown where Papa had first gotten work when he moved the family there from Hot Springs in 1908 after Mama died. He hadn't wanted to stay in Hot Springs and knew he could find work in Knoxville since they were still rebuilding the downtown after it had completely burned in a fire in 1897.

When they first arrived, Papa had bought two houses to fix up and they'd lived in one of them until he sold it. Papa continued to build and sell houses until he hurt his back and settled into the house he was working on at the time. When Loney moved in with him, she got a job at the Brookside Cotton Mill while Papa stayed at home and watched over the children when they were out of school.

I imagined the house would hold four people comfortably, or even six when you threw in Loney's children who lived with their father during the week and only stayed with her on the weekends. I was used to just Fletch and myself—and Fritz, of course—and I worried as we drove through the city that the house would be too crowded with two extra people in it.

I had no inkling just how crowded until I got to the house. Not long after arriving, I found myself counting down the minutes until I could go back to my mountain. It wasn't that I didn't enjoy seeing Loney and meeting her young'uns, visiting with Roy and Thee who both lived nearby with their families, and, most of all, spending time with Papa—I enjoyed that most of all—but even with those pleasures, my time in Knoxville turned out to be one of the most puzzling times in my life … and yet it was also one of the best.

CHAPTER SIXTEEN

Summer 1924

There are a lot of nooses on their family tree.

When I arrived, the first minutes were taken up with long hugs and delighted laughter, tears of joy and invisible tears of despair when I saw how much Papa had aged. He was impossibly old, his once strong back bent, and he had to use a cane to walk. I mourned the young, vital man who had loved nothing more than to spend time with his beloved wife and children and even now was crying unashamedly at the sight of his "Bessie-girl".

After Loney hugged Fletch, she tugged Papa's arm. "Papa, let Bessie go so I can have my turn."

Papa sniffed and stepped back and I was immediately engulfed in my sister's embrace.

It wasn't until Loney let me go that I saw the young boy standing behind Papa's legs, head down and shoulders hunched as if hoping no one would notice him. When he peeked up at me, I recognized him—how could I not—he was the spitting image of Papa. But what was he doing here? Shouldn't he be in Asheville with his mama?

At my raised eyebrows, Papa reached behind him and drew the boy out. Smiling, he said, "I reckon you don't recognize him. He was just a tiny little thing when you met him but this is my John Henry, Jack's oldest boy."

I felt such a strong sense of connection to this child, I couldn't speak for a moment then mentally shook myself. I knew in my soul this boy belonged to me. But the name surprised me.

"John Henry?"

"Yep, that's what I call him."

"I thought Jack was in Asheville with her husband."

"She was," Loney said. "She moved back to Knoxville a month or so ago when her youngest died. She's working at the cotton mill with me and Papa watches over the boy when she's working."

This was news to me. Although Jack and I had promised to write one another often, life had other plans and we hadn't kept in touch as we had intended. I had so many questions that needed answers but didn't want to voice them in front of this young boy, so I settled for, "Why didn't you say anything in your letters?"

"I wrote you but I guess the letter didn't have time to reach you before you left."

Papa stroked his handlebar moustache. "Um, Bess, don't you think we should talk about this later?" He looked down at the boy. "Say hello to your Aunt Bessie and Uncle Fletch, John."

The child shuffled his feet and didn't say a word. I wondered what was wrong with him. Was he slow or just exceedingly shy? Or was he scared?

I walked over to stand in front of him. "Well, John, you're a lot bigger than you were when we last saw you and I can't imagine you remember us since you weren't even talking, but I'm your Aunt Bessie and that's your Uncle Fletch."

He slowly raised his head, cocking it to one side as he looked at me and I knew with a certainty I couldn't explain then and still can't today. He was the reason I was here, nearly 200 miles from home, wishing only that I could go back to my mountain.

But it seemed I had something to do here before I could.

Fletcher stepped forward and gently ruffled the boy's hair. "Hello, John."

"H-hello, um, Aunt Bessie and Uncle Fletch," he said, cocking his head to the left again, his voice a mere whisper on the air.

My heart turned over and quite simply broke in two. I guess it was a little like what I'd heard mothers say about their babies: after nine months of carrying them inside their bodies and hours of ghastly pain bringing them into the world, the first time they held their baby it was simply love at first sight. It was a feeling I hadn't been blessed with since Fletch and I had never been able to conceive, and it was a feeling I'd often wondered about, sometimes ... well, honestly, most times, doubted. But one look at this child standing in front of me with his head cocked to the left, looking amazingly like I imagined Papa looked as a child, and I knew.

He was mine. God had sent me here because this little boy needed me.

I crouched down in front of him and pulled him into a hug. He, of course, squirmed to get free and I let him go with a laugh.

"Don't be afraid, John, it's just that you look so much like your grandpapa, or what I think your grandpapa looked like as a boy." I looked up at Papa. "Jack said you called him John even though his name is Raymond Earl. But why do you call him, what was it, John Henry?"

Papa beamed down at his grandson. "I told Jack the first time I seen him he weren't no Raymond Earl. That's a sissified name. Ray-mond Ear-l" Papa drew out the syllables and spoke in a high voice as if he was singing the words. "He don't look like no Raymond Earl to me. He looks like a John so I told her I was going to call him Little John and I didn't want to hear no more about Raymond Earl." Again the singsong voice and the drawn-out syllables. "The John Henry comes from him likin that old song about John Henry so much. He like to devil me to death wantin to hear that song all the time."

I smiled up at Papa. "And I reckon it doesn't have anything to do with the fact he looks enough like you to be your son?"

Papa shrugged. "Might as well be mine. His mother don't—"

Loney interrupted, laying her hand on John's shoulder. "John, let's show your Uncle Fletch where he and your Aunt Bessie will be sleeping. And then we'll see about getting us something to drink. I imagine they're parched after that long drive. Why, maybe we can even talk Fletch into telling us what it's like to ride in a motorcar across the mountains." She grunted as she picked up our valise from where it sat beside the door. "Sake's alive, Bessie, what did you do, pack the whole mountain in here?"

I laughed. "Only half of it."

"Here, I'll take that," Fletch said, reaching for the valise.

John didn't say anything, just followed meekly along behind Loney. Fletcher put his hand on the boy's back as they walked and the feeling the boy was mine, or more rightly, ours, intensified. I waited until they were out of the room before I turned to Papa. "All right, Papa, let's sit down and you can start by telling me why you feel John might as well be yours." I shook my head. "No, let's start at the beginning. Why in the world is Jack here instead of in Asheville with her husband?"

Papa sat down in a chair with a weary sigh and shook his head. "I don't know what to tell you, Bess. Jack showed up here in tears. She had John with her and she said her youngest had died and her husband got hisself killed in a train accident and she needed a place to stay. What would you have us do? Turn her away?"

"No, Papa. I'm glad you let her stay. She's family. But why didn't anyone write me about this? Our farm isn't far from where she lived in Asheville and I don't understand why she didn't get in touch with me. She could've come to stay with Fletch and me. We wouldn't have turned her away either."

"I know that, Bessie, but she has her reasons. Don't know why but she didn't want you to know she was living with us. Told us all not to tell you, that she'd tell you in her own way when the time was right."

"But why? Why couldn't she tell me?"

He scratched his head then stroked his moustache. "Ask me, she's a little bit scared of you. You're the older sister she never really got the chance to know. You moved away when she was just a baby and only came to visit a couple of times. And, well, your Aunt Belle held you up as an example to her."

This surprised me. "Aunt Belle? She didn't approve of me for the longest time, and certainly not when Jack was born." I waved that away. "Scared of me? Why would Jack be scared of me? She was fine when Fletch and I visited her in Asheville after John was born."

He shrugged. "Don't know the answer to that one, Bessie but I can tell you your Aunt Belle certainly did approve of you. Why, didn't she see the way you practically raised the young'uns after your mother died—"

"Papa, that's not true and you know it. Elisi was the one who raised them with your help, of course, and mine, too, but it was Elisi, not me or you who shouldered most of the burden."

"She helped, I won't deny that, but it was you. I only wish you could've stayed around longer and raised Jack."

"Loney did a fine job with Jack. Besides, Loney's the maternal one, not me. She didn't need my help when it came to raising those young'uns."

"Mayhap you're right but she spoiled that girl rotten and you know it. I tried to step in a few times to discipline her but Loney wouldn't never let me. Ask me, if'n she'd taken a switch to Jack's backside a few times the girl would've turned out better. But Loney mollycoddled and fussed over her and now look what's happened."

"What has happened, Papa?"

"She's never home, doesn't have two minutes to spare for that boy in there. Leaves him with me almost ever' night and goes out on the town wearing dresses that hardly cover her knees. It's disgraceful the way that girl dresses and the men she goes out with aren't worth spit. Fancy clothes, slicked down hair and sissified ways."

I had to smile at that. "I remember a time when you thought men like that were the best thing for your daughter and tried more than once to see to it that I married one of them."

"A feller's allowed to change his mind, ain't he? 'Sides that lawyer fellow I brought home was a good man." He harrumphed. "You just didn't want me to pick a husband for you. And you didn't listen to me, did you? You went ahead and married Fletcher Elliott, the opposite of what I wanted for you."

I sighed. "Let's not go down that path again, Papa. Fletch is my husband and I love him and would appreciate it if you showed him some respect."

"I respect him, never said I didn't. He's got the gumption to go after what he wants and he's willing to work for it. He's a good man, just not the man I wanted for you. Hell, Bess, you should have better."

I bristled then took his hand and held it. "He's the man I want and he's given me more than I ever dreamed. You know me, Papa. You know I wouldn't be happy living a life of luxury with fancy clothes and a big extravagant house. I have what I need, more important, I have what I want. I wish you could accept that."

He grumbled something under his breath and I sighed, knowing I would never convince him.

"All right, Papa. Let's get back to Jack. I have no earthly idea why she would be afraid of me. She seemed fine when Fletch and I visited her in Asheville." I shook my head. "Never mind, I'll talk to her and find out myself. As for Jack, she's a young widow, Papa. It isn't unusual for her to want to go out on dates with men. Do you want her to be alone for the rest of her life?"

"Of course I don't but she needs to take care of that boy in there instead of dumping him off with me and Loney. Loney's got her own young'uns to take care of, she shouldn't have to shoulder the weight of Jack's, too. Not that John Henry is a burden to anyone but, well, it just ain't right."

"I happen to agree with you on that but surely Loney doesn't have to handle it all alone. Jack takes care of him sometimes, doesn't she?"

"No, she don't. She's too busy running around with them

fancy men of hers, and when she's here at home, she spends all her time in the parlor listening to that damn Jim-dog. Half the night, she's got that thing going and a buncha people in here laughing and carrying-on. Long about ten o'clock I get fed-up and yell at her to turn the damn thing off and send them people home, it's bedtime, but she don't listen."

I looked at him questioningly. "Jim-dog?"

He gestured to an odd looking contraption sitting on a table in the corner. I'd only seen them in pictures but the horn on top made it instantly recognizable. "Hell, Bess, that Victrola Phonograph over there." He shook his head. "She's got a perfectly good piano in here but she never plays it. Just turns on that damn Jim-dog and either dances or sings along or, hell, who knows what she does? All I know is I can't get any sleep with that damn thing going all night."

I understood his frustration but not why he didn't just get up and turn the thing off himself. "So, she plays the phonograph all night. Why don't you move it in her room with her?"

"Because then she'd be invitin them people back in her room and I ain't havin that kind of nonsense going on in my house. Besides, John sleeps in there with her and that boy needs his sleep more than I do. He's a young child. Your mama always said it was important for young'uns to get plenty of sleep."

I smiled, remembering Mama insisting we go to bed practically before dark and take at least one nap during the day, something I had always fought tooth and nail.

Papa shook his head and sighed. "Damn, Bess, I miss your mama. The good Lord knows I could use her help especially when it comes to her youngest daughter."

"She's your daughter, too, Papa," I reminded him.

"Don't you think I know that?"

I patted his shoulder. "I'm sure you do, Papa. And I can understand why she's worrying you but it seems to me playing a phonograph all night and going out on a few dates isn't something to worry about."

"Hell, Bessie, if you could see the men she's going out

with, you'd worry, too."

I laughed. "Oh now, Papa, they can't be that bad." I started to add how he'd been wrong about Fletch but I caught myself in time. There was nothing to be gained beating that dead horse again. Papa and I would never see eye to eye when it came to my husband.

"Maybe you'd think different if you saw them, Bess. One of them came around here the other night driving some kind of fancy car, a Buick he called it, and it had curtains in the back windows. Curtains! I told Jack to get her backside back in the house. There warn't no way I was going to let her go out with a man that had curtains in his car."

I couldn't help it, I laughed at that.

Papa frowned and then huffed out a disgusted breath. "I don't know why I'm telling you all this. It ain't going to change anything."

"Papa, whether you like it or not, Jack is a grown woman, she's been married and had two babies and if, as you say, she's spoiled rotten, I can't see anything we can do to change that at this point in her life. She's almost twenty-four years old, for pity's sake." I softened my voice. "You have to realize you have no say over what she does anymore, Papa, and the sooner you accept that the better it'll be for everyone concerned."

He held up his hand and whispered, "Little pitchers have big ears." Then he turned toward the doorway. "That you, John Henry? Come on in here. Don't be afraid of your Aunt Bess. She ain't gonna hurt you."

Hurt him? Why would Papa say something like that? I wondered but would save my questions for later when the boy wasn't in hearing distance. Little pitchers did indeed have big ears.

When John peeked around the doorjamb, his eyes immediately went to me, as if checking to make sure I hadn't turned into a monster. I smiled at him, hoping to set him at his ease but his eyes had moved to his feet and I wondered again if someone had hurt him in some way, either physically or emotionally.

And my heart turned over. It was a feeling I was to get

used to over the next few days … and into the future.

When Jack came home from work, she greeted me in what I can only describe as a hesitant manner. No big hugs from Jack, just a tentative smile and a somewhat weak "Hello" before she went off to her room to get cleaned up. She didn't come back out until Loney called her for supper.

I tried to talk to Jack as we ate but her answers were always rushed and consisted of only one or two words. As the meal progressed, I understood Papa's frustration more with every minute. It was like pulling teeth to get her to answer, much less look at me, when she did. As soon as we finished, she jumped up and started clearing the table, saying she had plans to meet friends, and though I waited up, she still hadn't returned by the time I went to bed.

The next morning, she left for work before I got up and I didn't see her again until dinner that night.

It was a bittersweet meal for me, eating with my family around me and knowing that tomorrow Fletch and I would return to our small farm on the mountain. I missed the farm animals, my garden and working with my herbs and plants, the quiet of my everyday life, and Fritz. I couldn't wait to get back to my home.

Roy, Alice and their children and Thee and his wife Myrtle went home directly after the meal because Roy and Thee had to be up early for their jobs at the railroad. We waved them off and went into the parlor where Papa and Loney sat in the rocking chairs by the window and Fletch and I sat on the small sofa.

Gene and a neighbor friend were tossing a baseball back and forth in the front yard while Loney's daughter Bessie and a friend from across the street played a game of hopscotch on the sidewalk. Their high-pitched squeals and giggles mixed with the deeper tones of the boys' banter drifting through the open window made me smile, thinking about my school yard at recess time.

John perched on Papa's lap, silently playing with Papa's watch chain. I had noticed he had a tendency to somehow become smaller whenever Jack was around as if he hoped she wouldn't notice him and assumed Papa's lap was where he felt safest.

Papa and I were talking about the time we'd lived in Hot Springs when Gene slipped in and sat on the floor at Loney's feet, a smug smile on his face.

He watched as Jack flounced into the room, her hair in waves, her dress above her knees and multiple strands of beads around her neck. Looking at him, I thought he resembled a cat that had just caught and consumed a long-pursued canary.

Papa laughed as he recalled the time I stood up to a Yankee and challenged him to a fight because he had kicked his deputy Theodore Norton when he was down.

"Damn, Bess, I liked to not've got you out of that one with your skin in one piece." He shook his head. "You sure could get up to some high jinks, girl, and you usually managed to drag me in with you."

I smiled. "I was only trying to keep you young, Papa."

"More like send me to an early grave."

"You're still here, aren't you?"

"Yep, I reckon I'm tougher than anybody thought."

Jack now stood at the door, an impatient look on her face. Papa glanced her way. "Well, aren't you going to sit down, girl?"

"I don't have time, Papa. I'm meeting some friends. I won't be out late, I promise." She blew him a kiss and turned to leave.

Papa sat up straight. "Wait a damn minute. You've been out every night this week. Don't you think you should stay home with your boy for a change?"

"But, Papa ..."

"And this is your sister's last night here. You need to stay home."

"Well, if I'd known they were coming, I wouldn't have made plans."

"Hell, girl, what about your boy? You need to take care of him. You ain't a mama to him. Seems to me you'd rather be anywhere but here seein to him."

Jack cut her eyes to Gene who now sat at attention, his

eyes watching her, and I thought again of a cat feasting on a long desired canary.

I watched as she seemed to come to a decision. She drew a deep breath and stood straighter, staring at Papa. "Well, since you think I can't take care of him and Gene don't want him here anyway, maybe it'd be best if I just take him on down to the Baby Store."

Gene's smile stretched until I thought it would split his face in two.

I didn't know what the Baby Store was but my stomach sank to my knees at the announcement. Loney's gasp and Papa's roar gave me a clue. "What the hell you talkin about, girl?"

Jack squared her shoulders and repeated, "I'm taking him to the Baby Store tomorrow and leaving him there. They'll find someone to take him."

I looked over at John, cowering in Papa's lap, tears rolling down his face. He winced when Papa yelled, "Oh, hell, no, you're not taking my John Henry anywhere. He stays right here with me."

My face grew hot with anger. No child should hear their mother say such a thing. I held out my hand to the boy, intending to take him out of the room, but Loney, who'd remained strangely silent during all this except for her initial gasp of surprise, stood up and said, "Let me have John, Papa. I'll take him out on the porch. Gene, you come, too."

I didn't know whether to be relieved she was getting the child out of the room or to be thoroughly angry at her seeming acceptance of Jack's plans. Had the years changed her that much? And her son, Gene, oh, he was enjoying this too much if the grin on his face was any indication.

This situation was baffling and I didn't know what to make of it or how I could stop it. I watched as Loney took John's little hand and walked with him out onto the porch and once again my heart turned over.

Jack ignored this, her eyes on Papa. She shook her head. "No, Papa. I'm his mother and I say where he goes. I can't take care of him anymore and I think the best thing to do is to let the children's home over on Central take him."

Papa's face was turning dangerously red and I knew I needed to say something. But what? What could I say to my sister then? I was completely flabbergasted and, in truth, furious with her. And I suspected Gene had obviously known this was going to happen and, even more obviously, approved whole-heartedly.

I stood up and went to stand in front of her, reaching out my hands to take hers. She stepped back away from me.

"What is this all about, Jack?" I said, "Why would you want to give up your child?"

"She ain't giving him up," Papa said, "he's staying right here with me." He speared Jack with an angry look. "You just get that notion out of your head right now, little missy. You hear me?"

Jack narrowed her eyes at him. "He's mine and I'll do what I want with him and you can't stop me."

"Jack," I started but she cut me off with a slash of her hand.

"No, I've made up my mind and you're not going to talk me out of it. He's going and that's that."

Well, I had wanted her to say more than two words to me and now that she had, I didn't like it one bit. I also hated the fact that John had heard his mother say she didn't plan to keep him. Didn't she realize what she was doing to her son?

I simply could not understand why she would do such a heartless thing. "What are you thinking, Jack? You'd give up your only son, the only child you have left? And for what? So you can run…" I stopped myself, knowing that anger wasn't the answer. It would only make her more determined and I just didn't have the heart to go on. Who knew how much damage this would cause and my adding to it wasn't going to help.

With the exception of my brother Roy when we were children, I had never in my life physically attacked a person but my palms actually itched now with the desire. If I thought I could have knocked some sense into my sister's head, I would have boxed her ears good, but I had a feeling there was no stopping her, no turning her in another direction.

When I turned back to Jack, she stood watching me unblinkingly, with her shoulders ramrod straight and her hands clasped loosely together in front of her, her face pale and so hard it made me think of a marble statue. It was obvious she was serious about this, and if she did what she wanted, that poor child would end up all alone in some cold, uncaring orphanage. I couldn't let that happen. I remembered Elisi's words to me in my dream, "When the time comes, you must stand up and do what you know is right for him," and I knew what to do

I turned to Fletch and he gave me a small nod, letting me know he agreed with what I was going to do.

Walking to Papa's chair, I placed my hand on his shoulder and looked at my sister. "We'll take him. John can come home with me and Fletcher, and we will raise him. He's welcome at our house for as long as he wants to stay. I don't understand how you can give up your child but we'll take him and thank you for the gift."

I expected Jack to protest or at least try to defend her actions—not that they could be defended—but she only nodded then turned around and walked out of the room.

I squeezed Papa's shoulder. "How did she get to be so unfeeling, Papa?"

"Damn, Bess, I don't know. To think that a child of mine would give up her little boy..." He shook his head. "The only things I know for sure is your Mama's pitching a dying duck fit up in Heaven right now and when she's finished being mad she'll be smiling down at her oldest daughter."

I could feel the tears building behind my eyelids but I held them back. I had to know one more thing. I opened my eyes. I took a deep breath. "Papa, did Loney know Jack was planning on giving up her child?"

He shook his head. "I don't know. I sure didn't know Jack was thinking about this. She ain't been the same since Ed died. I wonder sometimes if John don't remind her of him in some way, but I never would have guessed this was coming in a million years. Damn, Bess, this is a hell of a thing." He rubbed his hand over his face, closed his eyes and leaned his head against the back of his chair as he muttered, "Hell of a thing, Bessie-girl, hell of a thing."

I leaned down and kissed his cheek and smiled when his handlebar moustache tickled. And when he stood and wrapped his arms around me, I held on tight and let the tears fall.

The next morning, I was determined to get up before Jack left for work and have a talk with her. It wasn't hard to do since I hadn't slept much during the night. I slipped out of bed and dressed quietly, trying not to awaken Fletcher or anyone else in the house. I wanted this time alone with Jack, to try and determine if giving John to us was what she really wanted.

Going to the kitchen, I started a pot of coffee and sat down at the table to wait. It didn't take long, and when she came in and saw me, Jack only sighed.

I got up and poured her a cup of coffee. "Do you have time to talk to me before you leave for work, Jack?"

She took my hand as I sat down beside her, and when she turned her face to mine, I was surprised to see tears in her eyes.

"What is it, Jack?" I asked.

She hesitated then shook her head. "I'm, I'm sorry, Bessie."

"For what, Jack?"

"I know I came off as selfish last night and maybe even a little mean, to blurt that out the way I did. I love my son and I only want what's best for him." Her shoulders hunched and she cast her eyes down for a moment then looked back up at me and went on. "That's the God's honest truth, Bessie. I want what's best for that boy but I can't give it to him, not right now, anyway, and … and I'm really sorry for that."

I patted her shoulder. "I know it's a hard thing, Jack, and I can't claim to grasp how you can do it, but if you're trying to do the right thing for John, I think I can understand. But maybe you should think about it a little more before giving him up?"

She shook her head. "I've thought about it and thought about it and my mind never changes. I can't take care of that boy and I'm afraid of what might happen if I try."

I couldn't understand it but I could accept and maybe even forgive at some point in the future. "Fletcher and I will take him, we told you that last night, but I have to be sure in my heart it's what you want."

She nodded. "It is. I can't tell you how grateful I am to you and Fletch but I want you to know I'll never forget what you're doing for me ... or for him."

I wondered why she never called her son by his name but shook off that thought. This appeared to be what she wanted and, Lord knows, it was what Fletch and I wanted, so why question it? "All right, Jack, we'll take him and we'll love him and care for him. I just need to know if you can live with this decision."

She nodded again. I waited for her to speak but she only said, "I'm going to be late for the factory." She leaned over and hugged me, whispering, "Thank you, Bessie." Then she stood up and hurried out the door.

When Preacher Justice came to pick us up, I told Papa to keep John busy in the kitchen while I went outside to talk to the preacher. I asked him if it would be all right for John to come along with us on the trip and said if it wasn't we'd get a train ticket and travel home that way. I'm sure he knew something had happened, and judging by the frown on my face, he had to know it wasn't good but he didn't ask any questions and simply said yes.

When I brought John out, Preacher Justice welcomed him and asked if he was ready to go on an exciting journey over the mountains. John only cocked his head to the left, as if trying to figure out who this boisterous man was, and said, "Yes, sir," in a subdued voice.

And, of course, my heart turned over. The poor thing had to be scared to death. He was going to live with near strangers and couldn't know what was about to happen to him. His little mind had to be racing with questions. When we got home, Fletch and I would sit him down and try to answer those questions. I had a feeling it was going to be a long time before he felt comfortable with us but I would do everything in my power to reassure him that our home was his home and he was welcome in it anytime and for as long as he wanted to stay. And after discussing it with Fletch the night before, I was sure he felt the same way.

While Preacher Justice settled the boy into the back seat, I turned back to Papa and hugged him, whispering, "Don't worry about him. I promise Fletch and I will take good care of him and see that he's brought up with love."

Papa clung to me for a minute then pulled back and kissed my cheek. "If you need me, send a wire and I'll come right away on the train. Hell, I'll walk if I have to."

I smiled. "Of course you would but you won't need to, the train will be quick enough. He'll be safe with us, Papa, I promise you that."

He shook Fletcher's hand. "I thank you for taking care of my John Henry, Fletch." Then he turned to me. "This ain't an easy thing, Bess. Raising a young-un is sometimes like being pecked to death by a chicken. It takes a lot of work."

I couldn't help but laugh at that. "I spend nearly every day of my life with multiple young'uns. I think I can handle one more." Placing my hands on his shoulders, I gave him a little shake. "Do you trust me to love him and care for him, Papa?"

"'Course I do. I'm just goin to miss him, that's all."

He turned to the preacher's automobile and bent down to reach in and pat John on the head. "Now don't you go forgetting your grandpapa, John Henry. And you behave yourself for your Aunt Bessie and Uncle Fletch. I'll be coming over them mountains one day soon to see you and we'll have us a sing-along that'll rouse them mountain people up and set 'em to dancing until the ground shakes."

John reached up and grabbed Papa's hand. "I'll miss you, Grandpapa."

"I know you will and I'll be over here missing you right back."

I was never so glad of anything in my life as I was to see Knoxville behind us. I was more than ready to go home to my mountain and my quiet farm. I had felt crowded the whole time I was in Knoxville, almost as if I couldn't find enough air to breathe, and though I enjoyed visiting with my family, I wanted home. It was the place where I felt most comfortable.

I prayed John would feel the same way.

About an hour into our trip, the stress and sleepless night caught up with John. He curled up against Fletcher and went to sleep which gave me a chance to tell Preacher Justice the whole appalling story. When I finished, he only scratched his chin and didn't say anything for several minutes. I had almost drifted off myself when he said, "This is a terrible thing, Bessie, a mother giving up her child for no valid reason." He shook his head. "I think my sermon this Sunday will be about building a fence around Hell."

I looked at him but he didn't offer an explanation, instead, said, "I haven't asked you yet, Missus Bessie, and if you don't want to say, I understand, but how do you feel about all this, about what your sister did? And how do you feel about suddenly having a child to take care of?"

I thought about it for a minute and took a deep breath. I wanted to get the words right, to explain in a way that would leave no doubt in the preacher's mind that I accepted and even welcomed this change in my life. "You know how the mountain people are always saying God works in mysterious ways?"

He smiled. "That they do and that He does."

I nodded. "Well, I guess this is the proof of that saying."

"How do you mean?"

I rested my hand over my heart. "I'll tell you a secret, Preacher Justice. I've had my share of falling outs with God. Sometimes I'd get so angry that I'd raise my fist to the sky and curse him for all I was worth." I shook my head. "There were times I thought I'd never forgive Him for one thing or the other. But it seemed He's more stubborn ... or maybe, He's more tolerant than I am. He would just wait patiently and I always came around to His way of thinking eventually and He always opened His arms and took me back in the fold.

"Anyway, I spent most of last night praying, seeking an answer to whether I'd done the right thing for that young boy back there." I checked in the back to see John still asleep, leaning trustingly against Fletch, and smiled. With his eyes closed and his face relaxed, the boy looked so innocent and pure, and my heart turned over once more. Fletcher returned my smile and nodded as he had the night before. Turning back to Preacher Justice, I found him looking at me instead of at the road in front of him. "Don't you think you should look at where you're driving, Preacher?"

He jumped then turned his eyes forward and mumbled, "Sorry, Missus Bessie."

I laughed. "Don't mind me. I just want to make sure we get home safe. You see, I'm kind of eager to start living this next part of my life, now that I have the child I've wanted for so long. Fletcher and I are going to teach him so many things. We'll get to see him grow up bit by bit and become a man." I waved my hand. "But that's neither here nor there and doesn't really answer your question, does it?"

He shook his head, careful to keep his eyes on the road in front of him. "No, I reckon it doesn't but I think I understand. You want him, then?"

I patted my hand where it rested over my heart. "Oh, more than I can tell you, Preacher Justice. My heart is filled to bursting with love for that boy. I never knew a person could love another person so much. I love my husband and my Papa, my family but this ... this is different, somehow. I don't know if I can explain it, it just is." I smiled. "And my heart is also filled to bursting with gratitude to my God. That, and more than a little bit of wonder at His mysterious ways."

"That mean you're happy about this situation?"

"Oh, yes, happier than I've ever been. That boy back there is mine and Fletch's. It doesn't matter that he didn't come from me and Fletch. Directly from us..." I couldn't stop smiling. "I understand now, Preacher Justice."

"Understand what exactly?"

"God didn't see fit to bless me with a child in the customary sense, no matter how much I prayed for it. But if you ask me, He's given me something better. He's blessed me with a child of my heart."

Books in the Appalachian Journey series:

Whistling Woman, Appalachian Journey Book 1

At the turn of the 20th century, Bessie Daniels grows up in the small town of Hot Springs in the mountains of Western North Carolina.

Moonfixer, Appalachian Journey Book 2

In the dawning years of the 20th century, Bessie Daniels leaves her home town of Hot Springs and travels over the mountains with her husband Fletcher Elliott to live in the Broad River Section of North Carolina.

Beloved Woman, Appalachian Journey Book 3

In the second decade of the 20th century, major world events resonate even on secluded Stone Mountain where Bessie Elliott lives with her husband Fletcher.

Wise Woman, Appalachian Journey Book 4

Traditionally, a Wise Woman is a woman who possesses knowledge, passed down through generations, of time-honored folk medicines. They deal with all kinds of illnesses and medical conditions, often using practical herbal remedies, drawing on plants and the rest of the natural environment, which they know well.

Acknowledgements

We would like to extend our gratitude to the following people:

Our dad, Raymond Earl "John" Tillery, for the many stories he has told us over the years. He is the primary reason we decided to write about our great-aunt Bessie and great-uncle Fletcher and we can only hope we're doing his fascinating stories justice.

Our great-aunt Bessie and great-uncle Fletcher who lived the lives we're writing about. Although we didn't know them long, we feel we've somehow grown closer to them as we write these stories and sincerely hope they're enjoying it as much as we are.

Our cousin, Jackie Burgin Painter, renowned historical author for her book "The German Invasion of Western North Carolina, A Pictorial History." Thanks again, Jackie, your books are solid gold to us!

Our cover designer, Kimberly Maxwell, for the hours of hard work that resulted in our beautiful cover. Your talent and creativity are nothing short of amazing!

Our husbands, Mike Hodges and Steve French, who, once again, successfully navigated the sometimes precarious path of being married to an author. Thanks for understanding our need for "alone time" when the writing muse calls. We love you guys!

Last but certainly not in any way least, we'd like to thank our readers who are such an inspiration to us every single day. Thanks for the encouragement, support, and lovely comments on our blog and Facebook page. In turn, you've brought us laughter, tears (of joy), and are the force which drives us to continue telling the story of our amazing great-aunt and -uncle. We can never thank you enough!

Most of our research on this book came through online sources, and while those are too numerous to list here, there are a few print books we'd like to acknowledge:

First, as mentioned above, Jacqueline Burgin Painter's wonderful and informative book, "The German Invasion of Western North Carolina, A Pictorial History."

"Medicine of the Cherokee, The Way of Right Relationship" by J. T. Garrett and Michael Garrett.

Peterson Field Guides "Eastern/Central Medicinal Plants and Herbs" by Steven Foster and James A. Duke.

And finally, a special note to the family members we've connected with on the Internet and via e-mail: the stories we have used in the Appalachian Journey series are stories we've heard from our dad, Uncle Ken, and in a few cases, directly from Aunt Bessie herself. We have done our best to stay true to the telling but, in some cases, we took the liberty of changing the scene, character, and/or the time in order to help the story flow. We have, in *Beloved Woman,* made our dad about ten years older than he actually is (sorry, Daddy!) and we've placed historical figures in places we can't know for sure they actually were. We also, in the case of a couple of members of our family who don't come out looking very good, told the stories as we heard them without glossing over the truth to make those family members look better. We apologize if we've offended any descendents of the Elliott or Daniels family.

About the Authors

CC Tillery is the pseudonym for two sisters, both authors who came together to write the story of their great-aunt Bessie in the *Appalachian Journey* series. Tillery is their maiden name and the C's stand for their first initials.

One C is Cyndi Tillery Hodges who writes paranormal romance based on Cherokee legends under the pseudonym Caitlyn Hunter. To find out more about her work, visit http://caitlynhunter.com.

The other C is Christy Tillery French, a multi-published, award-winning author whose books cross several genres. To find out more about her work, visit her website at http://christytilleryfrench.webs.com.

For more information on the Appalachian Journey series, visit http://whistlingwoman.wordpress.com or follow us on Facebook at http://facebook.com/appalachianjourney.

Made in the USA
Lexington, KY
31 July 2016